Ten Times Have The Lilies Blown

Mary Erickson

PublishAmerica

Baltimore

First printing

ISBN: 1-59129-621-8
PUBLISHED BY PUBLISHAMERICA BOOK PUBLISHERS
www.publishamerica.com
Baltimore

Printed in the United States of America

For my children,
T. J., Cathy, Tim, Don, and Laurie,
and for my sister, Elsa

ACKNOWLEDGMENTS

I want to thank my husband, Alex, an enhanced recovery petroleum engineer, who assisted me with the technical knowledge needed to develop the story; Barbara Torke for supplying me with invaluable information about the Weldon Valley where she grew up; and Don Sheridan, my computer guru. I am grateful to my friends and family, who critiqued my manuscript and gave me advice and encouragement. These include my sisters, Laura and Anne, and good friends, Jeanne, Kathryn, Bev, Sandra, Penny, Kathleen, and Janet. Many thanks also to Publish America for making it all happen.

Author's note – The characters in this novel are fictional, as is the town of Platte Valley, where these characters lived their lives and dreamed their dreams.

I WILL paint her as I see her.
Ten times have the lilies blown
Since she looked upon the sun.

-Elizabeth Barrett Browning
-"A Portrait"

Chapter 1 - Lori

In the dream Lori is ten years old. She is locked in a dark room and gropes the walls trying to find a door. She tries to call for help but no sound comes out. Her mother's brother and his family, who live in Des Moines, are visiting. Lori is afraid of her two boisterous male cousins. When she tries to tell Mother, she is scolded. "Nonsense. They're our guests and it's up to you to see they have a good time. Take them outside and show them around. They'd probably like the tire swing."

Frank and Ray take turns on the swing. After about a half an hour they are bored. Lori tries to think of some games the boys might like, but everything she suggests doing is met with smirks and jeers. "Them's dumb girlie games," they say in disgust.

Frank, the older boy, who is twelve, has a better idea for a game. He says, "Let's blindfold someone, turn 'em around and lead 'em somewhere. Then they've gotta' guess where they are."

Lori is chosen by the two boys to be the first player to be blindfolded. Her family lives on a farm just at the edge of town. The property originally belonged to her grandparents. They had indoor plumbing installed, but there's an old outhouse at the edge of the property still standing. No one has used it for years. The two boys lead their cousin into the outhouse and leave. By the time she's able to remove her blindfold and try the door she can't get it open. She hears them laughing outside and begs them to open it. Finally it gets quiet. Lori tries the door again. Somehow they've managed to lock it. The inside of the old building is dark and musty. She feels her skin crawling with spiders, although she doesn't know if this is just her imagination. Lori screams repeatedly. Finally someone opens the door. Her eyes are almost swollen shut, but she hears her father's gentle voice.

When Lori opened her eyes, it was Larry she saw, not her father. And she was in a bed. Where? She tried to sit up, but her head started spinning, forcing her back down. Larry, who had been sitting on a chair by the bed, was on his feet.

"Lori, how do you feel? You were yelling in your sleep—something about being locked in a room by Frank and Ray. Who are they?"

Lori's throat was so dry she could hardly get the words out. "Could I have some water, please?" she asked.

Larry walked around to the other side of the bed. He poured some water from a pitcher that was sitting on a white, plastic stand. The stand was high, like the ones they use in hospitals, and Lori knew where she was.

He pushed a button, moving the top of her bed up, and handed her the glass of water. She sipped it slowly through one of those plastic straws that bend in the middle.

Lori had questions for Larry but was having trouble formulating what they were. "Frank and Ray are my cousins," she told him. "Once when I was a little girl and they were visiting us they locked me in an old outhouse. It was a terrifying experience. I used to have these nightmares a lot when I was a child but this is the first time I've had the dream as an adult."

Larry laid his hand on hers. "Do you remember anything, Lori? Anything about how you got here?"

"No, the last thing I remember—oh God, I was at the oil field and Blake was there, and…" She couldn't say it, not yet. "But, I don't understand. I know this is a hospital but how did I get here?"

"I brought you here. I got over to your house about two o'clock yesterday afternoon." At her look of surprise, he checked his watch and said, "Yes, you've been catching up on your beauty rest. You've been asleep for about twenty hours now. Anyhow, you pulled into your driveway a few minutes after I arrived. I'd been sitting out in front of the house in my patrol car waiting. You drove right past me like you didn't even see me, which I thought was strange. And then when I saw you getting out of your car, I high-tailed it over. I could tell something was wrong. I've seen a lot of drunks since I've been in law enforcement, and if I hadn't known better, I'd have sworn you'd been somewhere and tied one on. When I got closer I could see from your eyes you were in a daze, almost catatonic. I don't know how you ever made it home."

The events of the previous day were starting to come back, the gunfire,

Joe falling to the ground.

"Dr. Bob checked you over. Said you had obviously suffered a severe shock of some kind. He said you'd probably be all right after a good night's rest. It appears he was right."

"Do you know what happened out there, Larry?"

"Yes, I questioned you before you drifted off. Your answers were garbled, but I was able to determine your condition was connected with something out at the Wyatt lease."

"Blake killed Joe. And it wasn't to protect me."

"Yes, I figured that out, Lori, once I'd found the note on his body."

"But Blake took the note out of Joe's pocket. I saw him."

Larry seemed puzzled for a moment, but then a look of comprehension crossed his face. He placed his hand awkwardly on her shoulder. "I should probably check with Dr. Bob first, but there's something else that happened out there, Lori, after you left. "It wasn't Joe's body I was talking about. It was Blake's."

Lori looked at Larry blankly, trying to make his words register. Then she said in a resigned voice, "He turned the gun on himself then, the gun he used to kill Joe."

"No, although he had the means on hand. He didn't even try to get rid of the gun, a thirty-eight, just threw it in some brush next to the gazebo. I think he might have been in a slightly confused state himself and wandered around for a while. We found his body at the project site. His truck was also found there, parked in back of the maintenance building. He'd gone into the building and opened a valve, releasing a combination of natural gas and hydrogen sulfate. The H2S is extremely lethal. It didn't take long, Lori. He just went to sleep."

Lori was unable to respond. She closed her eyes and could feel herself drifting off again. Then, after a few minutes, she said with an effort, "He let me walk away. He was going to kill me, too, strangle me. I said I wasn't going to make it easy and just turned and..." She couldn't get the last words past her tongue.

Larry's voice seemed to be coming from somewhere far away. "I'm going to leave now for awhile. I'll notify Dr. Bob and the nurse that you were awake and coherent."

Lori had more questions but was too tired to protest. She had a vague recollection of Dr. Bob being there, taking her pulse, and of nurses coming in and out, but in-between she drifted off to sleep. She didn't mind, as she knew she wasn't ready to face the painful realities that lay ahead. So much had happened in such a short time. Less than a year ago her life had been pretty dull. She wondered idly if she was now the subject of the front pages of the *Denver Post* and the *Rocky Mountain News*. When and how had it all started? Counting backwards Lori realized only seven months had passed since the day Blake Johnson had returned to Platte Valley — the event that changed her life forever.

Lori Wyatt looked up from her desk at the Platte Valley Library into the most cherubic face she had ever seen. It held a pair of huge hazel eyes, fringed with copper eyelashes, a pug nose, a cute little mouth, and was punctuated by about a million freckles. It also held a look of expectation.

"May I help you?" she asked with a smile.

"I'm doin' this report on dinosaurs, but they can't be just any dinosaurs, just this certain kind called Torosaurus," the angel, posing as a small boy, said. "It has the largest skull of any land animal but is the most ignored dinosaur," he added in a singsong voice, sneaking a look at her to see if she was impressed with this knowledge. "Anyhow, I need some stuff—books on it, so I can do my report."

"You seem to know a lot about the Torosaurus already," Lori said. "What's your name?"

"Michael Lawrence Reardon, but they call me Rusty."

She smiled. His nickname seemed inevitable. Must be Cindy's boy. It's hard to believe that he's in the second grade already. Seems like only yesterday that he was born. "I'm happy to meet you Rusty," she said. "My name is Miss Wyatt."

Rusty nodded and looked at her uncertainly, apparently wondering whether any comment was expected from him. Lori changed the subject. "Well, Rusty, it seems that you already know some things about this ignored dinosaur. I'll admit that I wasn't aware of his existence, but now I'm anxious to learn more about him, too."

"My grandpa told me about him," he said proudly. "He tells me lots of stuff. We go fishing a lot, and he tells me things."

She was glad the little boy's life had some semblance of normalcy. His family had been plagued by so much tragedy, starting with his grandmother's murder. Some people said that it's what had affected Cindy, who was eight years old when it happened. She'd turned wild as a teen-ager, winding up pregnant at sixteen. Lori didn't know who the father was. Some said Cindy didn't either. She'd left the little boy with her dad to bring up when he was just a baby. Lori wasn't sure if they even knew her whereabouts.

She got up from her desk and came around to where Rusty was standing. "Well, why don't we go over to the computer and find out if there's some information on this dinosaur?"

The library's two computers sat side by side on a counter midway between the fiction and children's sections. A third was on order and would to be placed by the reference section when it arrived. Rusty seemed to be totally absorbed as Lori explained how to find a book. "Can I try it now?" he asked, his face eager.

Lori stepped aside and watched him expertly go through the steps she'd just shown him. He confided that lots of the children now had computers in their homes but that his grandpa hadn't gotten one yet.

"The school has some, though, doesn't it? I thought I read in the *Daily News* that the bank had bought new computers and had donated the old ones to the school."

"Well, yeah. I mean they got some but I don't remember how. Mostly they're for the fifth and sixth grade. The second grade, that's the grade I'm in, doesn't hardly ever get to use them. That's 'cause there's not enough to go around."

At least they'd bought some computers, and that's a good start, Lori thought. It probably made sense to let the older children use them. She thought that she'd also read in the paper that they planned to buy more as the funds were made available from the school district.

The library was small by big city standards, but Lori was proud of its selection of books. Of course, as the town's librarian, she'd been instrumental in ensuring their superior quality, while working with a limited budget. She loved the challenge. The walls above the cases in the children's section were filled with artwork contributed by the elementary school children. The late morning sun streaming through the windows enhanced the brightly colored pictures.

With her help Rusty was able to find six books on dinosaurs. Two of them had information about the Torosaurus. Once Rusty had broken the ice, the other children came over and asked her to help them.

The teacher began rounding up her class and heading them toward the door, but Rusty hung back from the rest. "Thanks for helping me," he said.

"You're welcome, Rusty. I hope you're able to write a real good report with the help of those books. You certainly picked an interesting subject."

Rusty hesitated, standing on one foot and then the other, as if he were debating whether to say something more.

"Can I help you with something else?"

"Well, it's just—I was thinking, maybe I could come by sometime and do some other stuff on the computer and maybe you could help me."

Lori's heart went out to the little motherless boy. "I'd like to, Rusty. But these are for everyone to use so they can find the books they're looking for, just as we used them to help you find your books. That's why we have to have them available for other people."

His little face fell.

Oh dear, this is not going well, she thought. But what can I do? Suddenly, she had an idea. "I have a P.C., that is a personal computer, of my own. Maybe your grandpa could bring you by my house sometime, and I could show you some stuff—things. But it would have to be in the evening or on Sunday when I'm not working."

"I'll bet he could," Rusty said excitedly. "That'd be really cool. Man, wait 'till I tell Cody. He's my best friend."

Lori had a sudden vision of spending her Sundays giving computer classes to the entire second grade class of Platte Valley Elementary. "Well, I'd really rather this would be our secret. You see, some of the other children may ask me to give them lessons also, and I think it would be nice if it were just you and me, don't you?"

Rusty's face lit up. "Yeah. I mean yes ma'am. I won't tell anyone, except maybe I should tell Grandpa. Okay?"

"Of course. You'll have to tell your grandpa if you want him to bring you to my house. You'll need to let me know ahead of time when you can come, so I'll be sure to be there."

"I bet he could bring me over this Sunday. I'll ask him as soon as he gets home tonight."

Lori noticed the last of the children were marching out the door. "That would be fine," she said. "Now you'd better hurry as your class is leaving."

The little boy turned, verifying the truth of Lori's observation. "Whoops. Now I'm in trouble," he said, but his face didn't match the anxiety in his voice. "See you on Sunday," he yelled over his shoulder, his back weighted down with the books in his *Lion King* backpack.

Lori smiled after him. He was certainly an argument against teenaged abortions. Maybe she could help to fill a void in his life. The thought filled her with a feeling of warmth. The chimes on the clock brought her out of her reverie. Whoops, she thought, borrowing Rusty's buzz word, I'd better hurry or I'm not going to make it in time to meet Sarah. Lori had a standing luncheon date with her friend every Wednesday. She kept her jacket and purse in the storage room back of her office and hurriedly retrieved them. As she headed out the door, she turned the sign hanging on it around, moving the hands on the cardboard clock to read "Back at one o'clock."

Walking the short block to the diner, a half block up Miller Boulevard and a turn to the right on Main, she hardly noticed her surroundings so familiar were they—Brooks Drug Store on the corner, Isley's Grocery Store, Johnson's Farm and Implement. It was the out of the ordinary things that caught her eye, like the squirrel racing up the cottonwood and the tinges of yellow edging its leaves, a visual reminder summer was coming to an end.

As she turned the corner onto Main, her mind drifted back to Rusty and his upcoming computer lesson. Who would have thought a year ago she'd be giving computer lessons to anyone, even if it will be to a seven-year old. The library had bought the new computers about a year and a half ago and with their purchase, Lori felt her small town was moving into the twenty-first century and that she was playing a big part in it.

She'd even worked with the people from the library in Fort Morgan to get the books converted over to the new system. Lori had felt a little nostalgic at first. After all, the old card catalog system had worked just fine for years, and it had made her world seem a little shaky when they'd converted to computers.

It was the same kind of feeling she'd had the first summer after Dad's death, when she'd looked out at the fields beyond the house and instead of tall waves of corn stalks and rows of beans, she'd seen only a sea of alfalfa. She was only nineteen then and had planned to return to college. Realizing there would be no one to plant and harvest the crops, she had the fields planted with alfalfa. Her neighbor, Mr. Jacobs, who had a dairy farm, had agreed to buy the alfalfa for a token amount. The agreement was that he'd irrigate the crop, as well as harvesting and baling it. There wouldn't be much income from the venture but at least the fields would be put to good use. This change had been necessary so she might move on. Just as the changes at the library were necessary, she reasoned, so the town could move on.

And she was quite proud of the new knowledge she'd acquired. Like many people her age, and especially those who'd grown-up and remained in Platte Valley, she'd not only been computer illiterate but had also been a little afraid of the new technology. Now, she even had her own computer.

She thought it would be fun to work with Rusty. He was so cute and seemed anxious to learn. And it would be nice to share her knowledge with someone. Her mother certainly had no interest in learning. As she had expected, Charlotte Wyatt thought her daughter had lost her mind when she started shopping for a computer. But Lori stuck to her guns. After all, she planned to use her own money. Eventually, she thought she'd sign up for an internet service.

"Hello, Melora." The voice interrupted her thoughts.

"Hello, Mrs. Gibbons," Lori responded to the greeting of the matronly lady coming out of the drug store. Phoebe, unlike many women today in her age group, had held onto the notion that a lady should never wear trousers. The floral print dress was her uniform. Lori was certain she remembered it, or one very similar, from her childhood. The woman wore thick beige stockings, which Lori suspected were support hose, and a perky little hat, which somehow seemed at odds with the grimace that made itself at home on her face.

"Haven't talked to your mother in a couple of days. Last time I talked to her she was doing poorly," Phoebe stated in an almost accusatory manner. "Tell her I'll give her a ring. Just haven't had the time what with all the canning I've been doing."

"I'll do that, and thanks for keeping in touch with her. She does so look forward to your calls." Lori didn't want to get caught up in a long conversation. She had neither the time nor the patience to listen to the woman's gossip. Phoebe's gleeful manner of delivering her stories irritated Lori, and she was afraid she'd respond with an unpleasant remark. Before the woman could say anything more, Lori added, "I've got to run. I'm meeting Sarah for lunch." She hurried down the street, leaving Phoebe with her unuttered words frozen on her tongue.

As she walked past the window of Dora's Diner, she noticed Sarah was seated in their usual booth and knew she must be late. Since Lori was the better organized of the two, it was usually she who arrived first. Her best friend since childhood, Sarah wasn't exactly beautiful. Her face was too round and her nose turned up a little too much. Even as a woman in her thirties, she had an impish look to her. "Cute as a button" had often been used to describe her friend. Lori was maid of honor when Sarah had married her high school sweetheart just after graduation. Jon was well over six feet tall in his stocking feet, the only qualification he'd needed to be the basketball star at their small school. Sarah, on the other hand, was only an inch or two over five feet. It had been a storybook kind of marriage with Adam's arrival two years later and the birth of April when Adam was barely two.

Oh, maybe Sarah did lament now and then that she wished Jon would watch his beer intake, and perhaps the small potbelly on his once lanky physique attested to the truth of Sarah's complaints. But she was as apt to grumble about her own waistline, expanded a little more with the birth of each child. In spite of everything, they still acted like a couple of love-struck kids most of the time.

Lori's own waistline had remained trim, a condition she attributed partly to genetics and partly to the fact she'd never had children. If her life had been different, she, too, might have had children and knew she'd gladly add five inches. Sarah with her out-going personality had usually been the leader of the two girls. Lori had often wondered why someone as popular as Sarah bothered with her at all.

Chapter 2 – Lori

Dora's Diner was about what you'd expect a restaurant in a small town on the plains to look like. Unlike the newer chain restaurants, it wasn't large. About ten booths lined the walls on either side of the room with three scarred, round tables in the middle. Rather than going to the trouble to have them replaced, Dora had covered them with green and white checked, plastic covers. There was a small vase of plastic flowers on each table. Oil paintings of purple mountains or deer suspended in time lined the walls, which were darkened from smoke from the kitchen and from the diner's smoking patrons. In Lori's opinion these paintings were mediocre art at best. On the wall behind the cashier faded yellow cartoons were tacked, some of which Lori was sure had been there when she was a child. Dora, now in her sixties, still cooked most of the food, and it was superb; probably the reason the diner was always crowded. Then, too, the only other places in town open for lunch were a small pizza parlor and Sam's Bar and Grill, which offered sandwiches only. For those who wanted an evening out on the town, Delong's Supper Club was the place to go, but this establishment was open only on weekends. Of course, even small towns weren't immune to modern trends and recently a couple of fast food places had "sprung up" on the highway leading into town. These were usually filled with kids.

Lori ordered her usual soup and salad, but Sarah opted for the "special" of meat loaf with whipped potatoes and corn on the cob, locally grown. Lori noticed, though, that once the food arrived, Sarah just picked at her lunch. "Guess I wasn't as hungry as I thought," she said with a small smile.

Lori had been busy talking about the children's library visit. No matter what her mood, after a visit from one of the classes, she always felt better. She had been telling Sarah about her offer to give Rusty computer lessons, but now she looked at her friend with concern. "Is there something bothering you?" she asked.

Sarah gave a little shrug. "Oh nothing drastic. Just a case of the blahs."

Lori looked at her friend helplessly. It was so unusual to see Sarah depressed.

She wished there were something she could do. Sarah was the one who was always going out of her way for her friend. It had been that way since they were kids; always making sure Lori was included if there was to be a party or just a group going into Fort Morgan for the evening. She had a sudden inspiration. "Why don't we plan a little trip to Denver?" she asked. "Do some shopping, have lunch, maybe visit the art museum. Kristen could handle things on Saturday at the library. We may even want to stay over and come back Sunday."

"I'd like to, but I can't get away just now. Maybe once the harvesting is done I'll have a little more time."

"I think that may be your problem, what with your job and then having all that extra work on the farm, it's getting to you. Can't Jon spare you for just one day?"

Sarah gave a small smile. "We'll see," she said.

The two friends hugged before they each went their separate ways, Lori to the library and Sarah to the office of one of the town's two physicians. As she walked back, Lori thought about her friend. If she really wanted to go to Denver, Lori knew all she had to do was bat her eyelashes at Jon, and he'd not only tell her to go but give her carte blanche with the credit cards. She smiled to herself as she thought about Sarah's persuasive powers and how she'd used them through the years. Back when they were kids she'd gotten her quiet, studious friend involved in some crazy antics. Like the time one Halloween, when with the help of some boys from their class, they'd loaded some old toilets from the school onto Jimmy Hollingsworth dad's truck. The school was being renovated, and Sarah couldn't miss this great opportunity to distribute the toilets around town, specifically onto the front porches of some of the town's dignitaries.

Lori was still chuckling to herself as she walked up the library steps. The rest of the afternoon went quickly, as she was extra busy. The children's visit had put her behind schedule, and it was quitting time before she knew it. After the one other employee, a high school student who worked afternoons, left for the day, she locked up and with a quick glance at her watch, set off toward home at a brisk pace.

Lori owned a car, a Ford Taurus, which she'd bought new several years ago, but she seldom drove it to work—only when the weather was really bad. The car was used for grocery shopping or for taking her mother places. Then there were the occasional trips to Denver or to Jackson Lake, the favorite spot for recreation in Morgan County. Platte Valley had only about three thousand population, and this number included those who lived on outlying farms. The home she shared with her invalid mother was on the outskirts of town, which made a walk of just over a mile. Most of the homes in town were old, dating back to another time, a time before television and all the other modern technology. There were a few small subdivisions springing up, where modern, ranch-style houses dotted the countryside, laying waste to farms, which had stood for over a hundred years. In a way Lori was glad that many viewed living on the plains as inferior to residing in the mountains just an hour away. The quiet way of life enjoyed by the inhabitants of Morgan County, many the descendants of original settlers, was less threatened by the "progress" taking place throughout the Rocky Mountain region. She supposed only families such as hers, who had their roots buried deep in the land, could understand and appreciate the simple lifestyle offered by Platte Valley.

Checking her watch again as she picked up the mail, Lori saw that it had taken the usual fifteen minutes to reach home. She felt the walk to and from work contributed to the good health she enjoyed and probably accounted for her still slender figure.

The Wyatt house was one of the older ones in town, a two-story white clapboard, which her grandfather had built for his bride. Lori noticed that some leaves were beginning to fall from the huge cottonwoods that lined the sidewalk to the house.

After removing her cap in front of the hall mirror, she ran her hands through her brown hair, cut in a short pageboy style. Easier to maintain, she claimed. Just a quick shampoo when she took her morning shower and a go-over with the blow dryer were the only attention she usually gave her coiffure. For church on Sundays or a rare evening out, she plugged in her curling iron and turned up the ends a little.

Her best features were her eyes, which were large and framed with dark lashes. Chocolate brown, Dad had called them. Although she wasn't aware of it, her eyes sparkled when she smiled. A casual observer would often fail to notice her other features, which weren't so remarkable—a nose, a little too pointed, and rather full lips. Her skin was unusually smooth for a woman of thirty-five. Noting the sprinkling of freckles across her nose, which she'd hated as a child, she thought again of little Rusty Reardon. Hope he doesn't hate his freckles, she thought.

"I'm home, Mother," she called out. With her failing health, Charlotte Wyatt spent less time attending to household chores or working in the yard. She now filled her days reading or watching television. Lori laid her cap and purse on the hall table and poked her head in the living room. The room was empty, which meant her mother was probably upstairs resting—a sign she wasn't feeling well.

Charlotte had the large master bedroom on the south, overlooking a pond surrounded by huge spruces and flowering shrubs. Just to the left of the pond was a flower garden that contained a medley of perennials. Lori's father had put in the garden, but the task of nurturing the new life that exploded each spring had soon fallen on Lori. She had never really thought of tending the garden as a chore, however. Her father had taught her how to gently pull up the weeds surrounding the tiny new buds. Working in this little plot of land reminded Lori of him. It seemed John Wyatt had approached all facets of life gently. By late spring each year a rainbow of color emanated from the garden to greet the viewer's eye. In more recent years the most frequent spectator was Charlotte, who viewed the garden from her position by the bedroom window. Today, though, the drapes were tightly closed.

The furniture in the room was old-fashioned but good. "You can't go wrong with oak," was one of John Wyatt's precepts. He and Charlotte had bought the bedroom suite as newlyweds. As with most other things, John had been right. Since his death, Lori sometimes reflected on her dad's sagacity. To her, it seemed the only times John had used poor judgment were in matters involving his wife, whom he adored.

"Are you not feeling well?" asked Lori as she entered the room.

"I'm having one of my migraines," Charlotte replied. "It came on right after lunch. My stomach got upset first. I think there were too many onions in that soup you made. You know they don't agree with me so why you insist on putting them in, I don't know," she added in a plaintive voice.

Lori snapped on the bedside lamp. Her mother was propped up on several pillows with a wet washcloth over her eyes. Like Lori, she had always been slender, but in the last few years she'd lost a lot of weight, and her skin hung loosely on her small frame. Her hair during the past few years had also turned quite white, and as if to add to the picture of a woman in pain, hung in pitiful clumps around her lined face.

"I didn't put any onions in the soup, Mother. It must have been something else, or perhaps you have a touch of that flu that's been going around."

Lori laid her hand on her mother's shoulder. "Why don't you try to get up?" she pleaded gently. "I'll fix you a nice cup of tea and a slice of Melba toast. Then we can take a little walk. The crisp air will make your head feel better." She grabbed Charlotte's robe off the chair by the bed and held it out to her.

"I don't feel like eating but maybe a cup of tea then," Charlotte answered with an air of resignation.

As Lori helped Charlotte into her robe and down the stairs, she chatted amiably, trying to get her mother's mind off her ailments. "It was the children's day at the library. They're so cute. Some of the things they ask! Emily Hamilton's son, Jordan, you know the youngest one, asked me if we had any books on white slavery. He said he'd heard his Uncle Al talking about it— said he didn't know there were white slaves, as well as black. He thought it would be an interesting subject for a report. I steered him in a different direction. He decided to do a report on President Lincoln and how he freed the slaves. I'd no more sent him on his way with a stack of books when Rebecca Hollingsworth wanted to know if we had any books on 'clustered' nuns..."

"I heard her Aunt Janice is in town again," Charlotte interrupted. "Seems she just shed her latest husband. How many times has she been married now? Is this the second or the third? From what I understand she doesn't even bother to take her husbands' names. I suppose she figures it's too much bother, since she won't be married that long."

"I think she's just been married twice," Lori replied.

"Well, whatever," Charlotte stated with disgust. "She's not even thirty yet. But with the Hollingsworth money, it's easy for her to just dump them whenever she gets a little bored; then run home to Daddy. Phoebe Gibbons said she's driving a brand new Monte Carlo. Probably Old Man Hollingsworth gave it to her to cheer her up. Poor little thing." This last was delivered with a note of sarcasm.

Lori pulled out a kitchen chair for her mother, trying to hide her look of exasperation. "We don't know why she left her husband, Mother," Lori tried to keep her voice calm. "For all we know he could have been a real bad apple, alcoholic or abusive."

"Not according to Phoebe," Charlotte stated with conviction. "Says she heard it nearly broke his heart—that he's a good man, worshipped the ground she walked on. She just got bored. That's it in a nutshell!"

Lori could have asked where Phoebe Gibbons received all this confidential information. The Hollingsworths and Gibbons had never been that close socially to her knowledge, but she thought it pointless to get into an argument.

She noticed, as her mother ate a slice of Melba toast, a scrambled egg, and applesauce, that she didn't mention her headache again. Charlotte did, however, beg off going for the walk since she was "feeling too poorly." Lori didn't press the issue. She was just happy to see her mother do more than pick at her food for a change.

While Charlotte finished her dinner, Lori made a quick trip to the living room. As she put a log in the fireplace and lit a fire, she made a mental note to have Mr. Jacobs deliver a new supply of wood. Over the weekend she'd brought in what was left from last winter, anticipating that with the already crisp nights, it was time for the winter ritual of a roaring fire in the evening.

"I have the fire going, so if you want to go into the living room, I'll join you as soon as I've cleaned up," she said cheerfully when she returned to the kitchen.

During the day the kitchen was the brightest room in the house. The ceilings had never been lowered as was the style, and this room was no exception. It would have been more practical to go with the modern trend, which helped conserve fuel, but the Wyatts felt the spacious effect of ten-foot ceilings was worth the added expense. The cupboards and woodwork were painted white and the walls were hung with white wallpaper, accented with bright green ivy. Crisp white organdy curtains trimmed in green framed the windows.

But with the nightfall the cheery atmosphere of the room vanished. Shadows draped themselves in lonely patterns across the walls. Lori noticed it was already quite dark out, another signal that summer was drawing to a close. Perhaps the coming of winter was contributing as much as anything to her feelings of discontent.

Even though she knew the warmth of the living room awaited her, Lori took a little longer than necessary to finish the dishes. From the sound of the television she knew her mother was already watching one of her programs. She knew Charlotte liked to watch them with her, that after being alone all day she needed companionship. But sometimes she wished their conversations could be a little more stimulating. The old feelings of guilt bobbed into her mind. *How can I be such a terrible person? I'm young and in good health. I wouldn't be here if it weren't for Mother. And giving birth to me was a great sacrifice.*

John had wanted a family but was afraid his fragile, little wife wouldn't be able to stand the trauma of childbirth. Charlotte's one pregnancy had been accidental, and she had almost died when Lori was born, something Charlotte didn't try to hide. In fact, in the days following her husband's death, she seemed to make a point of bringing the subject up.

Lori had just started her second year of college at Boulder when she'd been called home. Her father had suffered a massive heart attack and had died within minutes. Lori had thought then and since of the irony of life. Her mother was supposedly the one with a weak heart, due to a bout with rheumatic fever as a child.

Lori had idolized her father, and her need to stay busy was a blessing. Everything had fallen on her young shoulders. There was the estate to settle, as well as making arrangements for the crops to be harvested. She'd spent long days tormenting herself about the farm her father had worked so hard to preserve. Although she loved the land almost as much as he, her dream was to become a writer, to work on a large city newspaper. So once the crops were harvested and sold, Lori had talked to her neighbor about the leasing arrangement.

In addition to the farmland adjacent to the house, the estate included almost two thousand acres of raw land north of town, which had been acquired by her grandfather. The surface of this land had always been leased for grazing. In addition to the herds of cows that occupied the area, some fifty oil wells were spaced across the fields, about a third of them now no longer producing.

When Lori's grandfather leased the mineral rights, he had retained a base royalty of twelve and a half percent and her father had inherited this royalty. Then when John died, the land had gone to Charlotte along with the farm, but John stipulated in his will that the oil royalty should go to his daughter. Although the money realized from leasing the eighty acres of farmland to their neighbor didn't amount to much, Charlotte made enough off the larger grazing leases to live comfortably enough in the small town of Platte Valley. And because of the oil royalties, Lori would be able to continue her education.

With the estate settled and with everything at home finally under control, she made plans to return to school the following semester. When it came close to the time for her to leave, however, Charlotte literally seemed to fall apart. Lori hadn't been able to get her mother out of bed without a lot of coaxing. Charlotte had been totally dependent on her husband all those years and was terrified of being left on her own. Once again Lori had postponed her return, telling herself she would eventually be able to go back.

She knew her only hope was for her mother to become more self-sufficient, so she'd put a plan into action. Charlotte had never even written a check, so Lori patiently explained the rudiments of maintaining a bank account to her. She talked to Mrs. Jacobs next door about the possibility of enlisting her help. If their neighbor could do the weekly shopping and perhaps some cooking and cleaning, Lori felt her mother would be all right. Mrs. Jacobs had been receptive. She said since the kids were all gone, it would give her something to do and that she could use a little extra money to buy things for her new grandchild. Mrs. Jacobs' daughter, Beth, had just given birth to her first child and in so doing had given her mother her first grandchild. It was hard to believe that little Jared was now in high school and that there were three younger children at home.

Lori had finally admitted her plan wasn't working. As the months went by Charlotte seemed no closer to managing the household accounts than she'd ever been. And when Lori approached her about Mrs. Jacobs coming in to help, she refused to even discuss it, beyond saying she couldn't afford such luxuries and that she'd just have to do these chores herself. Since Charlotte didn't drive, Lori knew she wouldn't be able to manage this. So another semester had come and gone. Then one day when she was checking out books at the library, Jon's mother, Mrs. Moran, who was then librarian, asked if she'd like to come to work part time at the library.

It hadn't been a mistake, Lori reasoned. Books were her great love, and she enjoyed working with them. Perhaps her voracious appetite for reading had been an escape, the result of a lonely childhood, the knowledge that somehow she was different from other children. If it hadn't been for Sarah, who had taken the quiet little misfit under her wing, Lori would never have been included in anything.

Now, since Mrs. Moran's retirement five years ago, Lori was in full charge of the library and felt with her promotion she'd come into her own. She even felt her writing courses at the university helped in her work.

After placing the last clean dish in the cupboard, Lori joined her mother in the living room. They often viewed a game show together. Charlotte sat in a recliner that was a match to the one in her bedroom. After her husband's death she'd had his moved up to her room. After twenty years, they were still serviceable. The other furniture in the room had once belonged to John's parents. Lori's usual spot was an antique rocker, which had been re-caned a few years back. After the game show was over, Charlotte watched whatever the evenings potpourri of "sit-coms" happened to be, while Lori quietly picked up a book. Through practice she'd managed to block out the voices from the television. She knew her mother needed her company, but she couldn't digest a full menu of the mediocre programs, which were the usual fare.

Currently she had developed a taste for James Joyce. She had read *Ulysses* in college and had worked her way through it again; then moved on to his other works. She could, without even thinking, offer the proper response to Charlotte's running comments during a given program. For instance, an "I definitely agree," seemed to suffice quite well. Or an "I can't believe he (she) would do such a thing!" covered a whole legion of the actors' various escapades.

Tonight Lori found her mind wandering. The lines of Robert Frost's poem, "The Road Not Taken," kept running through her mind. Was her life really all that great or was she just fooling herself? It was true she loved her job, but circumstances had forced her into a role she had never envisioned. Instead of having a career as a journalist, leading an independent life in a city where this was possible, she was living in the house her parents lived in when she was born, working at a small town library, and acting as caretaker to a difficult woman. To the town's inhabitants she knew she was seen as a prudish little spinster. She'd even wound up in the profession usually associated with old maids.

And yet she'd never really had a choice. She sensed her father, because he loved his wife so much, had been blind to many of her faults. But more than that, he'd known it was his duty to carry most of the load and had he lived, he'd have continued to do so. With his premature death, it had been up to her to carry on. To do anything else would have been to betray him.

Later, as Lori lay in her bed, she was still mulling over the course her life had taken. But realizing such introspection was futile; she turned over and tried to think of more pleasant things. Her mind turned to Rusty. What a darling little boy! But then it dawned on her that meeting him could be the cause of her unrest. She was thirty-five years old. If she had married at the usual time, she could have had a son about his age. A tear slid down her cheek and burying her face in her pillow, she uttered a muffled plea, *Daddy, Daddy, why did you have to die? How different things might have been if you were still here.*

Chapter 3 - Blake

"Hi, Mitzi. You're looking younger and more beautiful all the time. What's your secret?"

Mitzi, secretary to the president of Pierce Petroleum Company, who was about forty pounds overweight, looked up from her desk. "Okay Blake, what do you want?" she asked good-naturedly.

The handsome face of Blake Johnson assumed an injured look. "I'm hurt that you'd think a sincere compliment may be a ploy to get you to do something for me."

Mitzi laughed. "You're good. If there were no mirrors to tell me I've gained twenty pounds since I saw you, I may just believe you."

"I meant every word I said. If you've gained some weight it's most becoming. Now, just to show you how wrong you are, I'm not going to say another word until the execution team, I mean the executive team in there, summons me."

He started to walk toward the plush furniture across the room, but turned. "Just one little question. You don't happen to know what this is all about do you?"

"If I did, I swear I'd tell you. But you know how those guys are. When they have these top level meetings it's all hush-hush."

"Okay," he said. "I'll just have to wait like a lamb going to the slaughter."

Blake walked over to one of the chairs in the executive waiting room and picked up a magazine off the coffee table. Opening it to a story about the hearings on the Clinton campaign abuses, he couldn't concentrate. He felt a little empathy for the President, since he was beginning to know what it felt like to be in the hot seat.

His eyes wondered aimlessly around the large room. Everything here spoke of money and power from the thick, trendy carpeting to the large brass wall hangings, the work of a leading contemporary artist. Up until now everything had gone according to plan. Since joining the company five years ago, he had steadily risen in its ranks, carving out for himself a place ever closer to the top echelons of the organization, to being one of those men behind the closed door. Although he was physically only a room's length away from this inner circle, he felt a great distance separated them. Ironically, a week ago, although he'd been thousands of miles from here, he'd felt much closer. Blake was in charge of the operations in Argentina, and things had been running smoothly until last Tuesday when Tom Ralston had come to his office.

"I won't stand for it," Ralston shouted in an angry voice. "What kind of a game are you playing? I paid you in good faith."

Blake was sitting at his desk, but Ralston refused the seat offered him, choosing instead to pace back and forth. "You told me the low bid was six million, and I underbid it by 500,000 thousand. And you still wind up giving the contract to my competition."

Tom Ralston owned a construction company. Today his ruddy complexion was several shades redder than normal. Blake had a fleeting thought that the man, who was overweight and subject to high blood pressure, might keel over right there in his office. It would certainly ruin his evening at the club if he had to stick around until the body was disposed of.

"How much did they pay you?" Ralston continued to yell. "Well, this time you've gone too far. I have my reservations made. I'm going back to the States and fill in the big boys about your operations."

Blake felt a cold sweat across his upper body but tried to assume a nonchalant posture. Ralston was tough, but he'd had a lot of experience dealing with clods like him. "You've got me all wrong, Ralston," he responded gently, as though to an unreasonable child. "I've always come through for you in the past but this time it was beyond my control. Those guys had me in a vise and were beginning to turn the screws. Stick with me and I'll make it up to you. We're starting work on this new project in the Golfo San Jorge basin the first of the year, and we're talking big money this time."

He got up from his chair and walking around his desk, put his arm on Ralston's beefy shoulder. "We've done business together a long time. It's been a mutually beneficial relationship, hasn't it? Just give it some time, think it over before you decide to do something that may be detrimental. And

I'm not talking about damaging for me. My bosses in Chicago are well aware of everything I do here. There are no secrets. They're very pleased with the way the project is being handled. What I'm trying to say is, as an old friend, I'm concerned about you. I can't in good faith do business with you if you try to undermine me with my company."

Blake could have sworn he had the man back in his pocket. The sagging jowls inhabiting Ralston's face had even crinkled into a semblance of a smile as he left Blake's office. Giving him the key to the company's suite in Buenos Aires for a weekend holiday had been a good touch. But two days ago Blake had gotten a call from Bill Grimes, Pierce's top aide, asking him to return to Chicago immediately. Grimes' voice had been cool.

Blake gave up trying to read the article about Clinton, tossing the magazine back on the table. When Mitzi's phone buzzed, he jumped. "Yes, Sir," she said into the receiver. "I'll send him in."

"We have now begun boarding for Flight 702 to Denver International Airport at Gate 57," said the generic voice over the loudspeaker. First class passengers may begin boarding, as well as those passengers with small children or those needing special assistance."

Blake picked up his attaché case and jacket and moved briskly toward the gate. As he walked, a number of heads turned his way, most of which belonged to females. It wasn't just his blonde, Nordic good looks, for he was by any standards a most attractive young man. He stood at just under six feet, with broad shoulders and a stomach that advertised the advantages of daily workouts and a sensible diet. But beyond this, there was an aura of confidence emanating from Blake. It came from somewhere deep within, an inborn trait worn as easily as his expensive Armani suits. He seemed unaware of the admiring glances coming his way, which added to his charming demeanor.

Or perhaps it was just that he was preoccupied. He had been given much food for thought during these last few weeks. He hadn't been fired, that word was not part of the vocabulary at the prestigious executive offices of Pierce Petroleum Company. Euphemisms such as re-engineering and downsizing were terms currently in vogue at Pierce.

He'd been called home from the company's drilling operations in South America and questioned about contracts with some of the companies on their projects there. It seemed, just as he had surmised, his efforts to appease Ralston had been unsuccessful. During the past few days there had been an investigation into some of the other contracts he'd made. The investigation turned up reported kickbacks he'd received for accepting contractors' bids.

Now as he boarded the flight to Denver, he was still in a slight state of shock. Where had the company been during the last century, for God's sake? he asked himself for the hundredth time. They've been players in the international market for years. Didn't they understand this was a common practice? No, Blake's confidence in himself and his methods hadn't been altered by the shocking decision of the board to quietly terminate him. Oh, they'd been real gentlemen about it, given him six months severance pay and a promise of good references, but it still meant he was out on the street at a time when it wasn't easy to find a position approaching this one.

But defeat wasn't a word in Blake's vocabulary. Even before the final decision had been handed down, the wheels in his well-calibrated mind were spinning—faster and faster down a road that could lead him to greater wealth than he'd ever have realized at Pierce.

Throwing his attaché case in the overhead compartment, he sat down and fastened his seat belt. He'd planned to do some calculations on his laptop during the trip, but he couldn't help noticing the attractive young lady in the seat next to him. Although he still had a lot to think about, plans to make, he decided he could use a pleasant diversion. "So what is a nice girl like you doing on a plane to Denver?" he asked with the dazzling smile usually reserved for members of the opposite sex.

The woman, who'd been absorbed in a book, looked up and coolly appraised the man who was to be her companion for the next two hours. Evidently she liked what she saw. "I'm just going to visit an old college classmate," she answered. "But since we aren't really all that close, I don't have to spend all my time with her."

Blake didn't miss the provocative way she looked at him, picking that moment to cross her long, nylon-clad legs.

"This is my friend and former classmate, Debbie. Debbie, Blake Johnson. He's traveling through on his way to visit his parents in Platte Valley," Denise explained.

The only light in the room he'd just entered, other than that emanating from the television set, was a lamp, so Blake was unable to get a good look at the young woman sitting on the sofa. He did get the impression that she was a little on the heavy side, and his interest, which had been slightly kindled at the thought of meeting another eligible woman, quickly waned. A large bulldog lying by her feet, raised his head for a moment, but like Blake, quickly lost interest and with a huge yawn lowered it to it's former position and closed his eyes.

"Nice to meet you, Blake, although I'm a little jealous. Here I am again on a Saturday night with just my dog, Jasper, for company. Denise blows into town this afternoon and already she has a date. It just isn't fair." Debbie gave a huge sigh. "Only kidding, really," she added. "Tonight's my night to do my nails and catch up on my mending. I look forward to it all week."

Debbie recommended the Buckhorn Exchange as a fun place to eat with good food. Blake remembered going there during his younger days and decided, since it was somewhere he was familiar with, this historic restaurant was a good choice.

After living away from the area for almost twenty years, he was open to suggestions. He'd picked-up his rental car at the airport and followed Denise's directions to Debbie's place without incident. But he'd noticed numerous changes due to the city's tremendous growth and didn't want to press his luck.

Henry "Shorty Scout" Zietz, one of Buffalo Bill Cody's famed bands of scouts, founded the Buckhorn back in 1893. Denise seemed enthralled by the atmosphere. The restaurant had a huge collection of animal trophies collected by the Zietz family and the walls of the Victorian lounge were adorned with Old West memorabilia. As they enjoyed cocktails and dinner, folk artists singing ballads of the West entertained them.

They both decided on baby-back pork ribs as an entrée. Then during after-dinner drinks, Denise gave Blake a brief autobiographical sketch. She was a buyer for Marshall Fields in Chicago. Recently, she'd ended a long-term relationship with a broker and seemed, from a few pointed remarks, to be trying a little too hard to replace him. Blake, on the other hand, had no desire for a serious relationship. It wasn't in his plans.

Denise wore a formfitting outfit that didn't leave one guessing much as to what lay underneath. As Blake sipped his vermouth, the pleasant libation began to do its work and he began to relax. I just might have to postpone my drive to Platte Valley, he thought. After what I've been through, I deserve it. And Denise will be going back to her job in Chicago, a city I have no interest in returning to any time soon. That should keep the situation from getting sticky. With a little luck I can get inside her panties tonight and be on my way in the morning.

"I almost took a later flight," he said, taking her hand and looking deeply into her eyes. "But I'm glad I didn't. I'm usually pretty cynical but I feel some things are meant to be. What I'm trying to say is that I enjoy being with you and don't want this evening to end."

Denise returned his gaze. Her look said she was open to whatever possibilities he came up with.

He figured if he could get a few more drinks into her, she would be ripe for the picking. "Guess we should have asked Debbie what the current hot spots are around here," he said. But remembering the plain, overweight girl settled in for an evening of television, he added, "Come to think of it, she doesn't seem the type to enjoy an extensive night life."

"My friend may seem like a real country girl," answered Denise, "but she's actually pretty sophisticated. She's a homebody more from lack of opportunity than from choice. But I'm not interested in discussing the deficiencies of Debbie's social life." Her eyes held a challenge. "To put it bluntly, I have my own digs at her place, private and upstairs. Debbie's room is on the main level. That is if you're game?"

"What are we waiting for?" he asked, as he signaled the waiter for the check.

When they arrived back at Debbie's apartment, Denise wasted little time saying goodnight to her roommate, who was watching *Saturday Night Live*. Blake followed her upstairs. As she switched on a lamp by the bed, he noticed the guest room wasn't large. Since a queen-size waterbed took up most of the space, there wasn't much room for any additional furniture. Debbie had managed to fit in a small dresser as well as a rocker, which Blake sat down on. He was in no hurry to make a move, preferring to let Denise take the lead. Unless things had changed within the last month or so, it wouldn't take her long.

Blake knew that women found him attractive, and most of the time, he basked in the knowledge. He was a healthy, young male, and the availability of women made it easy to appease his sexual appetite. But once in awhile this "talent" backfired. The wives of some of his colleagues and bosses had propositioned him, and a fling in the sack when the lady was good-looking held a certain excitement for him. Unfortunately, not all of these passionate ladies appealed to him, and he sometimes had to do some fancy footwork to gracefully ward off their advances.

Still, he wouldn't have traded places with some of his male friends, whom he knew envied him his allure for the opposite sex. He had never quite forgiven his parents for being less than wealthy, but he was at least grateful they'd given him the means to launch himself into the good life. Along with his looks, which seemed to give him an edge over an equally capable but less attractive peer, he'd been endowed with a keen mind and an aptitude for math, which had made him a natural for his career as an engineer.

Denise stood by the bed and stripped off her black mini skirt and sweater, revealing a sexy black bra and panty hose. An amused smile crossed Blake's face. Nope, old man, you haven't lost your touch, he thought, as he watched her quickly remove her bra and begin to peel off her panty hose. As she moved toward him, he realized she was taller than he'd thought as she sat beside him on the airplane. Aroused, he stood up and reached for her. Her body, as he pressed against it felt firm but supple, an appealing combination. He pressed his mouth roughly on hers and could feel the hunger in her as she responded, easing him toward the bed.

On Wednesday morning neither of them stirred until after ten. Blake had called his parents on Sunday and told them he'd be home later that day. But he kept putting it off. He couldn't seem to tear himself away from the recreation area, which doubled as Debbie's guest room. He rationalized that this was something he'd earned. He'd been too serious during the days following the loss of his job. But when he awoke, Blake felt it was time to "face the music."

"My mom doesn't worry me. I could be found guilty of mass murder, and she'd still be there for me, refusing to admit I've done anything wrong. But Dad's a different story." Just thinking about his father caused a tightness in his chest. He knew his father wouldn't be concerned that something had happened to him. No, his dad would be pissed at Blake for worrying his mother. In the elder Johnson's eyes, not showing up when one was expected was a sign of immaturity.

"But I don't want you to leave," Denise wailed. They'd just spent another pleasurable night in bed. Hadn't even bothered with dinner, other than to order in pizza. Debbie had left for work at seven that morning.

When Blake didn't answer, Denise sighed. "Well, at least let me fix you breakfast before I send you to the wolves."

She bounced out of bed and threw on a sexy negligee. After she left the room, Blake went to the bathroom to shower and shave. When he emerged, dressed in chino slacks and a blue cotton sweater, the aroma of frying bacon greeted his nostrils. He hurriedly threw his shaving kit in his suitcase and joined Denise in the kitchen.

Sitting at the table watching her move gracefully around the room as he sipped a cup of steaming, black coffee, he thought this was just the reprieve he'd needed. But now it was back to work—on with the plan.

"Why can't you stay just one more day?" Denise pleaded as she served his breakfast. She'd fixed waffles to go with the bacon.

Blake eyed her breasts, which were plainly visible through the thin negligee, with appreciation. It was his turn to sigh. "Because I told them I'd be home Sunday and by now Mom's probably fit to be tied. I should have called her when I decided to stay longer. You know how it is with mothers. There's no way I can postpone going home any longer. Besides, I think Debbie is starting to be a little put out. She wasn't her usual, bubbly self last night, you'll have to admit."

"Screw Debbie. As she said, she's just jealous, and I don't really care. I've met the most desirable man I've know in years, and I don't want you to go," Denise said with a pout.

"I said I'd be in touch, didn't I?" Why did they always have to get like this? A toss in the sack, and they think they own you. "I'll be back in Denver in a couple of days, and we can take up right where we left off. You said you could extend your vacation another week, didn't you? After I check in at home, I'll tell my folks I have to come back here on business." He got up and stood behind her, pressing up against her and giving her neck a little lick.

"Don't start that, or I'll never let you get out of here," she said with a groan.

Blake called home on his cell phone as he left Debbie's house and managed to pacify his mother. He could make up the most absurd stories and his naïve little mother usually fell for them. It was late afternoon before his rented Thunderbird pulled up in front of his parents' home. Betty Johnson was in the front yard spreading mulch on her flowerbed. When she saw Blake getting out of the car with his bags, she dropped her rake. "Dad, he's here," she yelled, "Our boy's finally home." Then she ran toward the car with open arms.

Bud Johnson didn't come out of the house when his wife called. After Blake had given his mom an ample supply of hugs, he followed her into the house carrying his suitcases.

Blake noticed the old cheap living room furniture was gone, replaced by new cheap furniture. He couldn't remember the wallpaper in the living and dining rooms, but supposed these rooms had been repapered since he'd left. The pattern was still too garish for his taste. He was impressed, however, to notice the old heavy, pinch pleated drapes were gone and that his parents, in a wild moment of abandon, had replaced them with modern vertical blinds.

He smiled to himself, thinking he was fortunate to have parents who were thrifty. Even though the farm implement store his father owned and operated had never been hugely profitable, his folks had, no doubt, managed to put some money back.

"Your old room is ready," Betty said as he followed her up the stairs. "We didn't do anything with it for the longest time. Then finally decided that even if, I mean when, you came home, you'd probably not want the old wallpaper with all the football pennants on it, anyhow. So we had it repapered. Penney's had this half-price sale, so we bought a new bedspread and curtains. We made it into a kind of guest room. Not that we have that many guests, just your Uncle Curt and Aunt Louise once a year. You remember, they always come in the summer."

He was only half listening to her. He had forgotten how she did seem to go on, and he was wondering about his father. "Dad is here, isn't he?

"Yes, after you called he took off work a little early. He didn't want to. You know what a workaholic he is. But I said, 'Bud Johnson, your son's coming home after being away all those years, and you certainly are going to be here.' He's probably out in the garage tinkering as usual."

"I'll go out and see," Blake said, throwing his luggage on the bed and giving her another quick hug.

He walked down the stairs and out the back door. The familiar path leading to the garage was lined with marigolds and pansies, the same flowers his mom had always planted. "Hi, Dad..How's it going?" he asked, as he walked through the side door.

Bud Johnson was standing at his workbench and didn't turn around. It looked like some kind of disassembled motor spread out on the workbench. "All right," he answered.

"It's good to be home. The old place never changes, does it?"

"Some things have changed. We're getting older."

Blake walked over to his father and stood beside him. Bud's physical appearance seemed to give testimony to his words. His hair was thinner than Blake remembered, his face heavily wrinkled. *It's been over ten years since I've seen him*, he reminded himself. The older man had never been large, but he seemed smaller now, perhaps because Blake now saw him at a different vantage point than as a child.

"Well, you're looking good." He felt the old awkwardness, which only

37

his father could arouse. He wanted to reach out and put his hand on the older man's shoulder but thought better of it. Bud's lips were drawn in a tight line, his back stiff and uninviting.

There was a long moment of silence, and when he finally did speak, it was to ask in a bitter voice, "What does bring you back, Blake?" This time he did turn and look at his son, his eyes cold. "Your mother's been pretty upset through the years. Her only son, and he can't bother to come and see her. She has a grandson she's never even seen."

Blake remembered the piercing look from his boyhood days, a look that made him flinch. But this time he wouldn't. He had spent many years learning the art of being in control of a situation. He did admit to himself that his dad was a tougher case than any of the big executives he'd had to deal with through the years.

"I wanted to get back, and I did send you and Mom tickets to come to Chicago several times…"

"Once. We came to your wedding and that was it. Not that we needed to be sent tickets, but as I recall when your mother approached the subject of a visit, she was put off with some excuse—'We're getting ready to leave for a vacation in Hawaii, or we just got back from Switzerland and haven't had a chance to settle back in yet.'"

"That wasn't all that was going on. My job kept me pretty busy. Someone had to pay for the vacations, which by the way weren't my idea. Then the last few years I've been working in South America. 'While the cat's away, the mouse will play,' they say. Andrea was having a great time from what I understand. It was a long bitter divorce. It took me awhile to recuperate, financially and emotionally, but I've slowly been getting back on my feet. Anyhow, I'm here now. And I want to spend some time with you, make up for the remissions of the past."

He didn't think this was the time to tell his father he was no longer employed. Not that he ever planned to tell him the whole story, just that his stay here in Platte Valley might be for longer than just a visit. Could, in fact, be permanent. Break it to him gently, in small pieces, he told himself. Then when I have him softened up, tell him I need some money to get started on my new venture. Convince him it will make them rich. He may have to sell the store, but so what? It's time for the old man to start thinking about retirement.

Bud merely looked at his son; then went back to what he was doing. He picked up a part and placed it against another one, beginning to screw them together. Soon he was completely absorbed in his task, seemingly forgetting his son's presence or that he even had a son.

Chapter 4 - Joe

The scream came from somewhere close by, and it was horrible. But what awoke him were the small animal-like sounds that followed. Someone or something was in terrible pain. At first he thought it was Norma, but as he sat up in bed fully awake now, he knew the noises had come from him. He was having the dream again, the one about her. In the dream she had been screaming, too, but then she stopped—as the man pulled the rope tighter and tighter around her neck.

Joe was covered with sweat. He got out of bed and walked to the bathroom. He filled a cup with water and sat on the side of his bed as he drank it. A small wind-up alarm clock stood on the stand by his bed. He had never set the alarm. In the outside world, where people bustled to this place or that and kept tight schedules, it was necessary. Here it was not. The face of the clock was luminous. The big hand was straight up and the small one was on the three. Joe sighed and lay back down, but he knew his night's sleep was over.

"You can go in now, Joe." Mrs. Groves smiled at the man sitting across from her. He got up from his chair and shuffled past her desk without returning the smile. He was a tall, slender man in his late forties with thinning brown hair. His features were even, his face almost handsome, but something was amiss. He had a nervous twitch, and his eyes, dark in color, had a haunted look to them, as if they had seen things no human should have witnessed. His shoulders were hunched in the green cotton suit he was wearing. It was the uniform for inmates.

The new doctor was standing at his office door. He held out his hand. "Hello, I'm Dr. Heffner," he said.

Joe didn't respond. He walked across the room and sat down on the beige couch, the same one that had been there for the fifteen years he'd been coming to this office. There were two other doctors who had used this office before Dr. Heffner. Each had told Joe they were there to help him get well.

Dr. Heffner sat behind a big desk with an open file on it. There were several pictures on the desk, one of a woman and two boys and the others of just the boys in baseball uniforms. The doctor was asking him something, but Joe was having trouble making the words into sentences. His eyes darted back and fourth from the desk to the large bookcases. There were probably hundreds or maybe even a thousand books in the cases. Joe had tried to count them as he sat in this same spot through the years, but he usually couldn't get past twenty before the noises started coming and made him forget what number he was on. He remembered other books with bright covers, the ones he'd used when he was a child in school. He'd liked reading back then, but mostly he liked the pictures. He'd made it to the ninth grade before they flunked him out. But then he'd gotten the letter from the draft board, and they sent him to Vietnam. He hadn't been able to read much since. The noises in his head made it too hard.

The books in the cases here had dark covers, blues and grays. They were all doctor books. Sometimes the doctors looked in the books when Joe said something and sometimes they said "Hmmm."

Joe's eyes traveled past the bookcases to the large window. This one didn't have bars on it, and it was easier to see out. He could see the tops of the big trees, the same ones he saw close-up when he went for walks on the grounds. He liked to be outside, especially now when the flowers were so pretty. They wouldn't let you pick the flowers, but they were pretty to look at.

When he stood by the fence, Joe could see woods off in the distance. He thought there were probably flowers in the woods you could pick, wild flowers like in the woods at home. But you couldn't get to them 'cause of the fences. They didn't even want you to touch the fences, and he always tried to obey the rules.

"Joe, please concentrate. Look at me."

Joe made his eyes move to the doctor. Dr. Heffner looked like a kind man. He had a small mustache and goatee, both dark like his hair but flecked with gray. He was average size, nothing much stood out about him except for the bright blue eyes, which were looking at Joe intently. What had the doctor before looked like? Joe suddenly couldn't remember.

"How have you been sleeping?" Dr. Heffner asked.

"I've been sleeping all right."

"I've read through your file. I understand that sometimes you have dreams that wake you up. Have you been having these dreams lately?"

Joe's face twitched. He was visibly agitated. "Yeah, the dreams is still real bad, and they wake me up sometimes."

"In the file it says you often dream about Vietnam. Is it always the same dream?"

"Yeah, the one where I'm in the fox hole, and the Cong comes through the trees at us." Beads of sweat appeared on Joe's forehead. His eyes began to dart around the room again, as if he were looking for some way to escape.

"The one where your buddy gets killed?"

"Yeah." Joe's eyes lit on the window once again.

"Would you go over the dream with me? I know you've told the other doctors, but I would really like it if you could tell me. It's the best way I can help you, even though it must be difficult."

Joe moved his eyes back to the doctor's face. The furrows in his forehead became visible, signaling his effort to comply with the doctor's request. Finally in a voice, which was almost a monotone, he began. "We'd been marching for two days. At night we'd dig the trenches, but you couldn' sleep, leastwise not for long. The leeches and 'skeeters was everywhere and then you was just scared. I think maybe on that night I must of slept some though."

"Sorry to interrupt, but was this the dream yet, or are you just leading up to the dream?"

"Just leading up to the dream."

"So what you're telling me is the way it was in real life."

"Yeah, it really happened like this."

"I see. Proceed then. You said you thought you fell asleep."

"Yeah, 'cause the first thing I knowed they was all around us, and everyone was yelling. Someone yelled 'Cong,' or 'fire,' or both. The noise was awful. There was so much going on, I didn' know he'd got hit. He was standing there right next to me. After it was over, I looked down and he was laying there, blood all over the place. He must of died right off. I never even heard him yell, or maybe I just didn' hear 'cause of all the noise. We was buddies ever since basic at Fort Carson. He was the best friend I'd had in my whole life. In my hometown, Platte Valley, my dad was a junk collector. The other kids didn' want to get too close."

Dr. Heffner was following along from the file. "But when you dream about him, it's different. He doesn't die instantly." It was a statement rather than a question.

"Nope. He has blood all over him like in real life, but he ain't dead yet. He's talking to me. He's asking me why I didn' look after him. He says I was his buddy and I didn' do my job. You see. I was older. I was nineteen, but he lied about his age to get in. He was just seventeen. I called him 'Lil Bro.'"

"But you did everything you could, didn't you?"

"Yeah, yeah I guess so. I can't remember. I remember being scared, more scared than I'd ever been. I just froze up. I don't remember if I fired my rifle. But I guess I did 'cause there was no shells left in it."

Dr. Heffner studied the file for a few minutes. "How about the other dream? Have you had that dream, lately?"

"You mean the one at the lake, where Norma gets murdered?"

"Yes, that dream."

Joe looked down and seemed to be studying his feet. Finally, he said, "Yeah, sometimes I have that dream, too."

"Is it still the same?"

"Yeah, it's always pretty much the same."

"Tell me about it."

He didn't like to talk about the dreams. It was bad enough during the night when he woke up in a cold sweat sobbing like he'd done last night. During the day he liked to forget about them. But he knew that Dr. Heffner was trying to help him. "I don' know what—how do I start it?"

"First tell me about how it was in real life, the part about how you happened to be at the lake."

"Okay. How I was out at the lake was 'cause I followed her out there. I'm on my bike, but I sees her get in a car with this guy. He picks her up at her house. I didn' know where they was going, and I couldn' keep up even though I pedaled real fast."

"Why were you following her?"

"I was following her 'cause I liked her and 'cause I thought she might be in some trouble. She was real nice. Most people in Platte Valley wasn't so nice to me, 'specially since I got back from 'Nam. They acted like they was scared or something."

"You knew she was married, didn't you?"

"Yeah, I knowed that. But she said that she liked me better than anyone, even her husband. And she was pretty. She said we could go out on a date sometime."

"How did you know she went to the lake?"

"I didn' for sure. I just guessed it. They was going that direction. I thought they had either went to Fort Morgan or out to the lake. I like it out there anyways, so I just decided to go on out there."

"And when you got there, you saw them?"

"I sees the car parked right in front of the lake. They was inside talking. I couldn' hear nothing."

"Did they know you were there?"

"Nope. I'd got off my bike and hid back of a tree, and I stayed there real quiet."

"Why? Why did you hide?"

"I don' know. I didn' know who this guy is. I knowed he wasn' from around Platte Valley. I wanted to see what was going on."

"You thought she had another boyfriend, someone whom she liked better than you?"

"No." Joe's voice grew louder. He was on his feet.

"It's all right, Joe." Dr. Heffner came around and put his hand on Joe's shoulder, easing him back down to the sofa. "Sit down," he said in a soothing tone.

"Well, maybe I did. And I didn' like it, but I was worried about her too."

"What happened next?"

"I could see them fighting. I could hear her yelling." A look of terror came over his face.

"Go on."

"She gets out of the car and was running and screaming real loud. She kind of stumbles and goes down, and he grabs her. She says to him, 'Please, please don't,' but he grabs her around the neck. He has this rope or something and chokes her for a long time. Then he lets go, and she falls on the ground and don' get up."

"What did you do?"

"I ran. I didn' even get on my bike. I just ran and ran."

"But in the dream, it was different?"

"Yeah, in the dream I goes over to her. The guy has got in the car and left. And I goes over and she's laying there, but she ain't dead yet." He stopped and put his hands over his face.

"What happened then?"

He took his hands off his face. His eyes were filled with tears. "She's saying something, but I can't hear 'cause she's just whispering, so I kneels down and puts my ear close to her mouth, and she says 'I was your girl, Joe. Why didn' you look after me?'"

Joe sat and sobbed. Dr. Heffner didn't say anything for a moment. Then he said in a firm but kind voice, "This dream is different than the way it happened in real life, Joe. You are the man who chokes her in real life. The man in the dream, the stranger, is really you. Until you can accept this, your chances of getting well are not good."

Joe jumped up again and started flailing his arms. "No, no, I didn' choke her. She was a nice lady. She was nice to me. I didn' choke her." His voice grew louder. "It was the stranger. He was a bad man. I tried to tell 'em, but they never did believe me."

He had started pacing around the room, fists clenched.

Dr. Heffner lifted the receiver from the phone on his desk. In a short time two orderlies appeared. They took Joe's arms and led him from the room.

Chapter 5 - Lori

"Hi there, Melora."

Lori looked up at the man standing on her porch. She hadn't realized it, but he had the same hazel eyes as those of the small boy standing beside him. The last time she'd seen him his hair had been about the same color as Rusty's, but it was now almost completely gray. He looked a little older than his forty-five years, perhaps because of the gray hair and because his face was a little more lined than some of his contemporaries. His build was trim and somewhat muscular, though, and he wore his uniform well. The silver badge of the Fort Morgan Sheriff's Department shined on his chest. Lori noticed the pleasing crinkles around his eyes when he smiled. Yes, he has a nice face, she decided.

"Hello, Sheriff. I see you brought Rusty." Lori smiled down at the little boy. "Hi, Rusty. Are you ready for that computer lesson?"

"I sure am," he replied, his eyes dancing.

"I thought maybe we'd just go through some of the things a computer can do. The thing is, most people only use a small percentage of things it's capable of. Most of us use the word processor a lot and then there's a spreadsheet program. You can make charts from the information you put on a spread sheet."

She saw she was losing him, so added, "Some of this isn't so interesting, but it's important to know. I thought after I showed you some of these things, we could play a game."

The sheriff grinned at her, knowingly. "I'll leave you two to get on with the lesson. I just wanted to make sure Rusty had gotten it right; that you really did say it was okay to bring him by. Sometimes his enthusiasm gets in the way of his perception of what was actually said. In other words I didn't want him to be making a nuisance of himself."

"Rusty did get it right this time. I'm enthusiastic about computers myself, and I'm happy to share what little I know with such an eager pupil."

"How about if you give me a call when you're finished? I'll be in my car this morning, but you can reach me on my radio by calling the dispatcher at the department." He handed her a card. "This is the non-emergency number," he explained.

Lori smiled after him as he walked toward his patrol car. He might look a little worn around the edges, but he seemed a much happier man these days. She remembered how he used to come to the library after his wife's death. He'd sit for hours pouring over the limited supply of law books. Lori heard he spent time at the larger library in Fort Morgan as well and even made trips to the law library in Denver. He'd been obsessed, as if he himself were the prosecutor in Norma's murder case, when at the time he was only a clerk at Johnson's Farm Implement Company. He'd been polite in those days, but Lori never saw him smile that she could recall, not even once.

"Um—I was just wondering where your computer is."

Lori looked down at Rusty, a little startled. She realized she'd been wool gathering. "I'm sorry, Rusty. I was just thinking how nice your grandpa looks in his uniform. You must be very proud of him."

"Yeah, I guess. Can we work on the computer now?"

"We sure can," Lori answered, leading him to her office in the back of the house.

"Did you hear the news about Janice Hollingsworth being back?" Sarah, who usually ran about five minutes late, had stridden breathlessly into Dora's Diner. She'd barely sat down in the booth across from Lori before conveying this news item.

"You forget, I have a direct line from Phoebe Gibbons through Mother," Lori answered dryly. "I'm sure Phoebe had her radar out to detect Janice as she drove into town. It was a couple of weeks ago, wasn't it?"

"Yeah, something like that," Sarah said, a little deflated. "Well, did you hear she's getting a divorce?"

"Yes. I heard that, too," Lori said in a tone of irritation. But seeing the hurt look on her friend's face, added, "I'm sorry, Sarah. It's just that I look forward to seeing you all week. We only have this one hour as a rule, so why do we have to discuss Janice Hollingsworth? I have to listen to this gossip at home. Phoebe seems to know everything that goes on with the Hollingsworths;

even that Mr. Hollingsworth bought Janice a brand new Monte Carlo. I have no idea whether any of it's true."

Just then, the waitress walked up to take their orders. "What's the special today, Pam?" Sarah asked the slender, bleached blonde.

"Fried chicken and its all you can eat, so I know that'll be your choice," Pam said with a smile. "And the soup today is Millie's famous vegetable beef," she said, looking at Lori, "which is probably what you're going to want."

"We come here too often," Sarah said with a laugh. "Maybe I should open up a restaurant so people would have a choice. Come to think of it, though, that may not be a good occupation for me since I'd be around food all the time."

By the time Pam left with their orders, Sarah had apparently forgotten her friend's irritation. "Where were we?" she asked. "Oh yeah, we were talking about Janice. It's true about the new Monte Carlo; at least that she has one. I saw her driving it the other day, nose in the air as usual. But I doubt if her dad bought it for her. He's so infatuated with his new, young wife, he pretty much lets her make the decisions. And I don't think she's that fond of her stepchildren."

Sarah paused to take a sip of water and Lori used the opportunity to try to change the subject. "Yes, that's what I've heard, too. By the way, how is the harvesting going?"

"Don't even ask. Jon doesn't get in to eat until almost eight o'clock now."

Evidently not interested in Lori's choice of a new subject, Sarah reverted back to the previous one. "I've heard he's even made out a new will, leaving everything to her. Of course, both Janice and her brother made out pretty well when their mother died. She had some family money of her own and had set up trust funds for them. Janice probably used some of the money from her trust to buy the car. That is one fancy set of wheels. I'll bet it took a real chunk out of her inheritance. The way she spends money, all those fancy clothes she wears—she's probably gone through most of it by now."

"It seems you have some excellent sources yourself." Lori started to add the words "of gossip" but thought better of it. She feared her good friend was rehearsing for Phoebe's job when she "retired" and thought this was sad.

"Working in a doctor's office, you hear things. Dr. Bob often runs late, and people like to pass the time just talking. I'm a good listener."

Lori reached across the table and laid a hand on her friend's. "None of this really matters to us, though, does it? I want to spend our time together talking about you and what's happening in your life. How are the kids? Do they like school this year? It's hard to believe Adam's already in high school. Sure makes me feel old."

"The kids are fine." Sarah, like most mothers, found it difficult to resist talking about her children and easily made the transition to this new topic. "Adam's following in his father's footsteps. He's on the basketball team, and April's a regular little scholar. Maybe asking you to be her godmother was a good move. In some respects, she's more like you than me. But she does like cool clothes and boys."

Pam brought their orders and they ate in silence for a while. "You can't beat Dora's chicken," Sarah commented. "Don't know what people around here will do if she ever retires."

Lori nodded in agreement.

A wistful look crossed Sarah's face. "You don't feel old 'till you're the mother of teen-agers," she said, laying down her fork. "It seems everything I do or say is out of the Stone Age. And if that's not bad enough, April thinks my clothes are vintage. But, of course, not like the cool vintage clothes she buys at Jill's Closet for big bucks. She wouldn't be caught dead in anything I own. To her I'm a first class nerd. I don't know, I feel so useless anymore. The kids are always off to their various activities or just hanging out with their friends. And Jon comes in so dead tired at night after working in the fields ten or twelve hours, he just drops off after supper. It's no wonder I like to gossip. Janice's life seems much more exciting."

"Life doesn't have to be exciting to be good." The thought crossed Lori's mind that she needed to convince herself as well as her friend. "Although you're going through a rough period, you have two beautiful children and a husband who adores you. I wouldn't be surprised if Janice doesn't envy you. Anyhow, I doubt if her life is all that glamorous either. In fact, I'll bet she's feeling pretty low right now. Divorce is awful, no matter who's at fault."

Sarah had been intent on what her friend was saying, her face serious. Now, however, her mouth turned up in a mischievous grin. "I don't think so, or else she's hiding it well. You didn't give me a chance to tell you. Guess who else is back in town?"

"I don't have the slightest idea, but I think I'm about to find out," Lori replied.

"Blake Johnson, although he's probably just home for a visit. He has a super big job at a huge oil company in Chicago. Anyhow, I was in the grocery store the other day and Karen Matthews, you know her, the gal who works there, said she saw Blake and Janice together last Saturday night out at Delong's Supper Club. Karen and her husband are taking dancing classes over at Sterling, so they go out to Delong's every Saturday night to practice their steps. Karen said they were dancing so close, Janice and Blake that is, you couldn't slide an empty envelope between them." Sarah giggled. "I don't know how anyone can dance that close to Janice with those big knockers getting in the way. Well, anyhow, according to Karen, neither Janice nor Blake looked exactly miserable."

Lori barely heard the last of Sarah's recitation. At the mention of Blake's name, she felt an odd sensation in the pit of her stomach, one she hadn't experienced in years. "I think we should be happy for both of them then." she said a little too quickly.

Pam brought them their checks and Lori, using this opportunity to recover her composure, counted out the amount she owed.

"Honestly, I don't know why I put up with you? You're just no fun at all," Sarah said.

Lori smiled at her friend affectionately. Sarah had made this same declaration over and over through the years. But she knew her love for her friend was mutual and would always endure.

Wonder what happened to Phoebe's radar system? Lori thought, as she waved good-bye to Sarah. *Mother didn't mention Blake was in town.* With his long absence, Lori had been able to put away the old, confusing memories. She quickened her pace, forcing herself to think of other things. As she passed Isley's, she noticed from their window sign they were having a sale on cereal and made a mental note to stock up when she did her weekly shopping.

Lori's afternoon was busy, as she had interviews with several sales people besides attending to her routine tasks. She didn't have time to give much thought to Blake's return, but walking home that evening, images of him again crept into her consciousness.

Blake had been a grade ahead of her in school. All the girls were crazy about him, except for Sarah and herself. Sarah, from the time Jon's family moved to Platte Valley when they were all in seventh grade, had eyes only for him. With her usual "steam roller approach," she set out to get him. Jon, however, turned out to be a willing victim. A quiet, easy-going guy, he was secretly smitten with Sarah.

Lori thought Blake was conceited. Sure he was gorgeous, but he knew it. He didn't have a steady girl friend through their high school days, preferring to give all the girls a chance to date him. Probably why he'd made a play for her. She thought now that in spite of this painful experience, she might have secretly been a little infatuated with him, something she'd never allow herself to admit during their high school days.

Her thoughts traveled back to that Sunday at the lake, Labor Day weekend, just before she was to begin her junior year.

"You're not going!" Sarah says in an incredulous voice. "I don't believe it. Why not? Everyone's going. There'll be lots of kids without dates. You can be with Jon and me."

It's Saturday evening and Lori has avoided calling her friend, knowing she'll try to talk her into going to the lake for their class outing. But Sarah calls her. Lori doesn't mind getting together with the other kids sometimes— like when a bunch of them go out to the drive-in for a movie or just to Brooks for cokes at the soda fountain. But the thing at the Lake would be for the whole day and a lot of the kids would be paired off. Lori feels shy in these situations and tries to avoid them. She's never even been on a real date, unless she counts the times in eighth grade when she went bike riding with Alan Hastings. Once she found out that Alan was sweet on her, though, she started to hide when he came by to get her.

"But I don't want to go," she says to Sarah. "Dad just took me to Denver to get my new school clothes, and I got all my new books. I want to go through them, get them ready for school." Lori realizes this excuse isn't going to float with Sarah and wishes she'd come up with something better.

"No wonder you can't get a boyfriend. Anyone who'd rather stay home two days before school's starting and look at schoolbooks is boring beyond belief. Besides if you really want to get your stuff organized, you'll have all day Monday to do it. As for me, I'm putting off that job as long as I can. With any luck I can cruise through the first couple of weeks without even cracking a book. Come on, Lori, why can't you act like a normal sixteen-year old just once!"

So as usual, Sarah wins. Jimmy Hollingsworth's dad has hooked up his tractor to a wagon, filled it with hay, and declares it a back to school celebration. When the kids balk at this misnomer, he says, "What do you mean you don't celebrate going back to school? This is a celebration for Mrs. Hollingsworth and me. At last peace and quiet will descend on the house again!"

True to her word, Sarah has saved a spot on the wagon next to her. Blake and his date, Tina Morris, one of the cheerleaders, are sitting across from them. Lori is enjoying the ride, talking and laughing with Sarah and Jon, when she glances over and sees Blake staring at her. She lowers her eyes, but every time she looks up, she sees his eyes still on her. Worse yet, he's started to hum a song in a low voice, which she realizes with embarrassment is "Beautiful, Beautiful Brown Eyes." Tina, whose eyes are unmistakably blue, is giving him dirty looks, which he seems unaware of or, if he notices, doesn't seem to care. Once when Lori meets his eyes, he winks at her.

She finds the whole thing disconcerting and finally solves the problem by turning around and looking at the passing scenery. Soon she is absorbed in the landscape and forgets Blake and everything else. The morning has been slightly cloudy, but now the sun is out brightly and she feels its warmth on her back. She even silently concedes she's glad Sarah talked her into coming.

Once they arrive at the lake, everyone starts unloading food, charcoal, ice chests, and blankets. Many of the kids brought swimming suits and towels and head straight for the rest rooms to change.

"Come on, Lori, lets test the water out," Sarah calls over her shoulder as she and Art join the other kids."

"Later maybe," Lori answers. "I think I'll just take a walk first."

"You can take a walk later. Jon and I'll go with you. Everyone is going swimming now."

"I'll be down in a few minutes, I promise."

"Okay, you'd better be," Sarah yells back.

Lori tucks her favorite poetry book under her arm and heads down a path towards the woods. This is one the best times of the year for her. Soon all the trees will be turning, signaling the end of summer. She also likes September because she loves going back to school. She likes most of the teachers, especially Mrs. Dixon, her English teacher. They seem to appreciate a student who is conscientious and eager to learn beyond just what's required. She does hate it, though, when they point her out to the other students as someone they should emulate. She never likes when attention is drawn to herself, and, besides, the other kids make fun of her, call her "teacher's pet" or even worse, "egg head."

She finds a secluded spot not too far down the path, hidden by the tall cottonwoods. She looks for a rock to sit on but realizes there are none. The land here, however, is irregular, and she spreads her jacket across a small hilly spot and makes herself comfortable. Opening her book, the pages worn thin, Lori is soon lost in a world of yesterday.

"There you are. I've been looking for you."

She brings herself back to the present with a start. Blake Johnson is standing there, looking down at her with a smile. He is clad only in his swimming trunks, a towel wrapped around his waist. His skin is the color of bronze, attesting to his many hours in the summer sun.

"Oh hi, Blake," she tries to make her voice casual. "Why were you looking for me?" She suddenly remembers he's brought a date to the outing. "Where's Tina?"

Blake laughs. "One question at a time. I was looking for you because I wanted to be with you. As for Tina, who cares!"

Lori doesn't answer, as she doesn't know what to say. She's always been shy around boys and finds herself especially tongue-tied around Blake. He's so good-looking, so sure of himself.

He sits down beside her. "So you like poetry, too," he comments. Taking the book from her, he flips through the pages as if he knows it well. When he comes to a page close to the front of the book, he begins to recite in a low voice, close to her ear.

I will paint her as I see her
Ten times have the lilies blown
Since she looked upon the sun.

Quiet talk she liketh best,
In a bower of gentle looks,
Watering flowers, or reading books.

He smiles at the look of surprise on her face. "Okay, now you know the truth. I'm a closet poetry reader. Blake Johnson, star of the wrestling team, class cut-up." He hesitates and looks at her with mock shyness. "And notorious ladies' man. But if you tell anyone that I read poetry, I'll deny it to the death. Don't want to ruin my reputation."

"The author of that poem, Elizabeth Barrett Browning, is one of my favorites," Lori says, looking at him as though she's never really seen him.

"Mine, too. But, come my fair Lori. See, I can write the stuff, too," he says, pulling her up. "Let's not waste the beautiful day, while we're young and life is fleeting." He laughs at himself with such delight that she can't resist a smile.

"You're so pretty when you smile. Your whole face lights up, especially

your eyes." He takes the book from her and lays it on the ground. "Let's go for a walk. We can have a discussion about the other poets we share a love of."

Thinking back on what happens next, as she did for many months and even years, it was as if it had all been a delicious dream, suddenly shattered into a million broken pieces.

They walk a long way until the shrieks of the swimmers become distant and finally disappear. They discuss Shelley and Keats and then easily slip into a discussion of their hopes and dreams for the future, hers as a journalist. He's always liked science, he says, is fascinated by the history of the Earth told in rocks and geological formations. He hopes for a career as a geologist.

But then he stops and, taking her by the shoulders, turns her toward him. His mouth on hers is the sweetest sensation she's ever known. First the kisses are gentle, but then grew more urgent, more passionate. He presses her down, spreading his towel beneath her head. Somehow, her blouse is open, his hands caressing her breasts; then his mouth is on them. She doesn't resist. It all seems so natural, so right. It isn't until he's trying to enter her that she suddenly comes to her senses.

"No, Blake, no, I can't!"

But he ignores her, keeps trying to spread her legs apart. She pushes him with all her strength, and he lies back with a glazed look in his eyes. "What? Why did you do that?" he asks in genuine surprise.

"Because I don't want to do this." She feels sudden hot tears on her face. "I'm not your girlfriend, not even your date. Why did you even bring me out here? What are you trying to prove? Was it a bet with some of the guys that you could get to the odd little book worm?"

His eyes are now clear and cold. "Yeah, that's it. Why not? You're a challenge. It's so easy with the other girls, it's not any fun."

She stands up, buttoning her blouse, fastening her jeans. "Well, it didn't work, did it? Nice try, though." Her tears are now those of anger and humiliation. "Go back and find Tina," she says. "She'd probably be grateful for such an opportunity with the great Blake Johnson."

As she walks hurriedly back toward the picnic area, she hears him laughing. "She's already had the opportunity," he yells, "and she was grateful. But you'll regret this tomorrow. You missed a great experience yourself."

She isn't sure, but, as she walks blindly on, she thinks she hears his voice in the distance reciting the words to Robert Herrick's, "Time."

Gather ye rosebuds while you may
Old Time is still a flying;
And this same flower that smiles today
Tomorrow will be dying.

Blake never approaches her again. But often in class or in the halls, she finds him looking at her. If she returns his gaze, he smiles in an intimate manner, as though they share some secret. Sometimes when she doesn't look away immediately, but returns his smile with a glare, he winks.

Even now, her face felt warm as she remembered. And yet, didn't she have to admit the times when he didn't look at her, when she'd pass him in the hall and he'd be standing close to some other girl, deeply engrossed in conversation, didn't she feel a small prick of disappointment?

As she passed the Taylors' house, their poodle ran out to greet her, wagging his whole body in anticipation of her greeting. "Hi there, Jojo. What's going on?" she said in a cooing voice. Why was she dredging up those old, uncomfortable memories? Look what a glorious day it is, and you're not even enjoying it, she admonished herself, as she noticed the bright sunlight speckling everything in its path.

"See you tomorrow, Jojo," she promised, starting across the street. He had followed her to the corner as always, watching until she was out of sight.

It's because he's back in town. What in the world is he doing back here after all these years? True, his parents do live here but as far as she knew, he'd only come back for brief visits while attending college in Golden and after that he'd never come back at all. So why now?

Dr. Bob walked in the room, interrupting Lori's thoughts. "How are you feeling now, Melora?" he asked, as he took her pulse.

"I'm not sure, Doctor. I guess I'm a little better."

"I'm aware of what caused your trauma, " he said, looking at her in his intent but kindly way. "It's a natural thing—a way of coping with a terrible shock until your body is in condition to deal with it."

Lori nodded her head. "Will I be all right then?"

Dr. Bob smiled. "From all your vital signs I'm confident you're going to be just fine. You've been doing the best thing you can for yourself by getting lots of rest. Now you need to get up and move around, slowly at first. The other thing is to try to get some food down. It's a little past lunch time, so I'll have a special tray sent in. Don't worry, it won't be steak, just something light for now."

After Dr. Bob left, an aide helped her to the bathroom. The image in the mirror over the sink seemed to be of someone who resembled her, but a much older version. Her face was drawn and there were dark circles under her eyes. She also noticed numerous small lines, which hadn't been there previously. But, she reasoned, *I feel years older than the last time I looked in a mirror. When was that? Yesterday? Yes,* now she remembered. She had checked her image in the full-length mirror in her room just before she left to meet Blake. How different that meeting had turned out than what she had anticipated. She had hoped for an end to her long weeks of pain, a grand reconciliation with the man she loved. Yes, she could admit it now. But instead she had been lured to a blood bath, one in which she had almost become a participant.

She forced herself to move, to walk slowly out of her room and down the long hallway, hoping to leave there if only for a time, those awful memories. With an effort, her legs wobbly at first, she managed to make it around the ward a couple of times. When she arrived back at her room, Larry was sitting in the chair by her bed, a smile on his face. And her black mood lifted a little.

"You look a hundred percent better," he said, helping her into her bed.

Lori thanked him, although she knew he wasn't being truthful.

"How is Rusty?" she asked.

Larry looked down but not before Lori saw the strained look on his face. "He's okay. He's worried about you, of course."

"It's something else, isn't it? Is it his mother?"

"I can't fool you, can I? Look, whatever's happened with Rusty and his mother, he'll be all right. He's a tough little dude. I'll tell you more about it later. Right now, though, let's just talk about pleasant things, like when do you think you're going to get out of here?"

"I'm not sure, but I'm okay really. In fact, I have some other questions about what—put me here."

Larry looked at her intently. "I know you do, but I'm going to obey the doctor's orders. I got chewed out for telling you about Blake's death before I'd okayed it with him. He says you survived it all right, but it could have set you back. As a law officer, I've found it's usually better to just get it out when I've had to inform someone of a tragedy. But I wasn't taking your condition into account."

Lori started to protest, but Larry had that look on his face that she'd come to know. He left shortly afterwards, telling her the best thing she could do for now was to try to get some rest.

She knew he meant well but found his advice not easy to follow. She was fully awake now and the unanswered questions kept rolling around in her head. In desperation, she reached for the television remote control and flipped through the channels, hoping to find something to interest her enough to block out the images. The afternoon fare was even less stimulating than the evening shows, though, and the soap opera she settled on lacked the ability to distract her. One big question was about Joe. If Larry had taken him back to Pueblo as Suzie, the sheriff's dispatcher had told her, how had he wound up out at the Wyatt lease on Sunday? But even her puzzlement over this dilemma couldn't blot out the image of Blake. How could she have been so gullible? Was it because her life had been so empty that she'd wanted – needed to believe his lies? There she was, single and childless, working at a profession usually equated with spinsterhood. Lori wondered if she was partly at fault for letting herself be victimized. This, after all, had been her pattern throughout her life.

Chapter 6 - Lori

"You've hardly touched your dinner, Mother. Can't you eat a few more bites?"

Lori had slow-cooked a roast in the crock-pot, along with some potatoes and carrots. This had always been one of her mother's favorites, and she was hoping Charlotte would do more than just pick at her dinner. She couldn't get used to seeing her mother so thin and pale.

"You treat me like a child, Melora. I ate all I cared for. It just wasn't very good. Don't know if it was the roast or how you cooked it. You never were very good in the kitchen. Always more interested in poking your nose in a book, for all the good it's ever done you."

Charlotte's words hit Lori like a physical blow. She hadn't quite finished her dinner either, but suddenly the food on her plate, which she had thought especially tasty, didn't appeal to her any longer. She got up from the table and started to clear the dishes. Then bracing herself, stated in a quiet voice, "If it weren't for my love of books I doubt I'd have my job at the library. When Mrs. Moran hired me she said she thought of me because she knew how much I loved books and . . ."

"That may be true, but if you'd been half as enthusiastic about learning to cook, you could have gotten a job over at the diner. Even if you were just working as a waitress, with all the tips those girls get, you'd probably be making more money than you do at the library."

Lori saw there was no use arguing. She didn't know why her mother was able to draw her into these debates. It was as if the old woman knew just what button to push and then purposefully set out to do just that. Taking a deep breath, she asked calmly, "How about a dish of sherbet? I bought orange and raspberry so you have a choice."

"Oh well, it really doesn't matter. Just give me a little raspberry. I see you've changed the subject as you always do when you don't have a good answer. I think you feel you're too good to work in a restaurant. Always had those high-blown ideas about going off to college and working at a newspaper. Well, your father and I never had any education past high school and we've done all right. Why didn't you at least get a job over at the Daily News? That's what you claimed you were going to school for, wasn't it?"

Without thinking, Lori retorted, "Because George Abbott can barely make a living himself on his little paper. He can't afford to hire anyone. Besides, I had a large city newspaper in mind. I don't think it would be very challenging doing a story on someone who spent the night in jail for drinking too much or reporting that so and so had out-of-town company on Sunday."

"That's very cruel of you, Lori, throwing up to me that you're stuck in this little town because of me--because I'm an invalid."

"I didn't mean it like that. Of course I don't blame you. To be honest, I don't think I'd do very well working on a big newspaper. I keep hearing about how competitive it is these days, how reporters use any means to get a story, even prey on others' grief." She put her hand on Charlotte's shoulder as she set the dish of sherbet in front of her.

But it was really her mother who had started all this, Lori thought. Why couldn't she defend herself against this woman? It's because she's an invalid, lonely and bored, and needs to strike out at someone. I'm here, so I'm an easy target. It did no good to argue. She could never win. She just couldn't let her mother draw her into these futile debates.

"It's all right. I just wish you'd try to be a little nicer. I'm stuck in this house all day with no one to talk to and then when you're here, you say such unpleasant things."

"You're right, Mother. I'm truly sorry and I'll try harder." Hoping once again to change the subject, she asked, "Did you hear from Phoebe, today?"

"Yes, as a matter of fact I did, and she had some interesting news. Said that Johnson boy is back in town. She hasn't found out why or for how long. She'll let me know when she does. And guess what? He's been seen with Janice Hollingsworth. Well, that's not too surprising, I guess. They're two peas in a pod. Both of them divorced and high rollers."

The confrontation with Charlotte had taken Lori's mind off Blake, but now as she cleared the dishes his image was once more vivid. She wondered how he and Janice had gotten together so fast. She'd seen Janice now and then when she came home for visits. A strikingly attractive young woman, she'd never be alone long. It dawned on Lori that perhaps the two of them had been in touch in Chicago, since they'd both been living there. But then again, Blake had always been a fast worker. He might have seen Janice at her brother's house. The two had been friends in high school. Back then, Janice had been a skinny little girl about nine years old. But now it would be only natural for Blake to be attracted to her.

Lori gave herself a little shake. What a waste of time even wondering about it. She hadn't seen Blake since his return and chances were she wouldn't if he was just here for a short visit. Why did he have this disquieting effect on her? She wished he'd stayed in Chicago.

Perhaps these feelings could be attributed to the slump she'd been in lately. She tried to remember if this was an annual thing. She looked forward to the first sprout of green each spring, to the longer days of increased sunlight. On summer evenings she sometimes spent an hour after dinner watering the plants and flowers. But with the fall days, she knew winter was just ahead, with its shortened days and long dreary nights.

A cold weather activity that would get her out of the house and provide some stimulation was what she needed. She had a lot more to learn about computers. But there were no classes in Platte Valley. She'd have to drive to Fort Morgan for these. She was tempted to check on some, even if bad roads sometimes kept her from making the trip.

As she put the last dish in the cupboard, Lori sighed. She realized this wouldn't work. Charlotte would never understand, would be hurt she was spending more time away.

As she joined her mother in the living room, a quick glance at the television set verified *Famous Quotes* was just starting. But she couldn't concentrate on even this program, which was a cut above the others Charlotte usually watched. She felt her mind beginning to wander again.

"I'm surprised you didn't get that one." Charlotte was looking at her reproachfully. "You're so fond of letting me know what an expert you are on English literature."

Lori looked up at her mother startled. "Sorry, I guess I wasn't paying attention. What didn't I get?"

She made an attempt to concentrate on the rest of the program, even redeemed herself by guessing right on Teddy Roosevelt's quotation, "Keep your eyes on the stars, and your feet on the ground."

When the program was over and *Code Blue*, one of her mother's favorites, started, Lori picked up her copy of Joyce and opened it, reading and rereading the same paragraph.

She thought of what Roosevelt had said. Her eyes had once been on the stars. But perhaps the problem was that her feet hadn't been on the ground. Her life had seemed exciting then, when she was finally realizing her goal of studying journalism. She recalled her days at the university. How long ago they seemed, when she'd dreamed those dreams of the untested young. She couldn't think of the university without thinking of Jeff. The two were intertwined in memories of her days at Boulder.

He was an intense young man not unlike herself. She was also zealous about her studies. It's what attracted them to each other. She remembered the first time she met him and how he'd pontificated about the future of news broadcasting. They were with a group of students who'd congregated outside a basic journalism class. The instructor had asked some thought provoking questions, such as "Why are you here?" and "Which way are you going?"

Jeff's serious demeanor was somehow at odds with his clothing—faded blue jeans with both knees out. "Newspaper reporting as we know it is a thing of the past," he'd said. "With all the technological advances being made news will be instantaneous. Satellites will carry it all over the world, and people will have immediate access through their television screens or through computers. It's equivalent to what the automobile did to the horse and buggy. No one will read newspapers. They'll be too slow."

After that day they'd drifted into a study group with a couple of the other students. But before long Jeff started dropping by the dorm when the study group wasn't meeting. They'd spent many evenings over beer and pizza, sitting on the floor in her small dormitory room or on the bed discussing their future careers. These discussions sometimes wound up in heated debates, but it had all been part of it, the burning quest to learn everything in this new stimulating environment. A whole big world out there, and they yearned to be a part of it. Knew they would for they could do anything.

Jeff was adamant that anyone who was serious about a news-reporting career should realize this trend and pursue a course of study in television communications, as he planned to. His face was so earnest as he tried to make his point, that face she was so fond of. Was it love? He wasn't that good-looking, at least not in the usual sense. He was too tall, too skinny, and his face had deep pockmarks, replacing the adolescent blemishes of his early teen years. It was his enthusiasm for life that made him so attractive, and Lori thought she probably did love him. But she couldn't let him sway her from her goal. It had been too long a part of her—the big city newsroom, the smell of the printing press ink.

True, most of her love for the written word had been fostered through the movies, although George Abbott had let her come in and watch while they printed the Platte Valley Daily News a few times, those times when she had pestered him unmercifully. She knew the printing press would probably go the way of the dinosaurs, replaced by computerized printers, but she didn't believe newspapers would ever be completely abandoned.

Because of Jeff, Lori's childhood in Platte Valley seemed far away, the memory of that lonesome little girl of someone else, although a child she remembered with fondness. She would never be the belle of the ball, but she'd become less introverted, less afraid.

It was Jeff to whom she lost her virginity. It wasn't wild passionate sex with him. At least, she didn't think so, remembering reluctantly that day at Jackson Lake with Blake. They were both so inexperienced. But it seemed so natural, an extension of their common interest. The fire was all spent on their heated discussions, their love making but the quiet consummation.

Then one crisp November day Lori received the call that would change her life, shatter her dreams. She had met Jeff at the student center for a study session as neither of them had a class that morning. Later, they'd taken a break from their studies to walk around the campus. It was a crisp, sunny day and even the trees, stripped of their summer wear, seemed to welcome the reprieve from the dreary days of the past week. The collapse of the savings and loan industry had thrown the country into a frenzy, and she and Jeff, tramping through mounds of fallen leaves, debated the probable causes. As they came to her dorm, Lori ran up to her room to exchange her heavy coat for a lighter jacket and found a note pinned to her door. The message said, "Call home, immediately. Urgent."

"Lori, what's wrong?" Jeff asked, his voice alarmed, when she returned to where he was waiting for her on the steps of the dorm.

"It's my father. He's had a heart attack."

"Is he going to be all right?"

"No. He didn't make it." She buried her head against Jeff's chest, sobbing uncontrollably. He didn't speak, just held her tightly.

Finally she backed away from him. "I'm all right. It's just such a shock. He's not—I mean he wasn't that old, barely fifty. And he's never had a problem with his heart, never had any health problems. Always bragged he hadn't been to a doctor in years."

She started crying again. "Dr. Jefferson was always joking with him. Told him he should come in for a yearly check-up and when he wouldn't, said he guessed our local veterinarian was checking Dad, since he was part mule. Oh, Jeff, what am I going to do without him?" She let him enfold her in his arms again.

"It'll be all right, I promise. You'll get through this. I'll come home with you if you want. Just say the word, and we'll do this together."

"No. I haven't told Mother about you and now isn't a good time. She'll need me, but it'll have to be just the two of us for now. You understand, don't you?"

"Sure. But I'll be here when you get back. You go home, help her with the arrangements, stay a week or two, but then get back here and throw yourself into your studies. It's the best way. And your dad would have wanted you to do just that. You've said how he encouraged you, how proud he was of you; that he didn't get to go to college himself because he was needed on the farm but that he always wanted you to get an education."

"I just don't know. I can't think that far ahead right now. I'll be missing so much with mid-term exams coming up in a few weeks. I may have to drop out this semester."

"Okay, don't think about it now. But you can do it. I'll help you cram. Just remember, you have to come back." There was a note of panic in his voice.

"I know, and I will. I just don't know when." Lori knew no matter what happened she couldn't lose Jeff. She realized he was more than a good friend, more than a lover. He symbolized everything new and wonderful that had happened to her since she came here. Without him, she could slip back into being the quiet little mouse she'd left in Platte Valley.

Lori hadn't told her mother about Jeff, but she had told her father. He'd promised to break the news to Charlotte about her young man and that she may be bringing him home for a visit over Thanksgiving. This was just last weekend, when she'd talked to him on the phone—their last conversation. She doubted if he'd done so. He usually took a few days to soften his wife up before he handed her anything that he thought might be unpleasant for her. And Lori knew her mother wouldn't like the idea of her bringing Jeff home. Even though this was the eighties, Charlotte's main concern would be what the neighbors thought, rather than to be happy her daughter had a friend.

Thinking about it now, Lori realized her dad had always acted as a buffer between the two of them. As far back as that day, the day of his death, Lori had had a premonition of what would happen with him gone, that it would always be just the two of them, her mother and herself. And she'd known at that moment how great her loss really was.

Over eight months were to pass before she saw Jeff again, and then it wasn't at the university. "You're where?" Lori asked in an incredulous voice.

"I'm right here in Platte Valley," Jeff answered. "To be exact I'm at a phone booth outside of, let's see, the name of this place is Brooks Drug Company."

She felt a thrill in spite of her misgivings. "Whatever possessed you to come to Platte Valley? I can't possibly see you—I mean it's not convenient right now."

"What are you talking about? Of course you're going to see me. Just give me directions to your house. From the looks of this place, it's not that big. I can probably be there in no more than five minutes. Right?"

"Wrong. I mean I do want to see you, but I'll come there. I can't get away just yet. Oh dear, how about in an hour?"

"Let's make that a half an hour. There's a diner down the street. It's almost noon, so I'll buy you lunch."

"Dora's Diner. The food is good but go ahead and eat. I'm—just not hungry." Where everyone in town will be on a Saturday, Lori thought. She searched her mind for an inconspicuous place to meet. Then it came to her— the school. Since it was summer, no one would be around. She gave Jeff directions. "You just go west on Main, make a turn on Cleveland, and it's in the next block."

"Okay, but why all the intrigue? You didn't get married did you?" He asked in mock horror, "to a jealous husband."

She giggled. "No, silly. "It's just that, well, this is such a small town, and everybody knows everything that goes on. You know what I mean."

"No, I'm not from a small town, remember. And if I were, I'd say screw everybody. But if that's what makes you happy, I'll meet you at the school."

"Who's on the phone?" Charlotte asked.

Lori jumped. "Just a minute," she said before covering the mouthpiece and turning around. Her mother was just coming into the room, still in her old chenille robe. She'd been to the doctor a few days ago, complaining of pains around her heart. Charlotte reported he'd prescribed more bed rest, so she was sleeping later.

Lori searched her mind desperately for an excuse to leave. "It's Sarah," Lori said, placing her hand over the mouthpiece. "She's having a problem with Jon again. Seems he stayed out until all hours with the guys. She thinks he doesn't love her. Wants me to come over and cheer her up."

Lori uncovered the mouthpiece and said, "See you soon," before quickly hanging up and running toward the stairs.

Her mother called after her, "She says 'jump' and you say 'How high?' Doesn't she think you have anything else to do with your time? Now that you're working at the library, there's a lot to do on weekends, and you know I can't do that much what with my poor health."

"I know, Mother, but I'll still have time to mow when I get home, and I can finish the laundry this evening. I think it's because she's pregnant again and so soon. She has her hands full with little Adam, and Jon isn't much help. He works hard on the farm but pretty much leaves Adam to Sarah. I'll just be gone for awhile."

Without waiting for any further comment, Lori ran up the stairs. As she hurriedly brushed her hair and put on lipstick, she promised herself she would stop by Sarah's afterwards. That way it wouldn't be so much of a lie. And Sarah had called her this morning earlier all upset. Everything she'd told her mother had been true—except the part about going to meet Jeff.

At that time, Lori was still driving her dad's truck. When she arrived at the school, Jeff's battered old Ford was already there. Her heart did a little dance at the sight of it with its numerous bumper stickers. The car was so ancient there was even an old sixties sticker on it that said, "Make love, not war." She hadn't realized how much she missed him until she saw his lanky form moving toward her, his familiar lop-sided grin.

"Hi there," he said. The next minute she was in his arms.

"Let's go for a drive," he said releasing her. "By the way, you look awful. You've lost weight."

"Thanks," she said with a smile. "There's a lake right outside of town. I'll show you."

When they made love, it seemed to fill a void for her. She hadn't realized how much she'd missed him and everything he represented. He was her witness to another life, the only person who knew that other girl—the happy, carefree one.

She hadn't gone back to being the timid little girl who'd left Platt Valley to pursue her education. She'd had to grow up fast, take on more responsibility than she'd ever known, at times be assertive in order to be taken seriously, always thinking of how Dad would have handled it. But something had gone out of her in the process—the exuberance usually associated with youth.

Jeff's hair, loose from the ponytail, lay across the back of the car seat. She looked at him with a feeling of possessiveness. He loved her. Everything would be all right.

"I've got to admit, this was the first time for me in my Ford. Not too comfortable, but it does have its charm."

"Your first time in your car? Does that mean there've been other times?"

"You've been gone a long time. I've been at the university, not a monastery. Come on, Lori. It has nothing to do with us and my feelings toward you."

"Of course. I'm being silly." But she felt deflated. Afraid her feelings would show, she looked straight ahead.

Jeff sensed her sudden coldness and pulled her face toward him. "I just had to see you," he said earnestly. "I haven't been able to talk you into coming back over the phone, so I had to come here and try."

"I have a job. Remember? I'm working at our library. I like it. I've told you, I don't think I'll be coming back."

"Because of your mother, right? How can you let that bitter old lady do this to you?"

"That's unfair and unkind. She's an invalid, and there's no one else to take care of her. It's my duty, what Dad would have wanted."

"No, it's not what he would have wanted, and you know it. What's happened to the girl I used to know, the one with all the spunk, the one who was so determined to have a career as a reporter? I don't even know who you are."

"You'll never understand. You've wasted your time coming here. You may as well take me home."

He turned on the ignition, shifting it into first so hard the gears shrieked, and headed back to town. By the time they arrived at the school, he'd calmed down some. Lori realized she didn't want him to leave on a bad note. Although she sensed this might be the last time she'd see him, she laid her hand on his arm and said, "Let's stay in touch, Jeff. Maybe I can come for a visit sometime or you could come back, plan to stay longer next time."

He turned toward her with a weak grin. "Sure. That would be great. I'll give you a call."

A phone call now and then was the only further contact they'd had. I wonder if he's happy, she thought, laying the book across her lap. The last she'd heard he'd married a girl from the university, an education major, and was working for a television station in Cleveland. They might have had children, and perhaps he too had settled for less than his dream, traded a job he really wanted for one that was secure. Lori didn't know. She'd finally lost track of him.

Chapter 7 - Blake

"You're not going out again tonight, are you?" Mrs. Johnson asked her son. She was standing at the kitchen sink peeling potatoes. "I'm fixing your favorite dinner—chicken with dressing and lemon meringue pie for dessert."

Blake had just walked into the kitchen. He tried to ignore the ugly new wallpaper, splattered with yellow teapots. It had been chosen, no doubt, in an attempt to match the gold refrigerator and stove, which had regretfully survived the grand redecoration project. Probably still serviceable, he thought. Even as a child he had hated them.

The aroma coming from the oven was enticing, though. He gave his mom a kiss on the back of her neck. "I was going to take a drive over to Jim's, but it can wait until after dinner since you just said the magic words. I sure haven't gotten many good home cooked meals since Andrea left. Come to think of it, I didn't get many while we were married either."

Betty turned to look at her son, a look of sympathy on her face. "I wish I'd known how bad things were."

"There was nothing you could have done. So why worry you by telling you what was going on."

Betty had placed the potatoes in a colander and was washing them. "What worries me now is the boy. He needs a father. I wish you could have worked things out for his sake."

"I see him as much as I can. I have season passes to the Cubs games, and I usually take him, that is, when I'm in the States."

"It's not the same. I suppose if you were married, you'd still have to be gone a lot, but you would be spending more time with him if you were living under the same roof."

Blake walked away from his mother and stood by the window, his back

69

stiff and his fists clenched. "It wasn't possible to stay married. How can I make you understand?" He paused a minute. Finally he said, his voice devoid of emotion, "The worst mistake I ever made was the day I saw Andrea across a room and, deciding she was the most beautiful woman I'd ever seen, walked over and introduced myself. Sure, she was gorgeous. I guess that's what made me so blind as to what she really was. I didn't wake up until we were married and had a kid."

Blake began to pace back and forth across the room, finally sinking into one of the chrome kitchen chairs. "From the minute we tied the knot, she went on a shopping spree that didn't end until I was practically bankrupt. Oh, at first I wasn't concerned, thought once she had her house in Oak Lawn and had it decorated according to her taste, she would settle down. And I was moving up the old corporate ladder so thought I'd be able to pay for the new house."

Betty turned the burner under the potatoes down and came to sit across from her son. She reached over and laid her hand on his.

"But then she turned to clothes and travel," Blake continued. "If we couldn't go skiing in the Alps or swimming in Hawaii, it just wasn't worth the effort. And, of course, one had to have the proper wardrobe. I've seen movie stars at some of these resorts who weren't as well dressed as Andrea."

"I didn't know any of this. I wish you'd told me. At least then you'd have had someone to talk to. When I met her at the wedding, I thought she was lovely. But I guess I didn't get to know her that well, just that one time."

"Her dad hired her the best lawyers he could find. He never wanted her to marry me in the first place, had the son of a big Chicago banker all picked out. She wound up with everything. As for Josh, she's tried to turn him against me. But I have visitation rights, and she can't stop me from seeing him."

His face was hard. "I don't want to talk about her anymore. She no longer even exists for me."

"Of course. I understand. But do you think you could bring Josh for a visit sometime? I'd love to meet him."

"That brings up a subject I've been meaning to discuss with you. Now that the divorce is over, I want to make some changes in my life. I'm thinking of leaving Pierce, striking out on my own. And if things work out the way I plan, I could be working right here in the area. I'd like to spend more time with you and Dad. I'd get my own place, of course. And Josh could spend the summers here with me. You may get to spend more time with him than you've bargained for. I'll probably enlist you for baby-sitting services."

Betty's eyes were shining now. "That's wonderful, son. I'd like nothing better than to have you living here in Platte Valley. It would be like old times, and I'd love to take care of Josh. I could make him cookies, and we could do lots of fun things."

Her voice became suddenly anxious. "But you have such a good job with Pierce. Do you think you could make it okay with your own business?"

"You know me. I'd never make such a move unless I thought it would be a good one. I've been planning this for a long time."

"Have you said anything to Dad, yet? He hasn't mentioned it to me."

"No, in fact I'd intended to tell you both together, but it slipped out. I want to spend some time with him, maybe go in to the store one of these days. I'll tell him then. He hasn't been exactly thrilled at my visit. Oh, he's been civil enough, but he's bitter because I haven't kept in better touch. Says I've hurt you."

Betty got up and walked to the stove, opening the oven door. "The chicken looks about done, and it's real juicy," she announced, as she poked it with a fork.

Then she walked back to the table and placed her hand on Blake's arm. "Dad can be stubborn and unbending, but he truly loves you." Her eyes were moist. "It's all a big cover-up. He feels rejected and pretends it's me he's bothered about. Of course I was sad when we never got to see you, but I looked at it differently. I figured you may be having problems and that you'd make it home when you could."

"Could you put in a good word for me, Mom? Tell him how bad things have been, that I didn't want you two to get involved, worry you."

His mother nodded in agreement. "I've already been working on him. You know I'd like nothing better than for you two to be close." She wiped a tear from her eye as she turned back toward the stove.

Blake got up to leave. "Please don't mention anything about my plans to him until I've had a chance to tell him myself. And don't let him know I told you first," he said, giving her a pat on the bottom.

"Mums the word. Now get out of here and let me concentrate on my dinner, unless you want burnt chicken."

When he left the room, Blake walked to the telephone in the living room, picked it up, and dialed. After a slight pause he said, "Hi. Just wanted to let you know there's been a change in plans. I can't do dinner but will be over later, probably around eight."

71

"So what came up that you had to cancel our dinner date?" Janice asked. She was sitting on the couch in the living room, her feet tucked under her. The stately old home, which had been in the Hollingsworth family for several generations, was one of the show places of the county. As if attempting to sweep away all semblance of the home's former mistress, the new Mrs. Hollingsworth, Tonia, had the home completely refurbished. Gone were all the dark mahogany pieces, many of which had dated from the eighteenth century. The new wife of Jim Hollingsworth, Sr. had opted for an ultra-modern motif. With the exception of the kitchen, plush white carpeting had been laid throughout, covering the lovely heart of pine flooring, once the pride of the former Mrs. Hollingsworth, now deceased.

In the living room there was a couch, chair, and love seat, all done in white leather, with glass accent pieces completing the arrangement. To relieve the austerity, Tonia had splashed vivid color around the room. The drapes and throw pillows were done in geometric patterns of aqua, red, and purple, and these colors were repeated in several large, exotic plant arrangements.

Blake had taken a moment to admire the changes, as well as the only other occupant of the room. Janice was wearing a bright red jumpsuit, which emphasized her curvaceous body and which made her appear to be part of the room's decor. Her platinum blonde hair was carelessly tied back in a red ribbon with loose strands framing her lovely face.

He answered her question about canceling their dinner plans with a simple "I got involved in a situation."

Janice gave him a simpering look. "I'm not prying, honestly. I just thought with Dad and 'Mommy' out of town for a few days, we might take advantage of the situation."

Blake smiled. "It's still early."

With a quick change of mood, Janice unwrapped her legs and stretched them lazily. "You're right. I'll just put some music on, and we'll have a sip of that wine you brought."

Watching the luscious sway of her hips as she moved across the room, Blake decided she was the sexiest thing he had seen in a long time. In fact, she made Denise, his recent conquest in Denver, look like a boy in comparison. He thought it was quite astonishing and a stroke of uncanny good luck that he had made this "find" right here in his little hometown.

A couple of days after his arrival in Platte Valley, he'd dropped by the home of Jim Hollingsworth, Jr. to pay his respects. Jim and Blake went back to high school days. Blake had a further motive for the visit, however. He wanted to sound out his friend about the oil field he was interested in. It had belonged to John Wyatt, but now that Wyatt was dead, Blake needed to know if it was still in the family. He could have gone over to the courthouse in Fort Morgan and looked through the records to see if title had changed. But people were awfully nosy in these small towns and Blake would just as soon keep his plans private.

When Blake had arrived at his friend's residence, a modern ranch-style house built on land adjacent to his father's place, Jim and Lisa were getting the kids ready for bed. The house, unlike that of the senior Hollingsworths, was simply furnished in a style that lent itself to that of a young family. There were tiny rocker chairs in front of the television and a miniature-sized table and chairs in the kitchen, along with the usual adult furnishings. When Blake arrived, toys were strewed from one end of the living room to the other, but Lisa quickly picked these up, apologizing for the mess. Jim excused himself while he read a book to the children, while Lisa fixed them a snack of ice cream and cookies. Nice family scene, Blake thought.

Jim had met Lisa while he was pursuing a degree in agriculture at Fort Collins. Lisa, who was studying to be a physical therapist, had postponed her plans for a career when she had married Jim. She told Blake she had no regrets, that being a housewife and mother was the most fulfilling life she could imagine. Blake felt a stab of envy for his old friend, who seemed to have fallen into a secure, tranquil life-style. It's easy enough when you have money, he thought.

While Lisa gave the children baths, Jim poured drinks for Blake and himself. Sitting in a comfortable recliner across from his friend, Blake seized the opportunity to question him about the Wyatt lease. Jim gave him the answer he was looking for, told Blake that as far as he knew the oil field was still owned by the Wyatts. Blake planned to check out this information with more certainty later. But since the status of the field's ownership was a major key to his plans, he had been anxious to learn what he could quickly. If he were to have to deal with a new owner, someone knowledgeable about the field's potential, it could complicate things. Jim's input had helped alleviate this concern.

As Jim was refilling Blake's glass, the children reappeared to say their "goodnights." Standing in front of his chair in their colorful sleepers they eyed Blake curiously. The girl, whose name was Rebecca, seemed to be about the same age as his own son; the boy, Travis, was younger. Blake made all the proper inquiries—How old are you? Do you like school? But his heart wasn't in it. As much as he gave lip service to the merits of the whole domestic scene, it wasn't for him. The little wife in the kitchen cooking dinner, dad playing with the kids—it seemed a deadly existence. Even with his own son, he found it difficult to communicate. Although he had made a weak effort to gain custody of Josh, mainly out of a need to antagonize Andrea, he was secretly relieved that she was adamant in her refusal to give him up.

While Blake was getting acquainted with Jim's family and trying to think of an excuse for an early departure, who should waltz in but "little" Janice, sans the braces and pig tails. Remembering the pesky little brat who had tried to follow the two teen-age boys everywhere, Blake couldn't believe the transformation. He hadn't thought of her in years but as he searched his memory bank that night, he seemed to recall she had had a crush on him. He had a nagging recollection that he and Jim had been pretty brutal in their efforts to "shake" her. Seeing her again that night, he hoped her memory wasn't as good.

Janice had hung around for the rest of the evening, which had become more interesting after her arrival, and they left together. As they walked toward their vehicles, Blake felt a strong sexual current between them. Being experienced in such matters, he knew he wasn't mistaken. He helped her into her car, which he noticed was a new Monte Carlo convertible. As they said their "good-nights," Janice made it clear she would be receptive to a call from him.

Driving back to his parents' house that night, Blake had reflected on the pleasant turn of events the evening had taken. He had come to Platte Valley with a goal in mind, one that would secure his future, and he needed to keep this purpose uppermost in his mind. But he was a firm believer in the old adage "All work and no play makes Jack, or in this case Blake, a dull boy." As he pulled into the Johnson driveway, his thought was that Janice would make a nice playmate.

Now, as he leaned back in the chair opposite her and sipped his wine, he knew the old Johnson charm was working again. Her whole demeanor was an unspoken promise of delights to come. As was his usual style, he masked his excitement with an air of nonchalance and waited.

"So what shall we do with the rest of the evening?" he asked. "Perhaps a game of Scrabble?"

"I did have a night of fun and games in mind," she said, "but Scrabble isn't on the list." Her lips curved into a wicked little smile, as she patted a spot next to her. "How about let's break in Tonia's new couch, instead?"

Blake didn't need a further invitation. "I've never fully appreciated these jump suits," he murmured softly, as he unzipped her garment in one swift movement.

"They're even handier when there's nothing underneath," she said, giggling.

Her full breasts had fallen free, as plump and delicious-looking as ripe fruit. Jim's skinny little tag-along sister—who would have imagined!

Chapter 8 - Lori

Lori often brought a lunch to work. That way, after eating her sandwich and a piece of fruit, she could then use her lunch break to take care of errands. The one day she deviated from this practice was Wednesday, when she met Sarah at the diner.

But today was just Monday, so after putting up the "closed" sign, she took her lunch from the small refrigerator in the back room and placed it on her desk. Another plus about working in the library was that she was never without reading material. She had picked out a book of short stories by Pearl Buck and read from it while she ate.

Charlotte had reminded her that morning that she was getting low on one of her prescriptions, and Lori promised to get it refilled if her mother called it in. So about twenty minutes later she closed the book, grabbed her purse and jacket, and set out from the library at a brisk pace. As Lori made the familiar walk downtown, she noticed the leaves were now a mixture of greens and yellows. She still loved autumn best, perhaps because the days at this time of year seemed more precious. All too soon the radiant hues of the season would be obliterated by the harshness of winter's ways.

With such thoughts on her mind, Lori didn't immediately notice the attractive couple coming out of Johnson's Farm and Implement Company until she was almost abreast of the store. There was no mistaking the young woman with her platinum hair, gleaming in the sunlight, and her chic outfit, a cut above those usually seen in Platte Valley. Janice Hollingsworth had her arm through that of her companion, a well-dressed man in his mid-thirties. When Lori had last seen him, he had been a good-looking boy of about nineteen, a mere preview of the strikingly handsome man she observed today. There was no mistaking who he was either.

Her first impulse was to turn and run or at least to turn toward the window and pretend to be looking at the shiny tractors within. It was true she had been seriously contemplating replacing their old tractor. The one she was using predated her father's death, and it seemed as the years went by it was breaking down more often.

But in the same instant she realized she was acting like a silly school girl, instead of a mature woman of thirty-five. And after all these years, Blake had probably changed, also. She doubted if he even recalled the incident at the lake. He probably didn't even remember her.

"Well, look who it is." Blake said with a dazzling smile. "My beautiful brown eyes. And they're still just as beautiful after all these years."

In spite of her effort at composure, Lori felt a warm flush move up from her neck. At the same time she noticed Janice, who'd had a smug smile on her face, suddenly stiffen. "I believe it's Blake Johnson, isn't it?" Lori asked, trying to appear nonchalant. "What are you doing in town after all these years?" Before he could answer, she nervously rambled on. "You're the town's success story, you know. Small town boy makes good. Big oil company executive."

"I think that's stretching it a bit. I've come back to see the old folks. I've neglected them for too long and just said to myself one day, 'Blake, my boy, here you are living the good life and more and more it seems just a rat race. I don't know, maybe it's a mid-life crisis, although a little early." He laughed. "Anyhow, I decided I needed to take some time off, get back to my roots. So far it's been great."

Janice looked at him with a knowing smile, but he ignored her. "I've had a lot of good talks with Mom, spent some time doing a few odd jobs around the place that Dad never seems to get to." Then, glancing to his left, added, "I came by today to get a replacement part for the folks' lawn mower."

Blake suddenly seemed to remember his companion. Turning toward her, he said, "I'm being impolite. You do remember Janice, Jim's little sister, all grown-up now."

Janice gave him a weak smile. Then turning toward the other woman, said, "How have you been, Ms. Wyatt?"

Lori felt the use of her surname by the younger woman was a deliberate attempt to emphasize their age difference. She decided she was not going to play the game. "I've been doing well," she answered with a smile.

"I hear you're still over at the library, ensuring the local yokels get a little culture." Janice's voice was condescending.

Lori ignored the other woman's tone. "Yes, I'm still there. We've been modernizing. We acquired some new computers last year and have expanded the children's section." Janice looked bored, so Lori decided to change the subject. "I assume you're just back for a visit, also, Janice."

"That's right. Spending some time with Daddy and my new mother." She laughed a little bitterly. "I'm not sure how long I'll be around. It depends on how things go here." She gave Blake a meaningful look.

There was an awkward silence. Lori glanced at her watch. "I'll let you two get on with your day. I'm just on my lunch hour and have to hurry over to Brooks to pick up some medicine for Mother."

"How is your mother by the way?" Blake asked with a look of concern. " As I remember she's never had very good health."

"She's not doing great. She seems to get thinner and more sedentary as the years go by. I try to get her up and around more, but she resists." Lori found herself smiling in response to his warmth. "But, goodness, I don't want to bore you with my family problems. It was nice seeing you again and you too, Janice."

"I'll drop in to see you one of these days at the library," Blake said. "Maybe now that I'm off the fast track for awhile, you could recommend some good books for quiet evenings in Platte Valley."

Janice's look was icy. "Good-bye, Lori," she said without feeling. "We don't want to keep you from your errands." She tried to grab Blake's arm and pull him away, but he shrugged her off.

Taking Lori's hand he said, "It's great seeing you, again, Lori, and I did mean what I said."

Lori's look must have registered her confusion. "About your eyes being just as lovely, actually more beautiful. You've improved with age." Blake laughed. "Maybe that isn't the right thing to say to a woman."

"Thanks," was all she could manage, as she hurried away before they could see the blush she knew was starting to spread across her face again.

The rest of the day went surprising well for Lori. Even Kristen, the girl who worked at the library part-time, commented on how nice she looked. "You must be wearing some new makeup or something. It really enhances your eyes."

During the days following Lori found herself looking up from her desk more, noticing who had come in the door. She'd taken a few extra pains with her wardrobe each morning. Had even taken a minute to put on a little eyeliner and lipstick.

By Friday afternoon she gave herself a good scolding. What are you doing Melora Wyatt? she asked herself. The first man who comes on to you in years, and you let it go to your head. If that was indeed what he was doing. He was undoubtedly just having some fun as he was doing all those years ago. Janice and he probably had a good laugh as soon as they left her last Monday. She could hear Blake telling Janice how he'd gotten a charge out of flirting with his odd, little classmate just to see her face redden in embarrassment. No, she told herself, Blake Johnson had not been a nice boy and now that he's all grown-up, it's doubtful he's changed. He's not even worth thinking about.

The scolding worked. Lori became so absorbed in entering data into the computer that Blake was standing right in front of her before she realized he was there.

"Hi, Brown Eyes," he said. "Morgan County is getting their money's worth with you, I see. I'll remember that now that I'm soon to be a resident and will, no doubt, be paying county taxes. Uh oh, guess I'm letting the cat out of the bag. No one's supposed to know about that yet."

"Oh, Blake, " she said. "Sorry, I didn't see you. Is there something I can help you with?" Lori was so flustered at his presence, his words about moving back to the area barely registered.

Blake didn't seem to hear. He walked over to one of the reading tables and picked-up a chair, which he placed in front of her desk. Straddling it, he looked around the large room. "I haven't been in this place since I was in school. It looks different, more inviting. Your touch no doubt."

Lori felt a sudden burst of pride at this compliment. "Thanks. I've tried to make it a place where people enjoy coming, especially the children."

"By the way, just as I pulled up and was getting out of the car, Larry Reardon drove by in his patrol car. I'd heard he was a deputy sheriff and assigned to this area. He recognized me and stopped the car for a minute to chat. That was a real tragedy about his wife. I haven't seen him since before it all happened. I was away at school at the time but heard about it from the folks."

"It's been a long time ago now, almost fifteen years. It happened the year I came to work at the library. Larry never really recovered, they say. The talk was that he adored his wife and for her to die the way she did devastated him. Their little girl was eight years old at the time. He brought her up with the help of his mother, who is a widow. I can't remember where she came from, but she just packed up her bags and came here to live with them."

"Probably from York, Nebraska. That's where Larry and his wife moved to Platte Valley from."

Lori must have looked surprised that he would know so much about Larry.

"He was working at the store for my dad back then, remember?" His wife, I can't think of her name, went to work at Dora's at one point. I guess it was after their kid started school."

"Her name was Norma, and she did work at Dora's. She was working there at the time of her death. It was brought out at the trial that Joe Isley used to come into the diner a lot. Some of the witnesses, guys who used to hang out at Dora's regularly, testified she was flirtatious with Joe but that she was just having some fun with him. I guess Joe took it seriously, and when he found out she was just playing with him, he followed her to the lake and killed her. As I said, this all came out at the trial. Whether it's true or not, the jury was convinced."

Lori felt a cold shiver run through her, even though with the sun streaming through the windows, the room was a little warm.

"I'll bet Reardon wasn't too happy with that theory, I mean that she was leading Joe on, even if it was just in fun." Blake observed.

"No, I heard he was upset about that. He did believe Joe murdered her, but not for the reason that was brought out. Guess he hated it that this would be the image people would have of her. He thought Norma felt sorry for Joe and that Joe mistook her friendliness. Then, when she rejected his advances, killed her in a fit of anger."

Some high school kids came into the library just then. Now that school was in full swing again, it was a favorite spot for some of the more serious students to work on their school projects. They nodded at Lori and Blake and went back to the computers.

They were both quiet for a moment, thinking about the event that had rocked their little town, making headlines across the state on a daily basis. Lori remembered how Larry had looked in those days. There'd been an almost fierce look in his eyes, and his mouth seemed to be set in a permanent, grim line, as though if he let himself smile, he would crumble. Such a contrast to the cheerful man who had been bringing his grandson by to use her computer these past few weeks.

She remembered that Rusty was coming for his computer lesson on Sunday. "By the way, Cindy, Larry's daughter, has a little boy whom Larry and his mother are bringing up. Cindy was only a teenager when she had him, and one day she just took off. Rusty is seven years old now, a real nice little boy. I've been teaching him to use the computer."

"Sounds like a great thing for you to do. But what do you think? I mean, about the murder. Did Joe do it?"

"I really don't know. I never knew his wife. I do have a lot of respect for Larry. He used to come into the library to use our law books after it happened. Our legal books are somewhat limited. We have the Colorado state statutes and a set of legal encyclopedias, and he used to pour over them. I think he may have gone into Denver, also, so he could use the more extensive law library there."

"Mom kept me posted on what was happening. Larry confided in her a lot. But I don't remember her telling me about him doing all that research. What was he trying to accomplish?"

Lori paused for a moment before answering, trying to recollect the details of this long ago event. "I didn't know him well, so he didn't say much to me when he came in. But the rumor was that Larry believed the investigation was sloppy. The prosecution did get their conviction. It seems the jury felt on the basis of the evidence presented that Joe had murdered Norma. But they found him not guilty by reason of insanity. He was sent to Pueblo. It bothered Larry that any time Joe could pass a sanity hearing, he could walk. Guess he thought he could do a better job if he were in charge."

"Yeah, as I said, my mom kept me up-to-date on what was happening. All that research must have been what sparked Larry's interest in law enforcement. After the trial, he quit his job at the folks' store and went away to study at a law academy. Now I guess he works for the sheriff's department and is assigned patrol duty in our area. By the way, is Joe's old man still around?"

"No, Henry died a couple of years ago. They let Joe come back for the funeral. He was under guard, and they took him back immediately. It was kind of sad. At least it was a nice funeral, since Joe's uncle paid for it and the burial. Henry died penniless, probably because of his drinking, which is undoubtedly what killed him. You may know this, but in the earlier years he worked with Luke at the grocery store. After his wife died, the story is that he started drinking heavily. Eventually, when it got to be a real problem, Luke bought him out. I heard he went through the money within a few years."

"It seems Luke Isley has done all right with the store," Blake observed. "But he'll probably be squeezed out one of these days when one of the big chains moves in."

"Isleys has been in the family for three generations, so that would be a shame. It's what they call progress, I guess."

Blake suddenly jumped up. "Wow, all this stuff is too heavy. I've got to run, but before I do, I was wondering if you could have dinner with me tomorrow night."

Lori was momentarily at a loss for an answer. She had thought Blake may actually come by the library some time looking for a book and had visualized this scenario—how she would be more confident on her own turf, would help him find a book by some obscure author. But this was totally unexpected. "I don't know," she said finally. "I'd like to, but I try to stay home with Mother in the evenings since I have to be gone all day."

"The library is closed on Sundays, I believe, so you can spend the whole next day with her. Remember us big executives aren't used to taking 'No,' for an answer."

In spite of her resolve, Lori's heart did a little flip-flop as he smiled.

"I'll pick you up around seven. I thought we'd run into Denver as they have a better selection of restaurants than here. They have more than two," he added laughing.

"Just kidding, but seriously it seems the only new restaurants in town are fast food and lets face it, the menus at the old independents like Dora's and Delong's haven't changed since I left town. Still not what you'd call the last word in fine cuisine."

Lori suddenly felt defensive. It irritated her that he should criticize the town he had left so many years ago without a backward glance. "It's really out of the question. Sunday is my day to catch up around the house, and . . . " She was talking to the air. Blake was half way across the room, heading for the door.

Chapter 9 - Lori

"Why do you suppose he asked you to go to dinner?" Charlotte asked.

Lori wished she'd called Blake and told him to meet her somewhere—anywhere but here where she had to answer her mother's prying questions. She'd just gotten out of the shower and was getting dressed when Charlotte came into her room.

"I honestly don't know why he asked me, Mother. Perhaps he just wants to touch base with some of his old classmates, needs someone to bring him up to date on where everyone else is and what they're doing."

"Well, you could have said 'No.' I don't like it. He's a divorced man and besides, he's all involved with that Hollingsworth girl. Phoebe says they're inseparable. It just doesn't look right."

"It's no big deal. It's not really even a date." She said this as much to convince herself as her mother. Otherwise she would be tempted to have Charlotte go to the door when he came and tell him she was in bed with a migraine.

"Then why are you taking such pains getting ready, curling your hair and putting on makeup? Things you normally don't even bother with."

"Because I usually don't go anywhere in the evenings. And I do curl my hair when I go anywhere besides work or to the grocery store." She didn't need this. She was nervous enough as it was. "I have to hurry. He'll be here any minute. Do you want to say 'Hello'?"

"Absolutely not. I don't approve of him or your going out with him. It's thoughtless of you to leave me alone all evening, so why should I put up a pretense by being sociable."

"You'll be fine for a few hours. And if you do have a problem, Mrs. Jacobs is right next door."

Lori was relieved to hear the doorbell. She sneaked one last glance in the mirror. She looked all right, she decided. Her black dress was several years old but one of those dresses that was always in style. Anyhow, she thought, it really isn't a big deal, is it?

As she walked past her mother, she asked herself again why she hadn't canceled out. At least a dozen times she'd picked up the phone to do so, but something always stopped her. Perhaps it was because she needed to put some of her unresolved feelings to rest. So many years had gone by. She was a different person now. And Blake had probably changed as well. Hadn't he asked about her mother with genuine interest? The boy she knew at seventeen wouldn't have been interested.

No, he had definitely changed. Sure, he had the same flirtatious manner, but she had sensed this was just a guise, that the man he had become was more like the boy who had briefly shown her that other side, the sensitive side who read poetry in secret.

As she started down the stairs, she looked back at Charlotte, who was standing in the bedroom doorway glaring at her. Impulsively Lori retraced her steps. "I'll be home early," she said, giving her mother a quick kiss on the cheek. Then she went downstairs to open the door.

"I can't get over how you haven't aged at all. Your figure is just as good as it was at sixteen, and you don't have a hint of a wrinkle." Blake was looking at her in that intense way that made her uncomfortable.

The waiter came to take their order and Blake asked, "Have you decided yet? If not, perhaps you'll allow me to order."

"Yes, please do." He'd taken her to The Broker, a popular Denver restaurant. Lori had heard about the place, but this was her first time here. The restaurant was situated in an old bank vault in what was once the Denver National Bank building. The booths were formerly the stalls used by bank customers for privacy to open their safety deposit boxes. Within a few minutes of being seated, the waiter brought them a huge basket of boiled shrimp as appetizers.

Lori was tempted to order only a salad after feasting on these, but she didn't know if this would be a faux pas. It wasn't as though she'd had a world of experience at proper dating etiquette. Not for the first time during the evening, she wished she were at home curled up with a book.

Blake ordered the Beef Wellington for both of them, explaining this was the house specialty. During dinner, Lori briefed Blake on what she knew of their old classmates whereabouts and what they were doing. He didn't seem all that interested, though, interjecting a few polite comments or questions. When the waiter came back to remove their plates, Lori's was only half-eaten.

"How about an after dinner drink?" Blake asked. "I'm going to have a shot of Brandy. Can I order one for you?"

"Perhaps a glass of white wine," she replied.

"I have some news I wanted to share with you, Lori," he said, as they sipped their drinks. "I guess I let it slip the other day when I was at the library."

She looked at him questioningly. Lori suspected he was referring to his statement about moving back to the area but didn't want to convey she'd given the matter much thought.

"When I said I might be moving back here. I'm seriously considering leaving Pierce and striking out on my own. I've contacted some investors about some fields in the Denver-Julesberg basin and it's looking good."

"Meaning some of the fields here in Colorado, as well as Nebraska and Wyoming."

Blake looked at her with surprise. This information was not something an ordinary person had at his or her fingertips. Then a look of comprehension spread across his face. "That's right, you're a librarian. You're a little scary, you know. Most women, at least the ones I've dated, aren't all that knowledgeable."

"Although I hate to confess it, I'm not a walking encyclopedia. We own some oil property north of town on which we receive a royalty. I learned a lot about the oil business from Dad and more after he died, when I was settling his estate."

"That's right, I'd forgotten. I guess at one time those wells were really producing a lot. Did your family own the field back in the boom days?"

"Yes, it's quite a story, but lets save it for another time. I don't want to bore you. You were saying you have plans to move back to Platte Valley. Will this happen soon?"

Blake ignored her question. "Being an oil man, the history of any field is of great interest to me. I have a general knowledge of the fields in this area, but don't know much about the one owned by your family. I'd really like to hear about it." He looked at her encouragingly.

"Well, the story my dad told me was that in the early thirties my grandfather, that's my dad's father, bought three sections of land north of town. He'd heard the area was being drilled for oil. Like his neighbors, he leased the land to a big oil company, and they put up some wells and started drilling."

"As I recall most of the wells didn't pan out at that time, right?"

"That's right. The oil boom was short lived. Some of the wells, including those on the Wyatt lease were shut down as the companies ran out of money. The oil was either deeper than what they'd thought or wasn't there at all."

"But eventually most of the fields in this area did produce big time, so your grandfather must have struck it rich. Right?" Blake asked.

Lori thought everyone in Morgan County must have heard the rags to riches, back to rags story about her grandfather. Blake was probably just being polite. "As a matter of fact he did, at least for awhile. About twenty years later, some oil people who told him they thought the oil was there, since the right geological conditions were present, approached Grandfather. They said that with the better technology of the day, they could get to it easier. He leased the land to them, retaining the customary twelve and a half percent royalty interest. They drilled some additional wells, bringing the total to forty-six. This time they struck oil. Grandfather's income from the royalties was almost five hundred thousand dollars the first year alone."

Blake whistled softly. "That was a small fortune, especially back in those days."

Lori nodded in agreement and continued. "Dad was twenty-two years old at the time. He'd always wanted to go to college, but there had been no money four years earlier when he finished high school. And besides, he was needed on the farm. The unexpected windfall from the oil could have made it possible for him to leave the farm for college, since his father could afford to hire outside help. But no one encouraged him to do this, so he continued working the farm."

"Back in those days it was rare for someone to go to college if they didn't enroll immediately after high school," Blake observed.

"Exactly. Added to this was the fact he was courting my mother. They married about a year later. And then, too, by this time he was completely in charge of the farm operation, since my grandfather had other interests. As it turned out, Dad's decision to stay on the farm was probably for the best. Within a few years most of the money was gone."

"How did that happen?"

Lori had never told this story to anyone, but Blake seemed genuinely interested, so she continued. "The story was that Grandfather had been a gambler. It was what had made him gamble on the oil speculation in the first place. He took the money from the oil royalties and invested it in the stock market. He got into commodities and futures and eventually lost everything but the farm and the oil field. The production by then was only about sixty barrels a day, a small fraction of what was being produced during the early years. Dad told me the loss of all his money had contributed to Grandfather's death. He just gave up the will to live."

Blake reached over and put his hand on hers. "I didn't mean to pry. This is family stuff you may not want to talk about."

"No, it's okay. I didn't even know my grandfather. This all happened before I was born."

"If my memory serves me right, there was a second oil boom in the seventies, when they came out with a new method of enhanced oil recovery," Blake said. "They found that by water flooding the fields, they could get out a lot of additional oil. In the old days you just drilled a well and got what you could out by pumping. But geologists always knew there was more oil down there that the pump wasn't getting. So when this new technology was developed, it was a real bonanza."

The waiter returned to their table, and Blake ordered her another glass of wine. "I'd better not have another one," he told the waiter. "I have to drive back to Platte Valley tonight."

"And this is definitely all for me," Lori said. "I'm not used to drinking, so I'm not sure what effect two glasses of wine will have on me."

Blake grinned. "Maybe it will loosen the little lady up to the point this city slicker can have his way with her," he said in a drawling voice.

Lori knew he was joking, but his remark put her a little off balance. She wished she were better at the light bantering other people engaged in. Instead she chose to return to the prior subject, which was more comfortable. "You were talking about this new method of oil recovery," she said. "They did water flood our field and it worked very well. I was only a child at the time, but Dad told me the story on this just a few years before his death. When he told me about it, I was quite surprised. We seemed to have all the necessities of life, but I'd never gotten the idea we were rich."

Lori had been looking down at the glass in her hand as she talked, swirling the wine gently. She was amazed how freely she was confiding in Blake. Wonder if it's the alcohol, she thought. When she looked up she saw he was watching her intently.

"And?" he asked. "Are you going to finish your story or leave me wondering if I'm sitting across from a heiress?

Lori laughed. "I'm sorry to say that's not how the story ends. Dad explained that he and Mother had used up most of the money years earlier on her medical expenses. She didn't think old Doc Jefferson took her seriously, so she talked my dad into taking her to several specialists through the years. The first two practiced in Denver. When they couldn't do anything for her, they flew to Switzerland for several months where she received further treatment."

Lori recalled the summer she had spent with her aunt and uncle in Des Moines. It hadn't been a great experience, although Frank and Ray, aside from a few taunts to the "little country bumpkin," largely ignored her. They had their own friends to hang out with and didn't see the need to include a younger, female cousin in their activities. This was fine with Lori as her memories of their visit the previous summer were still vivid. But she was terribly homesick. This was the first time she'd been away from her parents. She knew they were in Europe, but hadn't been told the reason for their trip or for her exile. Later she realized it was probably that they didn't want to worry her, but at the time she felt deserted.

"So that took most of the money?" Blake asked.

"Yes. And the shame of it was these doctors were charlatans, although Dad didn't say this. He just said none of them did her any good, but if they had, he would have hocked the farm to pay them when the oil money ran out. He really loved my mother a lot."

Lori felt a little embarrassed. She was sure by now the wine had loosened her tongue. "I don't know why I'm telling you all this. You can't be that interested, at least not in my family's personal problems."

Blake's eyes were warm. "On the contrary, I'm very interested. I think it's touching when a man loves a woman to such an extent." Then he smiled impishly. "I am sorry you're not a heiress, though. I'm in the market for one. Have to find some way to keep up my alimony payments."

His laughter was infectious, and Lori found herself laughing with him. She didn't know whether he wanted to discuss his divorce and decided not to pursue the subject, choosing instead to comment on his lament about her not being an heiress. "I guess it's never really bothered me that we're not rich. Mother and I don't lack the things we need."

Blake looked thoughtful for a moment. Then said, "Say, you may be interested in selling your royalty. It could be a good move for you. Of course, I'd have to look the field up in the state records over in Denver, do an appraisal. I know it's not worth an awful lot now, that some of the wells aren't even producing anymore. And beyond that, the state has a move on to plug these non-producers, which could be expensive."

Lori was surprised to hear he knew this. Just a few months ago she'd received a letter from Murphy Petroleum telling her that the state was insisting the non-producing wells be plugged. She'd called immediately, asking what all this meant. Mr. Murphy told her it was because of all the new environmental laws. He said, although he didn't agree there was a danger of the oil contaminating the fresh water, the law was the law. He, too, thought it would be quite expensive, but said the state had given them some time to comply. This would give them an opportunity to think of some alternatives.

When she'd asked what alternatives there were, he had been a little vague. He assured her that, although he wanted to keep her informed, none of this concerned her as a royalty owner. Any expense involved would be up to him as the working interest owner.

This had eased her mind, but she wasn't sure what this meant as far as Murphy Petroleum went. Murphy was a sole practitioner who'd bought the working interest from a larger company when the production went down. She wondered if his company had the assets to meet the state requirements for plugging the wells, and if not, what would happen. Lori decided to be candid with Blake and get his opinion.

"If Murphy doesn't have the assets, he'll probably just walk off," Blake said, "in which case the state would look to the larger company that had originally owned the working interest." He added in a casual voice, "There has been talk that on some of these deals where the money isn't there to plug the wells, they may eventually go to the royalty owners to cover the expense."

Lori must have shown her alarm, as he added in a reassuring voice, "I wouldn't worry about this happening until way down the line, if at all."

"Thanks for your input. At least I know where I stand."

"But you haven't answered my question," Blake said, looking at her intently. "You may want to take me up on my offer to buy the property and that would take care of all your worries about the state and it's plugging program."

"Regardless of what happens, I would never sell. I promised Dad," she said firmly.

"It was just a thought. It's really small potatoes, anyhow. Oh, sorry, I didn't mean that the way it sounded. But I'm looking at something much bigger. There's a guy who owns the working interest in the whole Adena field, the largest field in Colorado, and I'm working up an offer right now."

"Why would you be interested in it, Blake? With the price of oil up, we do make a nice little income off our royalty, but the Adena has similar properties, which means production there is down, also. And they probably have the same problems with the state wanting to plug the wells."

Was that a flicker of irritation on his face? But in an instant it was gone, and Lori thought she must have imagined it.

"Once you warm to a subject, you just open up, don't you? But this is a pretty complicated subject, and as Murphy said, there are alternatives. Let's just say, I don't hope to get rich, but if I can buy the interest at the right price, it will give me the means to stay in this area, which is really what I want to do, be able to operate right out of Platte Valley."

Lori suddenly remembered how the whole conversation about her oil wells had come about. "So this isn't just wishful thinking? You're really planning to move back?"

Blake had evidently gotten the waiter's eye and signaled to him. "Let me take care of this first and I'll tell you more about it," he said. He reached inside his jacket and produced an American Express card, which he handed to the waiter.

When the waiter left with Blake's card, he continued. "Neither of my parents' health is good, and I want to be around to help them. I know this is something you can understand, since your own mother's an invalid." He looked at her in a confidential manner. "We're in the same boat, Lori, so to speak."

As Blake came around to help her with her coat, she smiled warmly at him. She was pleasantly surprised at how much at ease she felt with him. He really isn't that self-centered, young man who left here so many years ago. He even wants to give up a promising career to look after his parents.

Chapter 10 - Lori

Lori glanced at Blake. His mind seemed to be on the city traffic as he made his way toward the interstate. He was so handsome. He had dressed casually in a tweed sports jacket and khaki slacks, but he looked as classy as if he had been attired in a tuxedo.

He must have sensed her looking at him, as he turned toward her and smiled.

"I never knew you were such a brilliant conversationalist. Or is it just a tape you play and now it's run out. You're suddenly awfully quiet."

"No, I usually don't talk this much. I guess it was the subject. Oil's had a big impact on my family's life."

"I need to watch for my turn, so it's okay if you don't want to talk, kind of refreshing. A lot of women never shut-up and it can be distracting at times."

He reached over and pinched her on the leg, sending a sudden, hot charge through her body and causing her to squirm. The feeling wasn't unpleasant, though, and Lori hoped in the dark he couldn't see how this small action had affected her.

She wondered again why he had asked her out. Her mother had been right about Janice. The word was they had been seen together a lot. Why would he be interested in her, when he had someone like Janice on the string? She'd seen how Janice looked at Blake that day in front of his folk's store. The thought crossed her mind that perhaps he really was just interested in the oil royalty, but this didn't make sense, since the royalty was virtually worthless. And he'd said he was more interested in the larger Adena field.

Her mind went back to the Wyatt field, which could have made her life so different had fate not stepped in twice and determined otherwise. When she was a child, she'd often ridden beside her father in his old Chevrolet pickup as he'd gone on errands around town. It had been during the days before mandatory seat belts, and he'd placed an old couch cushion on the passenger seat so she'd be tall enough to see out the window. Lori never tired of accompanying him on these sojourns, but her fondest memories were of the times when he'd turned the pickup north and taken the dusty, dirt road to the oil field.

As he and the one of the engineers discussed business, Lori found an abundance of things to occupy her. In the spring the field was covered with wild flowers, and she delighted in picking large bouquets of sunflowers, poppy mallows, and sweet peas. Near the seep ditches she'd found an abundance of wild tulips. Later she'd beg her father to let her go down to the little gazebo, nestled beneath a cluster of willows. Her grandfather had picked this site to build this little haven since there was a stream that ran close by to nurture the seedlings he'd planted there. Here as the trees grew, providing a barrier from the merciless beating of the sun's rays and the harshness of the winds that whipped across the plains, Grandfather would sit and dream his dreams. Or at least this is what Lori liked to think years later, as she dreamed her own dreams or engaged in games of make believe.

The willows could only do so much, and the years of harsh weather had taken their toll on the small, dilapidated building. Only a few flakes of faded red paint remained on the worn wood. But the little girl had an active imagination and had been able to envision the structure in its heyday, as bright and shiny as her Radio-Flyer wagon. The men finished their business and John was ready to leave long before his daughter had exhausted all the make-believe possibilities for her "castle" on the plains.

Dad had taken her back there as a young woman, when he'd told her the history of the field. He still had the pickup, but the cushion had long since been discarded.

"The reason I'm telling you this is because there's still oil in that field," he'd said. "The first time they drilled they couldn't get to it at all, but through the years as technology has improved, they've been able to get more and more out. I've had a chance to unload the field several times through the years, even make a small profit, but I'll never do it."

She remembered the serious look on his face as he'd continued. "Hopefully, one day they'll come up with even more advanced technology and be able to get the rest out. You'll inherit the land someday, and I want your promise to not let anyone talk you into selling it. Maybe you or your children will do better with the money than your grandfather and I did."

So far the field hadn't been a big money maker, but it had provided a comfortable living for her mother and herself. Lori soon learned after taking over management of the estate that the royalty interest and cattle grazing fees pretty much made up their sole income. The years when a small, independent farmer could make a living had passed, and in the five to ten years before his death, her father had barely broken even on his crops. But farming was all he knew, and he'd loved it.

She thought if her mother had known this truth, she'd have hassled her husband to give it up, to do something more productive. Charlotte had her own agenda of things she felt were important, like painting the kitchen cupboards or cleaning out the flowerbeds. John had a way of placating her, which Lori had never mastered. He would say in his calm voice, "I know, Lottie, and I'll get to it just as soon as the crops are in."

But he hadn't gotten around to it as fast as his wife would have liked, so when Lori was old enough Charlotte turned to her daughter to do these chores. She hadn't really minded, as she wanted to please her mother. She'd been this way even as a small child, perhaps because she sensed her mother's fragility, knew that when she was upset it brought on a bout that sent her to bed. So Lori wanted to do only those things that made her happy.

And, although her mother usually wasn't too free with compliments, Dad always had something nice to say. "Keep it up, and you can be a professional painter," or "I noticed when I came in from the fields how nice the flower beds look." These little words of praise had made it all seem worth the effort.

But Lori wondered after his death if another reason her father continued to farm, when it wasn't profitable, was that it provided an excuse to get out from under his wife's thumb. Lori had quickly put this thought from her mind, however, feeling a little ashamed of herself.

Once they were on the interstate, traffic was light. Blake turned and smiled. "I'm afraid I was bending your ear this evening. I guess all these big changes in my life are occupying my mind these days."

"Actually, I seem to have been doing most of the talking. As you said, once I warm up to a subject . . . ."

He looked over at her. "I was most interested in what you had to say about your field. Remember, oil is my line of business, and you are most knowledgeable."

Lori couldn't think of a response. She remembered his reason for wanting to move back to Platte Valley and said, "I am sorry to hear about your mom and dad. I hadn't realized they were in bad health. They're not that old, are they? And your dad still has his business."

"They're in their late fifties, which, as you say, is still young. But they've worked hard all their lives. Mom keeps the books for the store, you know. Anyhow, it's taken its toll on them. Dad has developed arthritis, no doubt from all the lifting. And Mom, like your mother, has a bad heart."

Lori was surprised she hadn't heard about Betty Johnson's heart problems, or for that matter that Bud suffered from arthritis.

"I'm going to try to persuade Dad to sell the business," Blake continued. "The guy who's working for him, Hal Osborne, is interested. I sounded him out. He doesn't have a lot of money, but he could probably get the bank to float a loan. He hinted his brother is pretty well fixed, he's a dentist or orthodontist in Denver, and may be willing to put up some collateral."

Lori pulled her jacket more tightly around her.

"You're cold, " he said, reaching over to adjust the heat.

"It's okay. I think I get cold more easily than some people. You're not interested in taking over the business, I guess."

"If it weren't for these bucket seats and the seat belt laws, I'd tell you to scoot over and I'd warm you up fast. Romance, while riding in an automobile, was a little easier in the good, old days."

Lori's attempt at a light-hearted laugh, caught in her throat and all she could manage was a weak "You're right about that."

"Back to your question about my taking over the business. The answer is 'No way.' It was never anything that lit my fire. I don't know if you remember, but Dad tried to get me to work there after school and weekends when I was in high school, but I was more interested in other activities." He smiled. "Girls, I guess. So that's when he hired Larry Reardon."

Blake was silent for a moment as he negotiated the turn off the interstate into Platte Valley. Then he continued. "Nope, it was never anything that interested me, but there are other reasons. There's no money in it, maybe in the past but not now. At least my parents were able to make a living out of it—were even able to put me through school. But the handwriting's on the wall. Farmers are in trouble, losing their farms. They're having to declare bankruptcy, and Dad is listed as a creditor, which means he's left holding the bag."

"I know what you mean. After my father's death, I came to realize we weren't making much off the farm. We'd have been in trouble if it hadn't been for the money from the oil property."

Blake glanced at her. "So you can understand where I'm coming from.

Not that I think I'll get rich with my oil operation, but it's something I know. It's where my experience is. And Osborne seems real keen on taking over the store. Maybe he can think of a way to turn it around. I don't know how. I'm just thankful he seems interested."

When Blake pulled up in front of Lori's house, he shut off the motor. "Well, here we are. Unlike Cinderella, you're home before midnight," he said.

"I had a nice evening." She really meant it. She even had a small hope he would ask her out again.

He leaned over and taking her chin in his hand, turned her face toward him. "I had a wonderful evening, Lori. As I said, if everything works out, I'll be staying around here for a long time. But there's something else I need to tell you. I plan on spending a lot of time with you, so you'd better make arrangements to work this out with your mother, get her used to the idea."

Lori didn't trust herself to speak. Her heartbeat had quickened at these words, but it was too much for her to take in. Why would he want to spend time with her? And what would her mother's reaction be? Then suddenly she was angry. This seemed to be the same old Blake, assuming she'd jump at the chance to be included in his plans. He hadn't even asked her if this was something she was agreeable to.

"As I said, I enjoyed the evening, but I don't think I'll be able to see you again, Blake," she said in a cool voice.

He seemed undaunted. "Come on, I'll walk you to your door." He jumped out and reached her side just as she was getting out. Pulling her up, he put his arm around her as they walked toward the house. Lori noticed there was no awkwardness in any of his movements and wondered what it would be like to be so sophisticated and confident.

When they reached the porch, before she realized what was happening, he'd turned her around and had both his hands on her shoulders, pressing her against the door. His mouth was on hers, his tongue forcing her lips apart. It may as well have been yesterday instead of twenty years ago. She felt the same surge of excitement, the same anticipation, as she had that day at the lake, feelings she'd never had with Jeff. She marveled at how strong he was and wondered if she could break away even if she wanted to. But she was no longer sixteen. She was a mature woman who'd spent many years convincing herself that this kind of thing would never happen to her. She'd even learned to be content, knowing the wild, passionate love affairs other women seemed to fall into so easily would never be a part of her life.

So she turned her head and tried to push him away. When he finally backed off, she asked, "What are you doing, Blake? I thought you asked me out just to catch up on things here in Platte Valley. Besides, I understand you and Janice are involved. I don't like to listen to gossip, but this is a small town and there's been a lot of talk."

His answer to this was a long, hearty laugh. Lori was glad her mother's bedroom was on the other side of the house.

"Janice Hollingsworth isn't my type," he said finally. "If I'd wanted a barracuda in my life, I would've tried harder to stay married to Andrea. Sure, Jim's little sister has grown-up very nicely, at least from a physical standpoint, but now, instead of the spoiled little brat she was when Jim and I used to pal around, she's a self-serving, scheming woman."

Lori couldn't hide her look of shock. "But why do you go out with her then?"

"As I said, Janice never does anything without a plan. At this point I don't know what that plan is. She seems to have set her sights on me, but I'm not rich enough to be a long-term interest. I think she's just back in town for the short haul, biding her time until she moves on to bigger and better things. I'm, no doubt, just a diversion to keep her from getting too bored while she's here. Anyhow, because of my friendship with Jim, it's been a little difficult trying to get uninvolved."

He put his hands on Lori's shoulders again, gently this time. The earnest look on his face was disarming. "Once she realizes I'm interested in you, she won't be a problem."

In an attempt to cover her confusion, Lori was a little more abrupt than she'd intended. "I'd better say goodnight, Blake," she said, placing her key in the lock. Then, without turning around, she quickly stepped inside, closing the door behind her. For a long moment there was only silence as she stood there hardly breathing. Then finally, she sighed with relief as she heard Blake's footsteps receding into the distance, and a couple of minutes later, the sound of his car engine as he drove away.

Chapter 11 - Blake

As Blake drove to his parents' house his mind was filled with the evening's events. He thought that all in all things had gone well. It had been a blow to learn Lori was adamant about not selling, but he'd planted a seed. Telling her the state may look to the royalty owners to pay for the well plugging had had an effect. He might have stretched the truth a bit, but he'd heard a rumor this could happen. Now if he could just keep chipping away until this supposition seemed more a certainty to her. But what if this didn't happen? She could be stubborn, and said she'd promised her dad she'd never sell. These people with morals were a pain.

But Blake had put a lot of thought into this. If Lori couldn't be persuaded to sell, there was always Plan B. He'd called his mom from Chicago a few weeks before he left for the sole purpose of finding out if Lori had married. Of course, he didn't come right out and ask her. But Blake was a master at eliciting information and with Betty Johnson it was easy. All he had to do was maneuver the conversation in a certain direction and his unsuspecting mother would soon supply the answers he needed. Somehow, it didn't surprise him that Lori had never married, a fact that fit in with his plans. In a strange sort of way she intrigued him, always had. She was certainly different from any other woman with whom he'd been involved. And he believed firmly in the old adage about variety being the spice of life. He was whistling softly as he rounded the corner to his parents' house.

"And you think an injectivity test would make the odds even better?"

"I'm convinced the area is a prime candidate," Eric Anders said. "The lab studies, as you know, indicate temperatures and pressures are high enough. I would say, without further testing, there's a ninety-five percent certainty the process will work."

"Could you hang on a minute, Eric?" Blake was using his father's study to make the call. He'd heard Betty, who'd been working in her flowerbeds, coming in the back door.

He laid the telephone down and went to the door of the study. "I'm on the phone. Be out in a minute," he called. Then he closed the door.

Returning to the desk he picked up the telephone, taking a deep breath before he spoke. "Sorry. That was my secretary. I told her to make sure I wasn't interrupted again. Now, where were we? Oh, yes, I need to know if you'd be willing to meet with some of my potential investors, present your findings to them."

"Of course. Whenever you're ready to go. Has the working interest owner agreed to go along? I can't remember the name of the company."

"Murphy Petroleum. It's a small privately owned company."

"Ah yes. Is this Murphy ready to go with the project?"

"I'm sure I can convince him, especially if I put up all the money. He has the state breathing down his neck, wanting him to plug those non-producing wells, and I doubt if he has the assets to comply. So my plan is to line up the investors before I approach him. This way he'll jump at my offer. It will be like throwing him a life line."

"Do you have any idea how much pressure the state is putting on him? You know if those wells are plugged, it will cost to open them back up and the project won't be as attractive economically."

"From what I can see, no one around here has done any plugging. After we get everything in place, the investors' and Murphy's go ahead, we'll need to make a presentation to the state. If we just give them a plan, they'll back off on making him plug the wells."

"Make's sense. Think you may have the right approach."

Blake's tension began to subside a little. "Glad you agree, Eric. Can you start getting something together?"

"I'll get to work on it right away."

"Great. I'll be back in touch soon."

Blake hung up the phone and leaned back in his chair, a look of satisfaction on his face. During his conversation with Anders, he'd been playing with some small plastic-headed stickpins, poking them into an old 1990 calendar covering the desk. Now he removed one more from the box and placed it in line with the others. So far, so good, he thought. No need to tell Anders about his plan to get with Murphy right away. Blake was banking on the possibility Murphy hadn't heard of the new enhanced oil recovery process. Or, if he had heard of it, was not convinced it had merit. Oil companies were traditionally cautious, choosing to stick to the old ways, and this would work in his favor. He was almost certain Murphy knew nothing about the successes a few, more adventurous companies were having with high pressure air injection.

Why settle for only a percentage when he could get the whole enchilada? No, Blake's plan was to buy Murphy out. The man would probably sell out cheap just to get out from under.

But he needed some money up front. For one thing he would have to pay Anders, and a consultant of his caliber didn't come cheap. Blake had a lot of confidence in his own abilities but was smart enough to realize his limitations. Anders was the country's leading expert on the air injection process, and Blake knew he needed him.

He'd considered offering Anders a percentage in lieu of a salary but decided to use this only as a last resort. It would be more advantageous in the long run to have Anders on salary, inflated though it was.

He rubbed the back of his neck, feeling the tension coming back. Relax, Blake, old boy, he told himself. This is just a game, and you've always been a winner. So you lost the last one, but that's rare. Besides, as he had reasoned earlier, getting himself canned by Pierce was probably a good thing. It had gotten him going on an idea he'd been toying with for several years.

He got up and walked to the window. Betty had left her lawn tools in the yard, obviously planning to return to her task. He heard sounds coming from the kitchen, which indicated she'd taken a break to prepare lunch.

The only solution was to step up the pressure on his dad. Blake figured a cushion of around a million would see him through the preliminaries. He wanted to be able to tell potential backers he was bankrolling part of the project himself. Investors were more likely to put up their own money when they saw the operator risking some as well.

That's where his old man came in. He'd been making some real progress with Bud, going to the store every day to help out. He could see his father softening toward him. But there was a big jump between mere cordiality and handing over your life savings. The first step was to convince Bud to sell his business. Then, with the money available, he would convince him of the logic of bankrolling his son's venture. Glancing toward the kitchen, Blake thought he knew of a way to soften his dad up a little faster.

"I didn't realize how much I've missed your cooking. You have to be the best cook in Morgan County." Blake was sitting at the kitchen table finishing off a lunch of meat loaf, mashed potatoes, and creamed asparagus.

Betty blushed with pleasure as she poured them both a cup of tea and sat down across from him. "Well, I have won a few prizes for my recipes at the fair. Last year I won a blue ribbon for my apple dumplings. Phoebe Gibbons thought her blueberry cobbler was a shoo-in and was she steaming! Oh, she didn't say anything, but you should have seen the look on her face. And what's more, she didn't even come over to . . ."

"I wish I'd been there," Blake said, cutting her off. He had other things on his mind.

He laid his hand on hers, feigning a look of concern. "I've been trying to talk Dad into retiring. It's time you two started enjoying life more, travel a little while your health is still good. I need your help in convincing him. I know Hal is interested in buying him out, and I think he ought to go for it."

Betty looked at her son adoringly. "You're right, Blake. And it touches me that you're worried about us. But Dad is stubborn. Thinks he can't afford to retire."

"You keep the books. I know you two have always been careful with your money. You must have a bundle stashed away."

"We have more than enough. With our IRAs and other bank holdings we've managed to accumulate several hundred thousand."

"That's great. And with the proceeds from the sale of the store, you'd have more than enough to live comfortably and even have a few extras. You ought to take a Caribbean cruise. I'll bet Uncle Curt and Aunt Louise would go again. The four of you would have a great time."

"Oh, they just raved on and on about it. They begged us to go with them, but Dad didn't want to leave the store even with Hal there, even though he's perfectly capable of running things. And they do plan to go again."

Blake's hand was beginning to cramp. He drew it back, but continued to look at his mother intently. He fervently wished his father were as easy to influence as she was.

Betty was silent for a moment, a rare occurrence. A wistful look came over her face. "The truth is, I don't think he'll ever retire. He grew up poor, you know, and no matter how much money we have, it's never enough."

"I told you I'm looking into some things around here. If they pan out, we'll all be so rich Dad will have no excuse for not retiring. And better yet I'd be able to stay in the area. As I said, I have visitation rights with Josh, and he could spend time here with us. I want so to have you get acquainted with your grandson."

He paused for effect; then plunged ahead. "The thing is I'll need some capital to get started. But the only reason I'd even consider asking you for a loan is because the project I'll be working on is risk free. And better yet, your money would be doubled in a year or two. By helping me, you two will be in a position to go on lots of cruises, even sail around the world if you want to."

"Oh, Blake. That would be wonderful. About the money, but also that you'd be able to live here. I've been thinking a lot about Josh. I guess before I tried not to, as I was afraid I may never get to meet him." She reached for a tissue in her apron pocket and wiped a tear from her eye.

Blake's face was a study in compassion. "I know I haven't been much of a son these past years, but I want to be here for you now. Help make up for the past."

Betty put the tissue back in her pocket and straightened her back. "I'll get started on Dad tonight," she said with a tone of resolve. "Once I set my mind on something, eventually he sees it my way. He says he gives in just to get a little peace. But usually the things I've insisted on have turned out well, like when I wanted to redecorate . . ."

"That's great, because I have to get going on this thing real soon."

"With both of us working on him, he doesn't stand a chance," she said, giggling.

"I'm to meet Malcolm Murphy. Is he here yet?" Blake was standing in the reception area at the Denver Petroleum Club.

"Yes, Sir. Please follow me," the host said, leading him to a table toward the back. When he'd made the reservation, Blake had requested seating where he and his client could discuss business without being disturbed.

Once he was seated, and they'd introduced themselves, Malcolm Murphy said, "I don't know why we had to come all the way to Denver to meet, but this is a real fancy place. This is my first time here. I guess us small town oil people don't travel in the same circles as you big city types."

Looking over his luncheon companion, Blake could well believe this. Murphy looked like a fish out of water. He was a balding, red-faced man in his fifties, attired in a cheap, out-of-style suit. The outfit might have fit him once but was now too snug for his stout frame. He wore the required dress shirt but rather than a regular tie, he sported one of those bolo things. Even so, he looked like he'd be more comfortable in a pair of old jeans and cowboy boots. Blake decided Murphy was an easy mark.

"Mr. Murphy," Blake said, "you know what a small town Platte Valley is and how rumors can spread. As a matter of policy I like to keep my business private. If you and I decide to do business together, I must insist our relationship be kept in the strictest confidence."

"Sure, that's fine with me." He looked at Blake expectantly. "What kind of business did you have in mind?"

But Blake wanted to set the pace, take control from the start. He picked up his menu. "I think we should order first. What would you like to drink?"

An hour and a half later Blake walked out of the club with a commitment from Murphy, sealed with a firm handshake. For a small pittance Murphy had agreed to let him take over the working interest on the Wyatt lease. With a little skillful prompting, the owner had admitted he'd been spending some sleepless nights wondering how to survive the state's aggressive environmental program.

It was as Blake had surmised. Murphy simply didn't have the assets to comply and had been considering walking off when things got too rough. Blake had convinced him that the contract, to be drawn-up within the next week, should for the present not be divulged to anyone. He had told Murphy he'd like to keep him on to take care of the lease. Blake's reasons for retaining Murphy were twofold. First, he'd need someone to check the wells, at least until the project got underway; and secondly, and more important, having Murphy still around would keep the locals from learning the interest had changed hands. He especially didn't want the Wyatts to know he'd bought the interest.

Murphy had balked a little about not telling the royalty owner about the sale. Said he didn't feel right about it, especially in view of the fact that John Wyatt had always treated him fairly. Now that his daughter owned the lease, he wanted to keep things above board with her, also. But when Blake had shown signs of withdrawing his offer, Murphy had become flustered and had quickly agreed with this provision.

As he drove back to Platte Valley, Blake congratulated himself on his ability to carry off this phase so smoothly. By buying Murphy out, he'd be able to pocket a larger share of the profits from his proposed project. He realized, as working interest owner, he'd have to foot all the operating costs, rather than splitting these costs with the royalty owner. This made Lori's twelve and a half percent royalty, in actuality, more like sixty five percent. Not a cheerful prospect. Time to move ahead with the next phase—the one that would eventually make Blake Johnson extremely wealthy.

Chapter 12 - Lori

"Good-morning, Sunshine. It's a beautiful day, way too nice to be indoors. How about if I pick you up in an hour, and we'll drive to the lake?"

It had been a week since they'd had dinner in Denver, and this was the first time since then that Lori had heard from Blake. She had begun to doubt his intentions again, to think he was playing a sick little game at her expense. All that talk of how he wanted her in his life and then no word from him.

A part of her had dreaded this call, afraid of the changes that may lie ahead for her, but another part had been even more afraid. She wasn't sure she could face the disappointment if he were suddenly gone from her life. Many times during the past week she had wished he'd never come back or if he had to come back, that he hadn't asked her out. Her life might have been a little on the dull side, but at least she hadn't jumped every time the phone rang. Now she found herself lying awake at night wondering why he hadn't called.

At the sound of his voice, the part of her that feared change took over. "Blake, I don't know if I can. I told you weekends are pretty busy here, and we're invited to dinner at Phoebe Gibbon's. Mother has been looking forward to it all week."

"It's only nine o'clock. If I come by in an hour, I'll have you home by three at the latest. Come on, the fall colors will soon be gone. We need to get out and enjoy them while we can."

To her consternation, she found herself saying, "Well, I guess if you're sure I can be home by three."

As Lori hung up she was wondering what had happened to weaken her resolve. She did have a lot to do. She was grateful Charlotte had decided not to attend church that morning, had said she wanted to rest up for the evening at Phoebe's. But it would have given me a perfect excuse to decline, she thought.

As she started toward her room, Lori's mind turned to the subject of what she would wear. Her favorite jeans were in the laundry. This was another chore she'd planned for the day, doing the weekly wash. How could she have let him talk her into changing her plans on the spur of the moment and for a drive to the lake of all places. But it was a lovely day. Who really cared if she put the mulch down in the gardens, and she could throw a couple of loads in the washer when she got home. I'm still young, she thought. I need to be more carefree, less responsible.

Suddenly, Lori realized Charlotte was standing in the doorway, an inquiring look on her face. She wondered how much her mother had heard.

"So you're going off somewhere with that man again," Charlotte stated, answering her daughter's unspoken question.

There was nothing to do but level with her. "Yes, Blake's picking me up in an hour. We're driving to the lake, but I'll be home in plenty of time to take you to Phoebe's." She hurried past her mother but not before she caught a glimpse of the look on Charlotte's face.

"But I thought you were going to do the laundry today and what if you don't get back in time to take me to Phoebe's?" Charlotte's shrill voice followed her up the stairs. "You've been acting so strange lately, it wouldn't surprise me if you got out there and forgot all about the time."

"I'll be home by three." Lori cut off any further conversation as she closed her bedroom door.

Blake was wearing tight-fitting Levi's and a white polo shirt. A yellow sweater, tied loosely around his neck, brought out the gold in his sun-streaked hair. Why did he have to look so sexy? And why after all these years did her stomach do flip-flops when he smiled at her or touched her as he did now?

"I'm glad you decided to come," he said as they walked toward his car, his hand lightly on her shoulder.

As they drove through town, Lori continued to silently question her attraction to Blake. No other man had ever had this effect on her. Was she so shallow that a man's physical make-up was what attracted him to her? Or was there something more about him, something deeper, which she'd first glimpsed those long years ago when he'd confessed his love of poetry to her. That day before he'd made a pass at her and turned a beautiful day into something ugly.

Lori spotted Phoebe coming out of Isleys, her arms loaded down with groceries. Phoebe apparently recognized Lori about the same moment and almost dropped her bags.

Lori's mouth curved in a small smile as she waved. She was certain she'd be the subject of Phoebe's latest gossip. She also knew this would be the first time in years, since her life was normally quite ordinary and boring, at least from Phoebe's perspective.

She stole another look at Blake. She marveled that she was sitting here beside him, and even more so that she was returning with him to that setting that had had such a profound effect on her. But that was long ago, when she was young and impressionable. And he has changed. She had to believe this, as the alternative was too awful. If he was still the same unprincipled person as that wild, young man she once knew, what did this say about her judgment?

Blake seemed relaxed and happy. "When I told Mom I had a date with you to go to the lake, she was so pleased she went right to the kitchen and packed us a picnic lunch. Then I stopped off at the liquor store and picked up a bottle of wine, so we're all set."

"Was she pleased you were going out with me or just that you were getting out to enjoy the day?"

"Oh, she said she'd prefer it had been Janice but that she was tired of watching me mope around."

Lori's reaction must have registered on her face. But then she saw he was grinning at her.

"Silly, Goose. Don't you know when someone's joking? The truth is Mom thinks you're a 'very nice young lady.' And she doesn't think too much of Janice by the way."

As Blake drove down the road to the lake, he commented on the abundance of campers at the trailer park to their left. "This place has sure grown up since I left," he said.

"I think a lot of the owners just use the place in the summer. It's pretty quiet this time of year."

Blake stopped the car in the parking lot and jumped out. "Come on, let's go down to the lake. We can come back for the lunch later." He came around and opened her door.

As they walked, Lori realized how happy she was, regardless of the reasons. She was going to have to quit being so introspective, she told herself—just enjoy what was happening. Blake had taken her hand, making her feel warm and tingly. And to think she'd almost stayed home to do laundry!

They stood looking out at the water, and Blake, as if reading her thoughts, said, "Now, wasn't this worth the trip out here?"

"Yes, I'm glad you talked me into it."

The cottonwoods were at their fall peak, the leaves a myriad of bright golds and rusts, as breathtakingly lovely as at any time she could recall. Or was it just that she'd never appreciated their beauty as much as today. Here, with Blake beside her, she felt she was living a dream, one she'd never allowed herself to have. Suddenly, Lori knew she'd always been in love with him.

A cool breeze emanated from the lake, and they were quiet for a few minutes, mesmerized by the gentle movement it created on the water.

Lori was the first to break the silence. "There's something that's been puzzling me, and please don't think I'm fishing for compliments. I honestly don't know why you want to spend time with me. I'm sure most of the women you've been with have been really gorgeous, and I heard your wife was beautiful. I've been told by you and one other person that I have pretty eyes, but aside from this, there's nothing outstanding about my looks."

"Oh, and who was that other person? Have you got another fellow on the string?" Blake asked, ignoring the first part of Lori's statement.

"No, I don't have anyone and haven't had for a number of years. It was my father who commented on my eyes."

He looked at her for a moment, as if formulating his words. Then he took her hand. "Don't you know how attractive you are? You're beautiful, and there's more to you than just being merely physically attractive. You're intelligent and caring and unspoiled. I don't know if it's because you never left this little town but just like Platte Valley, you belong to a time that's disappearing, a time when things were normal and—I can't think of the right word but secure will do. The way things are today, at least in the big cities, you get to moving so fast you miss everything that's important. And people are phony and devious and think nothing of stepping on each other just to get ahead."

He laughed. "Wow! I didn't mean to make a speech. What I'm trying to say is that I'm very attracted to you. What you are, all those things I said, make you one very sexy lady. If I'd been smart, I'd have come back here after college and married you."

Lori knew her face must be flushed. She freed her hand from his and took a step or two away from him, as if retreating to safer ground. "I don't know what to say. You're overwhelming me."

Her eyes were fastened on the rippling water as she spoke. "I know people in the city live more stressful lives as a rule. I think it's described as 'life in the fast lane.' But living in a small town doesn't automatically mean one is immune from vice, myself included. I'm not the virtuous person you seem to think I am. Just ask my mother. I'm often impatient with her. Probably the only reason I'm here in Platte Valley and not one of those big city-types you described is because of her. And at times I resent her for it."

"But you stayed. Most people in your situation wouldn't have. They'd have figured, and rightfully so, that they were entitled to their own lives. Besides, I doubt if you treat her all that badly."

When she didn't immediately respond, Blake added, "Anyhow, from what I've heard about Charlotte Wyatt, I think she can hold her own."

Lori was a little taken aback by Blake's comment but didn't care to have him elaborate. "Still, as I said, people in small towns can do some pretty awful things. Right in this spot one of Platte Valley's citizens murdered another one in cold blood."

Blake gave her an exasperated look. "Lori, I was trying to tell you what I see in you, and I don't think I'm mistaken. Of course, what I said is an oversimplification. But I know one thing, maybe because I've had a lot of experience in the big bad world, I'm a good judge of people."

He moved closer and turned her face toward him. "Lori, Lori, I am learning one thing about you I didn't know. You're very argumentative. So maybe I'm wrong, maybe you're a murderess or worse, but please don't destroy my illusions. I need to think there are still a few old-fashioned girls in the world."

"I'm sorry, Blake. I guess I'm not good at handling compliments. But isn't the reason for dating, if this is what we're doing, to get to know each other? I don't have many close friends with the exception of Sarah, and even she doesn't always know who I really am. To most people in Platte Valley I'm what you described, and I try to live up to this image. But there are times I feel like a real phony."

She shrugged her shoulders. "I don't know exactly what I'm trying to say. I know you've been burned, that you went through a divorce. I don't know the details and can only surmise that somehow your wife let you down. But everyone is human, and as such, not without flaws. I just don't want you to think I'm some kind of exception."

"Okay. You've told me all your dark secrets. But this is another thing I like about you, your honesty."

"I haven't told you all my secrets," she said with a small smile. "For instance, I'm not exactly an old-fashioned girl." She couldn't look at him.

"What I'm saying is I'm not a virgin. When I was in college I had a thing with a student I met there."

"My response to that confession is that I didn't think you'd been in a convent. In fact, I'm surprised there was just one. If we're going to start counting, I guess I'd better change the subject."

This time it was Blake who walked a few steps away. Then turning back he said, "I'm sure you remember that other day at the lake, because I do."

She looked up at him, not daring to breathe.

"The only part of that seventeen year-old kid who was really me was the part that discussed poetry with you. That arrogant little rascal, the one who tried to seduce you, was a fake. In those days I was just an insecure kid who could never measure up to my father's expectations. I guess I thought that getting girls in the sack would prove I was a man."

He smiled a little bitterly. "That hasn't changed. I mean my dad still doesn't understand or approve of me. But I guess I've gone beyond that. I don't need his approval anymore."

"I think I know what you mean. I've always felt I've been a disappointment to my mother. But I still care too much."

"Then I'm going to have to help you overcome that. I doubt very much that your mother approves of me, but since it's my intention for us to be married some day, we'll have to present her with a united front. Charlotte has a reputation for being a tough cookie, but, like the famous quote, 'We shall overcome.'"

Again Lori ignored his remark about her mother. This time because she was focused on what Blake had said about getting married. "Things are moving too fast for me. It's true we've known each other for a long time, but today is the first time we've ever had an intimate conversation. We're just now getting to really know each other."

"We know each other, Lori. And this isn't our first intimate conversation. Remember that other talk years ago, when the subject was also about our hopes and dreams for the future. I think we've always been soul mates. But anyhow, I didn't say we'd get married right away. I have to get my company going first."

Suddenly he turned and started running toward the car. "Come on," he yelled. "All this heavy talk has made me famished. Let's eat."

"Be sure to thank your mother for the lunch and tell her it was delicious." Lori said. They had returned to their earlier spot and had spread out a blanket to sit on. After feasting on salami and cheese sandwiches along with deviled eggs and potato salad, Blake had opened the bottle of wine.

"You say this is where they found the body?"

"Yes, some kids found her. From the state of the body they figured it had happened late the day before." Lori shivered, thinking about it.

"I shouldn't have brought it up. Sorry. It's been a great day and I don't want anything to mar it." He refilled their glasses and held his up in a toast. "Here's to many more days like today."

Lori clinked her glass against his. She wasn't sure how to respond, so she only nodded.

"Can you make time for me in your life, Melora Wyatt?" he asked.

His look was so appealing, she couldn't resist. "If you really want to see me, I'll find a way."

"Yes, I really want that, even after you've divulged your wicked past," he said smiling. "I've signed a lease on a house. As wonderful as Mom is, I'm beyond the stage where I can go back to being her little boy. I'll be taking possession in a week. This way we can have some privacy."

As if anticipating her reaction, he continued, "I'll admit I want you, Lori, but I'll give you all the time you need."

She looked at him with gratitude. "Thank you, Blake, but I don't think it will take all that long." This time it was Lori who impulsively reached for Blake's hand.

Chapter 13 - Lori

"Please don't take this wrong, Lori. Jon and I were Blake's classmates, too." Sarah's face had a pleading look. "If he's on the level, no one could be happier than we are. You know how much I've always wanted you to meet someone, to have your own home and children."

They were having their usual weekly lunch at Dora's, this time in a back booth where they could have more privacy. Sarah had insisted. She'd tried to get Lori to go out to dinner at Fort Morgan, but Lori had spent so much time away from home lately, she couldn't manage it.

"But I'm concerned you're moving too fast. We wish you'd just step back a little, spend a week or so away from him. For God's sake, Lori, this isn't like you. You've always been so—so sensible."

"I know I have, Sarah. And I won't deny that to those who care about me this change must be a little frightening. But you know what? The way I feel I can't lose on this, even if Blake turns out to be a real jerk. Even if after all his promises, he suddenly leaves town or finds someone else, at least I can say when I'm old and gray that I have experienced life."

Sarah smiled. "Kind of like the old saying, 'It is better to have loved and lost than to have never loved at all.' It goes something like that, I think."

Lori gave her friend a grateful look. "Exactly. Do you know sometimes in the evenings when I've been sitting there reading, while Mother was watching television, I've just wanted to scream—scream so loud she'd turn away from that damned television set and look at me. You heard me right. I did say 'damned', and I thought about using an even stronger adjective. But you know what? I don't think it'd have any effect on her. I doubt if she'd even hear me. Once she gets absorbed in one of those programs she's so addicted to, nothing I say or do would get her attention."

Sarah, who had been munching on a piece of fried chicken, started giggling and almost choked. She grabbed a glass of water and took a drink. When she'd recovered, she asked, "Sorry I just got a mental image of how to get her attention. How about taking off all your clothes, stick a rose in your teeth and dance in front of the television?"

Lori smiled. "I don't think she'd do anything other than to try to look around me. The point is I don't want to be like her. Oh, for me it isn't television, but we both know it's been books. I've used them as an escape all my life."

"Of all people, I should know this. It's ironic, for as long as I can remember I've tried to get you to take your nose out of a book and live, and now that you're doing just that, I'm trying to stop you."

Sarah reached across the table and laid her hand on her friend's. "I just don't want you to get hurt. You're more sensitive than anyone I know, and I'm afraid of what will happen if he's just playing some kind of game."

"You mean fragile, don't you? But I don't think I am. And besides, as I said, I'm willing to take that risk. There have been times when I've spent all those nights with Mother when instead of reading, I'd sit there and ponder things. One of the things I wondered about was if a person could go through an entire life without rocking the boat just a little. And it's almost become an obsession, this need to rock the boat just a little before I die."

Sarah smiled. "Honey, I think you can say you're rocking it so hard there's a danger it will capsize. By the way I've been dying to ask, how's your mother handling all this? I'll bet she's fit to be tied!"

"It's funny. Once I knew this was something I had to do, it's been easier than I thought. Oh, at first she pulled out all the stops, tried all the old guilt trips. But for the first time, and Blake has helped me to work through this, I've been able to see her clearly. All these years, even as a child, she manipulated me."

"Praise the Lord. You finally see it. I guess I'm going to have to give Blake a little more credit."

"And she did the same thing to Dad, although he was stronger than me. He loved her so much, but he'd only let her have her way to a point. Perhaps this was because he met her as an adult. But she knew how much I needed her to love me, and she used it. I'm even beginning to suspect that some of her illness is psychosomatic, just a means to keep me in line."

"She kept you from your dream of going to college, of becoming a journalist," Sarah said quietly.

"Yes, in the back of my mind, I think I've always known this, but I was never strong enough to fight her until now. Oh, don't get me wrong. I do love her a lot, and I even think she does have problems with her heart. I've talked to Dr. Jefferson, as you know, and he says her heart was definitely weakened by rheumatic fever as a child."

"I know. Remember I work for her doctor. Her records date back to the old days when his father was in practice. It's true about the rheumatic fever, but it's questionable it left her that bad off. And it's certainly not life threatening. This is, of course, just between you and me, since I shouldn't be divulging what's in her records. But from what you're saying, she isn't giving you a problem over Blake."

Lori picked at the remainder of her Chef's salad. "Once she realized it wasn't working, she seems to have given up. Oh, I get the silent treatment a lot, but I can handle it."

"If seeing Blake has done nothing but break the hold she's had over you, it's worth it."

Lori glanced at her watch. "I have to get back, but there was so much more I wanted to tell you. He's so different than I thought, Sarah. I'm not saying he hasn't made mistakes, married the wrong woman for one, but he's learned from them. And he's always been sensitive and caring. He just thought he needed to have this tough image. It has to do with his relationship with his father."

Lori sighed. "What parents do to their children! If I'm ever lucky enough to have children, I hope I don't make the same mistakes. Before we go, I want to show you a poem he wrote. He says he's been too busy to spend much time writing, but once in awhile he's used it as therapy when things got rough."

Searching through her purse, she found a folded paper and opened it. "He wrote this a few years back but said that he was thinking of me at the time. Shall I read it?"

Sarah nodded, her face attentive.

It's called "The Fractured Stem," Lori said. She began to read.

Once fresh as new friendship,
beginning to grow,
the rose bud
with fractured stem
has lost its crimson glow.

Like a promise broken,
which ends things too soon,
it never knows
what it has lost,
the beauty of full bloom.

"It's beautiful. Are you sure he wrote it?" Sarah asked.

"Blake's been reading and writing poetry since he was in high school. I knew this. I knew him a little better than you thought. We had an—incident back then I never told anyone about."

"Not even me, your best friend?"

"It started out as something beautiful, but it didn't turn out well. It was a very painful experience, and I was too ashamed."

Lori noticed the astounded look on Sarah's face. "Oh, he didn't seduce me, or at least he wasn't successful. But he hurt me. The reason I'm telling you this now is because of the poem. It's his way of telling me he regrets what happened."

She searched for the right words. "I think until he gave me this, I still didn't quite trust him. I was holding a part of myself back. But with this poem he has scraped away that last layer of the shell I'd built around myself."

"You've done a good job of convincing me, too. I'd love to get to know this new Blake, and I'm sure Jon would like to give him a chance, too."

Lori reached for Sarah's hand. "I'll tell him. I just know the four of us will be the best of friends in time."

"So what do you think?"

Lori looked around the spacious room. The home was one of the newer ones on the east side of town. Blake said the owners lived in Denver. They'd planned to commute back and forth but had found the drive was too much, so decided to rent it until they retired in a few years.

It was really a large log cabin rather than a house, set back from the road among large evergreens. The interior, including the ceiling, was done in knotty pine. There was a large fireplace on the north wall, which made the cheerful room even more inviting. Blake had furnished it with rugged, ranch-style furniture. There was even a large bearskin rug in front of the sofa, which Blake had managed to find somewhere. An oak bar off to the right separated the kitchen.

"It's wonderful. I don't know how you managed to furnish it so quickly."

"It wasn't easy." He walked over to the fireplace and took out the poker. "My main problem was keeping my mother at arm's length. I love and respect her, but she's operating under the delusion she missed her calling as an interior decorator. She's tried to be a little too helpful," he added as he stoked the fire.

"But I could spend an entire evening on that topic, and I have other things I want to discuss. Come over here," he said, as he sat down on the sofa next to the fireplace.

When Lori was seated next to him, she was at peace with the world. For just this moment she felt there was nowhere she would rather be, enjoying the warmth of the fire and being alone with Blake. She sensed he felt the same, as he didn't speak for a moment.

When he did, it was to say, "I signed a six-month lease. They wanted me to take it for a year, but they were willing to go along with my terms, probably because there isn't an abundance of people in the area wanting to rent. If you like it, I'm sure we won't have a problem renewing the lease."

"There are a lot of hurdles to get through before we can even consider getting married," Lori said. "One big one is Mother. I'd have mentioned this earlier, but things have been moving so fast. I know we've discussed how she's kept me under her thumb all these years, but she is my mother and I'm all she has. I can't possibly leave her alone."

"Lori, look at me," Blake said, turning her face toward him. "I know I've caused a rift between you two, and I regret it. But it was unavoidable. This doesn't mean I expect you to neglect her. This is a small town, and your mom is only ten minutes away. You can go over there as often as you like, and I'll help. I'll go by and do the lawn work. I'm getting a new tractor, at cost of course, and I notice the one you have has seen better days."

"If someone had told me a few months ago that you'd given up your jet set life and moved to this little country town, I'd have figured it was just one of Phoebe's baseless rumors. But you're really getting into this country life, even buying a tractor."

"Well, I have to keep the brush trimmed down around here, so I may as well do your mother's lawn as well. And if this astounds you, don't laugh, but I've also ordered a new truck and trailer, so it will be no problem transporting the tractor. I may even have to go the whole nine yards and get myself a cowboy hat and boots."

Lori doubled over in laughter at the thought of this. The next thing she knew she was in his arms. How could life have changed so much in the past few months?

Blake had kept his promise and had been patient with her, and now it seemed the most natural thing in the world that he was carrying her to the bedroom. By unspoken assent they both knew it was time. He undressed her slowly and gently, kissing her mouth, then her breasts. As he caressed each new area, she felt her passion grow until her whole body was crying out for him. She reached for his belt, clumsily trying to unbuckle it. Somewhere in the recesses of her mind, she was aware he'd mastered the art of love, and she was thankful. He expertly measured her response, just when to pause and when to move ahead. Then, just when she was on the brink of insanity, he granted her that glorious relief, while he simultaneously burst inside her. Afterwards, as she lay in his arms and wept for joy, she knew she'd never willingly let him go.

Chapter 14 - Lori

"I did real good on my report. Miss Abernathy wrote 'excellent' on it," Rusty said proudly.

Lori looked fondly at the little boy. "That's great. I know you worked hard on it, so I think you deserved a good grade." During the past couple of months the two had become fast friends. Rusty's grandfather had dropped him off faithfully each Sunday, usually right after lunch. Teacher and student had developed an easy routine. After working at the computer for an hour, Lori would reward Rusty's diligence by allowing him to play a game. After about thirty minutes she'd call him to the kitchen, where she'd laid out a snack. Today they were enjoying brownies, fresh from the oven. Rusty was on his second cookie, washing it down with a glass of lemonade.

"I get good grades on most of my stuff," he said between mouthfuls.

"You're really doing great on the computer, too," Lori commented. She sometimes felt she was benefitting more from these sessions than Rusty. Most of her knowledge of children had been theoretical, and it amazed her to realize how much more she was learning from an actual relationship with a child.

"Grandpa says he's going to get me a computer for Christmas. Well, not just for me. It'll be a family present. He says he wants to learn to use it, too. Do you think you could give him lessons?"

Lori smiled. "I'd be glad to give Sheriff Reardon some pointers, but I'll bet you'll be able to teach him yourself."

She had forgotten how much children squirmed. He was kicking the chair legs as he talked. "Yeah. I can't wait 'till Christmas. I think my mom's coming."

"Why, Rusty, that's wonderful." Lori was surprised to hear this news. "You must have heard from her then."

"Yeah, well I got a letter last summer. I think it was summer. No, that's right, it was when school was still on."

Lori tried not to show her skepticism. "And she told you she was coming for Christmas back then?"

"Yeah, I think she did. Can I have another cookie? I mean may I have another cookie, please?" He covered his mouth with his hand and said through spread fingers, "Whoops, I forgot I'm not supposed to ask."

"It's okay, Rusty. But it's nice you remembered to say 'please.'" Lori had to fight to keep a straight face. "This one better be the last, though. Your grandma won't like it if you don't eat your dinner."

"These are real good," he said between munches. "My grandma bakes me cookies sometimes, but they're not this kind. I like these better. Maybe you could give her the reci—what's that word for when you write down what's in something?"

"I think you mean recipe." Just then the doorbell rang. "It must be your grandpa. Go ahead and finish your snack while I go see." She left Rusty in the kitchen and went to answer the door.

"Hello, Sheriff Reardon. Won't you come in? Rusty is having some cookies and lemonade in the kitchen."

"That must mean the computer lesson is over, so I'm not too early." As usual there was a broad smile on his face.

He stepped into the house and followed her as she led the way to the kitchen. "I haven't been in this house for many years," he said. "I came out one time to visit with your dad not too long before his death. I think you were away at school at the time. Anyhow, he'd been in the store looking at tractors and I wanted to show him this new catalog that just came in." He paused. "That was a terrible thing, I mean his dying so suddenly. He wasn't much older than I am now. Everyone liked John Wyatt. He was a great guy."

Lori nodded. "It was a terrible shock. I never had a chance to say 'good-bye.' I still miss him a lot."

A moment of understanding passed between them. Lori knew he was thinking of his wife, who had also died suddenly and tragically. Then he broke the silence. "I don't know how to thank you for all you're doing for Rusty. You're all he talks about these days."

"I'm sure the big draw is the computer. But I enjoy him coming over here as much as he does. He's a wonderful little boy. You've done a good job."

"Well, it hasn't been easy. But my mother has been the person who's made the difference. I don't know what I'd have done without her there to look after him."

"I'm not trying to pry, but Rusty mentioned his mother was coming for Christmas."

A look of sadness came over the sheriff's face. "Rusty fantasizes about her. I've tried to level with him for his own good. He hasn't seen his mother for over a year. I took him to Denver a couple of times, and she met us at a restaurant for dinner. That's about all the contact we've had. I don't even know where she lives. She writes to him once in awhile, but there's no return address."

She noticed his eyes were a little moist. She looked away as she didn't want to embarrass him, although she was touched. What a good man he is, she thought.

He swiped his eyes with his hand. "I've never brought it up, but he keeps the letters under his pillow."

Lori didn't know what to say. She figured there was probably nothing adequate. She was older than Cindy, but perhaps the little boy saw her as a mother figure, and it was as much for this reason as for the computer that he wanted to spend time with her. "Guess we'd better go see if Rusty has finished his snack," she said."

As she started for the kitchen, the sheriff took her arm and held her back. His look was intense. "I wish there was something I could do for you to show my appreciation. I have some time off tomorrow, and I notice those leaves are piling up. How about if I come over and do some raking for you?"

"That's really nice of you, Sheriff Reardon."

"Please call me Larry."

"Well, the truth is, Blake is coming by this afternoon. He promised to help me rake them. It's such a beautiful day to get outside."

"I heard you were dating Blake Johnson but wasn't sure if it was true. You know how rumors spread around here." There was a question in his voice as he added, "Often unfounded."

Lori knew he was not the type to pry, that he was genuinely interested.

"Yes, Blake and I have been seeing each other." She said it casually, not wanting to elaborate.

"Well, I guess this time the rumors are true then," he said flatly, his mouth in a firm line.

Lori was a little taken aback. It seemed no one was enthusiastic when they learned of her relationship with Blake. Why couldn't anyone be happy for her?

Larry reached out and touched her shoulder in an awkward movement, as if this were something he had little practice at. "If there's anything else I can ever do for you, Lori, please don't hesitate to ask, even if it's just to talk. Anytime, night or day."

Lori masked her surprise. Why would she need someone to talk to, especially at night? She made an effort to make her voice light and cheerful. "Thanks for the offer, Sheriff Reardon, I mean Larry. I'll remember it, if I ever need to."

"I can't believe this weather is holding. Just think, in a month it will be Christmas." Lori turned to include the passenger in the back seat. It had been Blake's idea to take her mother for a ride. Earlier she and Blake had raked what would probably be the last of the leaves. They had taken time out to have a leaf fight, instigated by Blake, but she had been a willing participant. And all the while Lori felt her mother's eyes watching them from her bedroom window. But somehow Charlotte had lost the power to make her feel bad about herself. Often lately, Lori felt she was making up for her lost childhood.

During those times with Sarah in their younger days, when she had followed her into whatever mischief her friend could conjure up, Lori was so afraid of getting caught that it was never much fun. Like the time when Sarah, who had just received her driver's license, had driven her mother's car to school. The two of them had gone for a spin during the lunch hour, and Sarah decided they should skip their afternoon classes and drive out to the lake. Lori objected, but as was the usual case with Sarah, her protests were ignored. And, of course, their parents were notified. Sarah seemed unaffected by her parents' disappointment. Her biggest regret was that her driving privileges were revoked for the next month.

Lori thought she detected a small twinkle in her father's eyes, perhaps recalling the antics of his own youth, but her mother was livid with anger. It wasn't so much what she said, as what she didn't say. Lori was forbidden to associate with Sarah and was then given the silent treatment.

For a week Charlotte hardly left her room. Her migraines suddenly worsened. Although nothing was said, Lori got the message, as always. Her mother's illnesses were a silent reprimand, a statement of what happened when she failed to conform to the rules. In time, after she was chosen class valedictorian, John persuaded his wife to relent.

"Have you started your Christmas shopping, Mrs. Wyatt?" Blake asked. "I'll admit that I'm behind in that department." Lori knew he was just trying to make conversation, but there was no answer from the back seat.

The day was indeed warm for late November. The trees were now bare, but the landscape was still quite lovely as they drove along the familiar country roads, passing harvested fields, tractors and planters standing idle. Lori had always enjoyed inventing scenarios of the families inside the houses, most of whom she knew. There was the Moran place. She could imagine Mrs. Moran, busy in the kitchen getting ready for company. She knew Sarah, Jon and the kids, who lived on an adjoining farm, often went to his parents for dinner on Sundays. She needed to pin down Blake about a time they could get together with her friends. He kept putting her off. He was busy trying to get his operation off the ground but didn't want to discuss the details. "I'd rather spend my time with you discussing other things, like when you'll agree to become Mrs. Blake Johnson," was his reply the last time she'd inquired about his project.

Blake had become increasingly persistent, saying there was no point in wasting time. He thought Christmas would be the ideal time for a wedding and that they should skip the fanfare and elope. Lori agreed they didn't need a big wedding, that at their ages it wasn't something she had to have. She thought maybe a small gathering would be nice, just his parents, the Morans, senior and junior, Sarah's parents, and, of course, her mother. But Lori was pretty sure Charlotte would decline. And this would put a damper on what should be the happiest day of her life. In the end, she thought Blake might have the right idea about just going away to be married.

Blake's plan was for them to fly to Las Vegas for a couple of days and rent a suite in one of the big luxury hotels. They could get a license immediately and could be married at one of the many chapels along the strip. Just being in Vegas would be another new experience for her, one to add to her list of other fast accumulating "firsts."

Considering Charlotte's dim view of her daughter's relationship, Lori was surprised her mother had agreed to a ride in the country that day. It was probably that she was so desperate for company. Lori felt a twinge of guilt. Poor old lady, she'd all but deserted her lately. In spite of everything, Charlotte was virtually the only family she had left. She just wished things could be different with them. Perhaps they could forge a new relationship if Charlotte could just learn to bend a little. Otherwise she would remain a bitter old lady, eventually driving her daughter away. The fact that her mother was here today with them could mean the start of something, could be Charlotte's way of showing acceptance of Blake.

Lori gave Blake a loving look. His inclusion of her mother on their outing had been a peace offering, and she was grateful to him for his thoughtfulness. She marveled at her wonderful fortune. This beautiful man was soon to be her husband!

"Hey, isn't that your field over there?" Blake asked.

Lori looked out over the land to the left, dotted with oil wells. "Yes, that's our field. We ought to take a drive through it. Would you like that, Mother?"

"It makes no difference," was Charlotte's only comment.

Blake turned onto the dirt road. There was a small sign on the left that said Murphy Oil Company. The grass had begun to turn brown, making the cattle they saw along the way work a little harder for a meal. Lori had often envied the cows for their simple, serene life but only in the summer. Life on the plains could be bitter. The cattle owners usually loaded their herds up and took them home for several months in the winter. There they spent the cold weather beneath sheltered enclosures while fed daily rations of alfalfa. Since the herds looked thinner, Lori surmised some of the farmers must have already picked up their cattle.

A small dot off to the left about four hundred feet soon materialized into the shelter she had loved so as a child, old and weathered but still intact.

Blake noticed it, also. "What's that old building?"

"My grandfather built it. According to Dad, his father raised some cattle back then. He built it because he spent a lot of time out here. The setting is really quite lovely, don't you think? There's a small stream that runs just back of the building. I think he picked a good spot for his little 'home away from home.' When Dad brought me out here as a child, I imagined grandfather sitting there years earlier. He died before I was born, you know."

Lori was silent for a moment, remembering those days with fondness. "When we came out here, sometimes we'd have a picnic lunch inside the shelter. In fact, since we're here, why don't we go ahead and have our lunch?"

She felt a small thrill of nostalgia at this thought. This was the first time she'd been here since before her father's death.

While Blake had bagged the last of the leaf piles, Lori had quickly sliced some ham for sandwiches, and along with apples from their trees and some of Phoebe's bread and butter pickles, packed them in the picnic hamper. The apple harvest had been good this year, and ordinarily she would have had many of them pared, sliced, bagged and in the freezer, but this year she simply hadn't found the time.

"You have my vote," Blake said. "How about you, Mrs. Wyatt. Shall we have our lunch here?"

"You can eat where you like, but I'm not hungry. And I don't want to sit on any hard benches that are probably full of splinters. I'll just wait in the car."

Blake got out and opened the trunk. He lifted the reclining lawn chair that he had thrown in at the last minute, and carrying it with one hand, opened the car's back door with the other. "Voila," he said. "Madame can dine at ze alfresco retaurante in style."

Not waiting for an answer, he leaned the chair against the car and held out his hand to help her out.

Lori, observing this production from the front seat, thought she saw Charlotte's mouth curve slightly. At any rate her mother didn't protest further. The air was a little cool as they ate their lunch, but with the jackets they'd brought along, they were quite comfortable. Charlotte even ate half of the sandwich Lori handed her. What was more surprising, she even contributed to the conversation. They talked of various and sundry things, including cattle raising, the economy, and the state of the nation in general. Is it possible she's beginning to thaw just a little? Lori thought. All during the pleasant hour and during the ride home, the phrase "my cup runneth over" was Lori's unvoiced prayer.

Chapter 15 - Blake

Her blonde hair lay tangled across the pillow. Her face half-covered by the pale locks looked angelic, almost childlike in sleep. Hardly more than a child actually, Blake thought. But the sheet had slipped down exposing her luscious breasts and stomach, belying the truth of this.

"Get up, Slut. The coffee's on. I even fixed you breakfast. But then you have to get out of here. I have work to do," Blake said gruffly.

Janice stretched her catlike figure and opened one sleepy, green eye. "That's it, use me shamelessly and then toss me out," she mumbled, brushing her hair from her face. "Turn me over to the mercies of my wicked stepmother."

He pulled the rest of the sheet off her, planning to grab her leg and pull her out of bed. But the view was so appealing, he thought better of it and climbed back in with her.

Later, over breakfast, reheated in the microwave, Janice's playful mood suddenly changed. "I still don't like it, Blake. What am I supposed to be doing while you're courting and marrying Jane Eyre? I'm sick of this God-forsaken place. I want to go back to Chicago and start living again."

He looked at her with exasperation. She had slicked her hair back in the usual fashion, tying it with a scarf, but already a few appealing strands had pulled loose. The tight jeans and sweater she had poured herself into openly advertised every curve of her fantastic body. He knew what he felt for her was pure lust, rather than love, and resented it as a weakness. These feelings were not something he had bargained for in the beginning. He knew she was trouble but was starting to realize he didn't want to live without her.

"Why must we go over it again? Everything I'm doing is for us. If you'll just be patient, in a year or so we'll be tremendously wealthy. Then we can live in Chicago, or Rome, or anywhere else you'd like."

"But how do you know it will work? I know you have the little librarian eating out of your hand. Charming women is child's play for you. But the rest of it is what I'm worried about."

He refilled their coffee cups and sat back down. "I've been planning this carefully for a long time. So far everything is going according to schedule. The paperwork has all been completed making me the working interest owner, the compressors have been ordered, and just as soon as Lori and I are married, I'll start work on the project."

"How do you explain this to her? You say she knows nothing about you owning the working interest or about the air injection thing you're going to do. Won't she be suspicious?"

"Just leave all of that to me, my sweet. As you said, I have her eating out of my hand. I'll just tell her I planned it as a surprise for her."

"It just makes it so complicated. Why won't the money from the working interest be enough? You said you don't need her permission to do whatever you want to. Why do you have to marry her and how will this make you the royalty owner anyhow? Divorcing her won't do it. I ought to know about divorce settlements." Her face was bitter. "Since the royalty was hers prior to marriage, they won't award you a fraction of it."

He got up and ruffled her hair. "Yes, Jan, you ought to know about divorce settlements. It looks like after the first time, you'd have been smart enough to not sign a prenuptial agreement. If you hadn't made that mistake, we could be living off your settlements. There'd be no need for any of this. As it is, we have to do whatever it takes to regain our affluent lifestyles. Blake's eyes became hard and cold. "No, neither of us has been lucky in love and especially in the area of financial gain. But this little plan of mine will change all that."

"Yeah, well, I still don't understand. You haven't explained how you're going to wind up with the royalty interest and why you need it. Didn't you say it was only twelve percent?"

"Twelve and a half. First, that twelve and a half percent is actually much more than that in terms of profits. It can be as high as sixty-five percent. That's because the royalty interest owner doesn't have to pay for any of the expenses. As for how I get possession of the override by marrying her, I'd rather not go into that."

"Well, I don't see how that's possible, unless she were to die and you inherited it. And I don't think that's likely. She's not even forty and her health is good, isn't it?"

Blake turned and walked toward the bedroom without comment. He could feel her eyes following him. "Run along little one," he said. "I have work to do."

When he heard the door close, he went to the window and watched her retreating figure. *God, what a nice butt,* he thought. He knew he was a fool, but he also knew he would do anything to keep her and that doing so would be expensive.

The ringing of the phone distracted him. Walking over to the desk, he picked it up. It might be Anders. Blake had been expecting him to call. "Johnson Resource Company," he said in a businesslike tone.

"What kind of game are you playing now?" the voice on the other end answered.

His face turned hard. "What do you want, Andrea?" He knew the answer. "And how did you find me?"

"It wasn't too difficult. When they told me your phone had been disconnected, I called Pierce and was told you were no longer with the company. With Daddy's connections it wasn't too difficult to track you down. So now, my darling ex-husband, if you'll just pop that couple of months' back child support in the mail, I'll not be bothering you again."

"Okay, now that you've found me, I need to tell you I don't have the money right now. But I'm working on something that'll be bringing in a lot of money soon and then I'll get caught up. In the meantime, since your daddy is taking good care of you and Josh, why are you harassing me?"

"It's not my father's job to pay your son's expenses. If that money doesn't get here by the end of the week, I'm going to my lawyer. They are throwing dead-beat dads in jail these days in case you haven't heard."

How he could have ever felt anything for the cold bitch was a puzzle that eluded him. Must have been the beautiful green of her father's money that had been the attraction. A fat lot of good all that wealth had ever done him. He hung up the phone without replying.

Betty Johnson was sitting at her desk in the office of Johnson's Farm and Implement Company, deeply involved in the task at hand. She didn't acknowledge Blake's presence, and he surmised she hadn't noticed his arrival. It had always seemed incongruous to Blake that his mother could be such an "air head" on the one hand, but when it came to mathematical endeavors could hold her own with the best of them. Undoubtedly, he had inherited his aptitude for figures from her. So far she had resisted his father's suggestion that they purchase a computer. She said she was too old to change now and that she liked balancing figures by hand. Her only concession to the latest technological advances was the purchase of a calculator.

"Hey, Good-looking. If I can tear you away, I thought I'd take my favorite girl to lunch."

Betty looked up with a start, a big smile spreading over her face. "Blake, I didn't hear you come in." She jumped up and smothered him with a tight hug. "I thought maybe you were mad at me. I haven't heard from you, and I've been leaving messages on your answering machine every day." She looked at him reproachfully as she stepped back.

"I know, Mom, and I'm sorry. But I've been busy trying to get my business off the ground and that's been taking every spare minute."

"From what I hear, your business must be a certain young lady named Melora Wyatt." She beamed at him. "You know you can't keep any secrets in this town."

"Yes, Mom, I'll admit Lori does figure prominently in my future plans." He thought his mother would be surprised to know just how much his business depended on winning Lori's devotion. "I hope you approve."

"I'm delighted. She's such a nice girl, although I guess you can't exactly call her a girl anymore. Of course, when you're my age, it's all relative, and I'll always think of you and your generation as kids even when I'm in my nineties and you're in your sixties."

"I thought we could go over to Fort Morgan for lunch. If you can take a couple of hours off that is." Blake knew his parents did most of their banking there.

"Well, I'll just take the time. Did you say anything to Dad?"

"He was with a customer, but we'll tell him on the way out." He took her coat off a hook by the door and held it out for her. "Better bundle up. It's cold out there."

It had snowed the night before, and Blake had to drive slowly as the roads were icy in spots. But once they got on the highway, driving was fairly good since it was evident the snowplows had been out earlier. Blake had given up on his father selling the business, at least for now. He saw how stubborn the old man was and knew that even if he eventually came around, it would take time to make the transfer. Hal would have to apply for a loan for the financing, and that could take weeks. The only thing left for him was a loan from his parents from their liquid assets. With what they had in savings, several hundred thousand dollars is what Betty had said, he could get by for a while.

No, he needed money now. The situation had become so desperate he'd been having trouble sleeping. His last reserves were almost gone. He had used up most of them renting and furnishing the house, and his living expenses were becoming a mounting debit on his credit cards. The compressors were due in any day, and he needed money to pay for them, plus he had been stalling off Anders. And now this thing with his ex-wife; that was the last thing he needed right now. It wasn't that she even needed the support. She was just vindictive, but Blake knew her. She didn't make idle threats.

"He pulled off the highway at the Fort Morgan exit. "How does La Case Feliz sound? I hear the food is good there."

"That would be great. Actually, I'd have settled for cooking your lunch. You know how much I enjoy doing things for you, honey."

The perfect lead, Blake thought. He turned the car onto West Platte Valley. "I'm glad you feel that way, because actually I do want to ask you a favor, a pretty big one."

"You know I'd do anything for you. What is it you want to ask me?" Her voice was earnest, eager to please. The blue eyes so dynamic in his face were weak in hers. She looked at him through thick lenses, surrounded by puffy cheeks.

Mom has let herself go, he thought with a mild feeling of disgust. She must have put on thirty pounds since I saw her in Chicago. But this wasn't his first concern. "Let's go in and have a nice lunch first."

They ordered the day's special, a Mexican plate. Betty ate hers heartily, chattering between bites. "Dad and I are going shopping for a tree this weekend. I'm having a little party for my bridge club next week, and I want to get all the decorations up for it."

Suddenly she put down her fork. "You've hardly touched your lunch, Blake. Don't you like it? I think it's very good."

But Blake's appetite had dropped off. "It's fine. I ate a late breakfast, so guess I'm not that hungry."

The waitress cleared away their plates, his still half full, and poured fresh coffee.

"Are you sure everything's all right, Blake? Come to think of it, you're not looking well. Do you think you're coming down with something?"

If she could have reached across the table with her short arms, Blake was sure her hand would have been on his forehead by now testing for fever.

"Are you worried about something, Son? I'll bet you're upset about not seeing Josh more. He is going to be able to come for Christmas, isn't he? I've been doing a lot of shopping and found some roller blades on sale. I found them here in Fort Morgan at Alco. The salesgirl said we could exchange them if they don't fit."

"You shouldn't be spending your money on him. I'm sure he has roller blades and everything else he needs or wants. The kid is shamelessly spoiled."

Seeing her stricken face, Blake's voice softened. "I'm sorry, but I guess I am upset. It doesn't look as though he'll be coming for Christmas or any time soon. It's what I wanted to talk to you about."

Oh, honey, what happened?" Betty asked. Her eyes had filled and she rummaged in her purse for a tissue.

Blake opened his mouth to respond but before he could speak, his mother said, "They can't keep him from you. Didn't the court say you get him for Christmas?" Well, if they won't let him come, we'll get us a lawyer and . . ."

Blake reached across and touched Betty's hand. "It won't do any good. Let me explain what's going on."

Betty nodded, biting her lip.

"This is difficult, and I wouldn't worry you if there was any other way. But the fact is I'm broke and haven't been able to keep up Josh's support payments. Andrea's been making threats, and she's perfectly capable of carrying them out. She's even threatened me with jail. I can't enforce visitation rights when I'm in violation of a court order, so that's why I can't insist on getting Josh for the holidays." He looked down at the table, feigning a look of despondency.

"Why didn't you tell me? I can loan you some money. How much do you need?

"The truth? I need a lot. Oh, I could get by now with about ten thousand. But what am I to do when that's gone? If I'm ever going to get my business going, I have to have some capital. I'm talking roughly three hundred thousand"

Seeing her look of shock, he hurried on. "As I told you it's a sure thing, but Dad will never loan me that much money. I was a fool to ever think he would."

"I did try talking to him, but I guess you're right." She fiddled nervously with her napkin.

"Yeah, I can just hear his response. 'The kid was never any good and never will be. I went into debt providing him with a fancy education, and what has he done with it? I'm not about to throw bad money after good.'"

The look on her face told him he had hit close to home. It was pretty much the same thing he had heard when he had hinted to his father about a loan. He reached across the table again and closed his hand over his mother's. "Mom, please, would you get me the money without telling him? Your money's in a joint account isn't it? He would never have to know, since you handle everything. And I'll have the money back there in six months with a huge profit. We'd be helping each other."

She gave him a blank look, as if she was having trouble registering his words. But Blake knew in a moment, when they did register, this little, church-going lady would turn him down flat, so he hurriedly pressed on. "When I came back here, it was to try to make a go of it, so I could spend time with you and Dad, make up for all the lost years. I had everything planned out, and things are moving in the right direction. The thing is I had really counted on a loan from you and Dad."

He looked across the room for a moment, formulating his next words. "I'm so sure of the success of this venture, I was positive I could convince him. I've already sold people in the industry, sharp men who have the insight to see the possibilities, who are willing to put up big money." His next words had a bitter tone. "But not my father. My years as a successful engineer don't count for anything with him. He can't get past this image he has of me, still sees me as irresponsible. Sure, I was back then. I was just a kid, but I've grown up."

Betty's face showed her sympathy. "I'm sorry, Son. I've always wished things could be different between you and your father."

"They can be. If I can pull this thing off, I can prove to him just how responsible I am. This in itself means a lot to me."

It was time to play his trump card. "I guess I should never have quit my job at Pierce. The only thing to do is to go back to Chicago and see if they'll take me back. This way I can at least pay child support, although I doubt if I'll be able to see Josh even then. If they do take me back, I'll probably be sent right back to South America." His next words were delivered more slowly. "And I don't know how I'll ever be able to bring Josh here for a visit."

This time Betty couldn't hold back the tears. She removed her glasses and dabbed at her eyes. After a moment, her face took on a look of determination well known to Blake, and he knew he had said the magic words. "We have most of our money right here in Fort Morgan over at First Security," she said. "There's no need in delaying any longer. Let's do it."

Chapter 16 - Lori

Rusty's face was beaming. He'd just torn open Lori's Christmas present. Inside was a Jumping Julius computer game. It was designed for early elementary school students to help improve their reading skills. The salesgirl had assured Lori that this one was fun as well as educational. Each question had a predetermined number of spots the player jumped ahead if he answered a question correctly.

They were sitting in the living room. There would be no lesson today. Christmas was just a few days off, and Lori thought it would be fun to have a little party. Larry had been invited to stay and Charlotte joined them. Lori had baked sugar cookies, using cutters to make Santa and Christmas tree shapes. It was midnight before she had put the last brightly frosted cookie in the jar. She didn't really mind. It was for Rusty, and she enjoyed doing these little motherly chores. Her last thought before drifting off was that the old adage about living on love must be true. She seemed to be getting by on a lot less sleep these days.

"Now you have to open your present," Rusty said. He was so excited he was bouncing up and down as he talked. "Grandpa, where's the present? You didn't forget it, did you?"

Larry was seated in a chair opposite Lori and Rusty, who sat on the sofa. "No, Rusty, I didn't forget it." His eyes moved to Lori. "You'll have to give me back my jacket. I left it in the pocket."

After Lori returned with the jacket, Larry searched through the pockets while Rusty danced nervously in front of his chair. From the way Larry's mouth curved up in the corners, Lori suspected he was prolonging the search intentionally. Finally he produced a small package, which he handed to Rusty.

"I hope you like it. I picked it out myself," Rusty said, as he gave it to

Lori.

Inside the package was a necklace with a small gold locket.

"You've gotta' open it up," he pointed out.

When she did so, she found a small picture of Rusty. He had recently lost his two front teeth, but this hadn't prevented him from smiling broadly.

Lori was touched. "It's the nicest present I've ever received. I'll wear it always." She reached over and gave him a big hug.

Like most boys his age, Rusty wiggled away. "I was wondering," he said. "I mean Grandpa and I was wondering, if you and Mrs. Wyatt could come to our house for Christmas dinner." He glanced over at Charlotte as he said this. Then he looked down at his feet. "I guess probably my mom won't be coming 'cause we haven't heard from her in a long time. Anyhow, we'll have a lot of turkey and pies and don't want to waste them."

Oh dear, Lori thought, this is going to be difficult. "I'd love to come, Rusty, but I've made other plans. I'm leaving town for the holidays." She felt her mother's eyes on her. It was a good time to break the news to her as well.

"Do you have a kid in another town you're going to be with for Christmas?"

Lori smiled. "No, Rusty. I don't have any children. I was never married. But that's going to change, at least the part about being married. That's why I'm leaving town—to get married."

The silence that followed was only for a few seconds but seemed to last longer. Lori's eyes involuntarily traveled to where her mother was sitting. Charlotte's face had lost its color. She seemed to be struggling for words. Finally she said, "Excuse me. I'm going to my room." As she walked toward the stairs, without turning around, she added, "Hope you have a nice Christmas, Sheriff Reardon, Rusty."

Larry stood up. "Rusty and I would be delighted if you would still accept our invitation, Mrs. Wyatt." He paused for a moment, before adding, "even if Lori can't make it."

Charlotte looked a little torn. Lori knew her mother was fond of Larry. Finally, however, she said, "That's very kind of you, but I don't think I'll be able to come to dinner either." With that she walked up the stairs, cutting off any further conversation.

After a moment of awkward quiet, Rusty asked, "Who are you going to get married to?"

"His name is Blake Johnson. You may not know him. He used to live here but he's been gone for many years. His parents live her, though. They're the ones who own Johnson's Farm and Implement Store."

"Oh", was the simple reply. He looked as though he wanted to say something more.

It was difficult to interpret the expression on Larry's face. "Let me offer my wishes for your happiness, Melora," he said. Then he walked over and grabbed Rusty's knee. "We'd better be running along. We wanted to go look for a tree today, remember?"

"Yeah, but I wanted to play my new game first."

"I think we'd better shelve that plan for today. I'm sure Miss Wyatt has a lot to do if she's leaving town." He looked back at her. "I did understand you correctly, that you won't be getting married here in town before you leave."

"We decided against it. As you know Blake has been married before. He had a big extravagant wedding and doesn't want to go through that again." She saw from the look on his face that he didn't think much of this, so quickly added, "And as for me, I don't want a big wedding either. We're going to Las Vegas to be married."

"I see." Larry looked as if he, too, wanted to say something more."

"Can I talk to Miss Wyatt alone, Grandpa?" Rusty asked.

They both looked down at the little boy, as if they had forgotten his presence.

"Of course, Rusty. I'll be in the car."

Turning again to Lori he reached out his hand. "Goodbye Melora, and again congratulations." Then still holding her hand, he looked at her intently. "I just hope you're sure. It wouldn't hurt to wait awhile, would it?" His voice had a pleading quality.

"I'm sure, Larry. In fact it's probably the first thing I've ever been really sure about in my life. She looked down at Rusty. "You're welcome to stay and play with your new game. I do have to pack but I can do that while you're on the computer."

"Can I please, Grandpa?" Rusty pleaded. "I don't need to be there to help you with the tree. You always pick a good one."

"If you're sure," he said to Lori. "I'll be back in an hour or so to pick him up."

When the door had closed behind his grandpa, Rusty said, "I guess you love this guy, right? What did you say his name was?"

"Blake. His name is Blake Johnson. And yes, I do love him."

"Well, 'cause I've been thinking about something. I think my grandpa likes you." He hesitated, his brows knitted together, as if he weren't sure whether to go on. Finally his words spilled out in one long string. "I don't know if he loves you, but I'll bet he could. You're so nice and pretty, and my mom will probably never come back." He looked up at her. "So I was thinking if you and Grandpa got married you could be my mom." His lip had started to quiver a little.

Lori bent down and put her arms around him. "This is my day for nice things to happen. That's the best compliment I've ever received, Rusty."

"Well, anyhow, I guess I'm being real silly 'cause Grandpa is old and this other guy, Blake Johnson, probably isn't."

"Your grandpa isn't that old. He's older than I am, but that doesn't make a lot of difference if two people love each other. The thing is, although your grandpa loves you a lot and so do I, that doesn't mean that we love each other or that we should get married."

"Yeah, I guess." He looked as if he were considering this, then abruptly seemed to dismiss the idea "Do you think I could still come over sometimes, I mean after you get married? I'll still need to know things, even if I have my own computer."

"Of course you can. I won't be living here. I'll be living at Blake's house, but your grandpa can bring you there anytime. And even when you've learned more than I know about computers, you can still come to visit me."

He smiled, showing the large gap where two teeth were peeping through his gums. "I guess it's okay then, about your getting married, I mean."

After Rusty put his game in the computer, Lori walked up the stairs. She looked at the closed door to her mother's room and hesitated in front of it. Then she turned abruptly. Better to let her stew awhile. Besides, as Larry said, she had a lot to do. She opened the door to the hall cabinet, and taking out the suitcases underneath the shelves, carried them to her room. As she began to pack, her mind was on Rusty and his grandfather. She smiled a little. Here I've gone all this time without a man in my life, and I suddenly get two proposals, even if one did come by way of a seven-year old. The more she saw of Larry Reardon, the better she liked him. She wondered what would have happened if Blake had never come back. This is silly, she thought. I'm madly in love with Blake, and just because Rusty is fond of me doesn't mean Larry has any feelings for me beyond friendship.

The next morning as Lori was getting ready for work, Charlotte came into her room, which was unusual. Her mother seldom stirred until well after her daughter had left. Lori was dressed and was brushing her hair. She noticed her mother looking at the two suitcases by the bed.

"When are you leaving, Melora?"

"I was going to talk to you about it after I got home from work. Blake is picking me up at six o'clock tomorrow morning."

"How long will you be gone? I thought you had a job at the library, or are you giving that up?"

"No, Mother. We'll just be gone a few days. The library is closed for a couple of days because of Christmas, so I won't even miss any work."

Charlotte stood there for a minute as if considering what to say next. "I suppose you know that without a prenuptial agreement, your new husband will get everything you have should you die," she said flatly.

It took Lori a moment to digest this. How in the world would Charlotte know about prenuptial agreements? Lori, herself, knew about them only in a general way. And why was she even talking about such things? She fought to keep her voice calm. "I imagine you're right, but what are you trying to say, that Blake is interested in me for mercenary reasons?"

"You're standing in front of the mirror, Melora. Are you blind? Why else would someone who looks like a movie star want to marry you?"

Lori did indeed look, as she had many times in the past month, asking herself the same question. But then her eyes filled, clouding her vision. Even if it were true, that she was so hopelessly plain, so unattractive, no man worth having could possibly want her, Charlotte's words had been cruel and hurtful.

She waited until she had composed herself to answer. Her voice was cold. "And I suppose a successful man, who has worked as an oil executive and is now starting his own company, is marrying me for my small retirement fund and an oil royalty that is virtually worthless."

Lori turned and looked at her mother and for the first time in her life felt genuine hatred. "Oh, that's right I have a twenty-five thousand dollar life insurance policy through my job. Blake probably plans to talk me into making him beneficiary and risk the electric chair by murdering me."

Charlotte looked a little uncertain, a new experience for her. "I only wanted to warn you for your own good. As it stands now, since you're not yet married, I would inherit whatever you have. With my poor health I won't live much longer, so it really doesn't concern me. Besides I don't need much to get by on."

Her face took on an injured look. "I was just trying to look out for your best interests, since you apparently are so mesmerized by this unscrupulous man you are unable to do so yourself."

"I know you don't like Blake. I'll admit you're not the only one who has doubts about him. Most of the people in this town don't understand why he would fall in love with me. But they don't know him, not who he is today. He's changed. And because he's changed, he can see something in me apparently you never have. I'm not talking about physical beauty. It's something that goes deeper than that."

She searched for words to describe Blake's love for her, which he declared frequently. He told her he was attracted to her simply because she was different. Other women, he said, were boring, talked of nothing but clothes and hairstyles; or if they did get off these subjects, it was only to engage in idle gossip. But being with her, he said, was exciting, just spending a quiet evening at home discussing everything from world affairs to poetry. Lori felt a warm glow remembering how he'd said "You're the type of woman a man never tires of being with."

Lori sighed knowing Charlotte wouldn't understand and said simply, "We have something special together. I wish you could be happy for me, but I guess that isn't possible. Now, I really do need to hurry or I'll be late for work."

Charlotte moved aside as Lori walked over to the bed and picked up her blazer and purse. But she ignored her daughter's dismissal.

"I called Bill Caldwell. I've wanted to make a will for years but kept putting it off. I read something in the newspaper that says everyone should have one. So he's coming out today. Of course, I'm leaving everything to you." She paused, for effect Lori supposed.

"He said it would all go to you even without a will, but it could save time, that without a will everything gets tied up in the courts. Just out of curiosity I asked him about your situation. He said you can leave half of your assets to someone else but that half has to go to Blake. Not that you have that much— just the royalty and it's not worth much these days. But your father wouldn't have wanted it to go to an outsider. I never knew why he gave it to you anyhow. I guess he was afraid I would sell it and to tell you the truth, I was very hurt he didn't trust me."

Lori knew that was just what her father had thought. She also knew her mother's main reason for calling the lawyer was to learn the status of the law concerning spousal inheritance rights. Having a will made was just an excuse for making the inquiry. But in spite of her earlier feelings, she suddenly felt a pang of sympathy for Charlotte. What would it hurt to pacify her? She was so happy she could afford to be a little charitable. It may even pave the way for her mother's acceptance of Blake.

"I think you're right in making a will. I agree everyone should have one, so I'll go ahead and make an appointment to have mine done. But it will have to wait until we get back."

Charlotte was looking at her expectantly. Lori continued. "And since it's not worth that much anymore, the royalty wouldn't be more than half my estate. I'll tell Bill I want it to go to you."

Chapter 17 - Lori

Lori had seen movies set in Las Vegas but nothing had prepared her for the real thing. Driving along the strip with millions of lights in every shape, size, and color was a feast for the eyes beyond imagination. Each new casino, planned by the industry's financial wizards, had been erected bigger and splashier than the last until it was unfathomable what they would come up with next. Her favorite was the Mirage where they were staying. Every thirty minutes a volcano erupted on the grounds in front of the hotel, the brainstorm of technological geniuses.

They had arrived earlier that day. Blake had reserved the honeymoon suite, and although Lori assumed it would be nice, she was unprepared for just how spectacular it was. It was huge and lavishly furnished. Live flowers and plants were everywhere, even in the bathroom. The flowers, like the fruit arrangements, were works of art and matched the décor. Lori knew a bit about art, and the paintings on the walls were not cheap prints, but originals.

When she protested about the cost, Blake explained that he would be the one to worry about that, and, besides, everything was relatively inexpensive in Vegas. He told her the hotel owners purposefully kept their costs low, knowing that people would spend money gambling in their casinos. Lori had tried her hand at the slot machines for a while but quickly lost interest when she didn't win anything. She marveled at how many people frequented these places, all of them feeding money into the machines, and from what she saw, few of them winning.

After she'd used up her rolls of quarters, she walked over to where Blake was playing blackjack. She noticed all the chips in front of him as she stood behind his chair.

"I'm up almost seven hundred dollars," he said. "It looks like we'll be able to really do the town tonight."

"I noticed they have a huge buffet right here that's quite inexpensive."

"They also have a really ritzy restaurant, and that's where I'm taking you." He winked at the dealer. "I want to spend my last night of freedom in style," he explained. "This young lady has agreed to become my wife tomorrow."

The dealer, a middle-aged, stocky guy, whose nametag identified him as "Mack," offered his congratulations. "Hopefully, your fiancée will bring you good luck," he said, grinning broadly at them. As he spoke he continued to deal the cards to Blake and several other people. Lori marveled at how his flying fingers never misdealt.

Looking around at the circus-like atmosphere, she felt as if she'd been transported to another planet. This must be what is known as cultural shock, she thought. It had been only this morning that their plane had left the ground in Denver, but it seemed like days ago. Once they were in the air, some of her nervousness had subsided. Up until that point she was afraid something would happen to stop them. She had visions of a policeman seeking her out at the airport with the information her mother had suffered a heart attack or that something else equally devastating had happened.

They were to be married in L'Amour Chapelle, one of the numerous chapels that dotted the boulevards. They had gone to city hall earlier and obtained their license and then on to a walk-in medical center close by to get their blood tests. It appeared nothing stood in their way. She had given the number of the hotel to Mrs. Jacobs, who had been enlisted to look after her mother's needs. Lori had, however, firmly emphasized that Charlotte was not to have the number. She hoped she hadn't shocked her neighbor, but she didn't want anything to mar her wedding day. She tried not to think of the look on her mother's face as she'd stood on the porch with Mrs. Jacobs, watching them drive away.

Lori reasoned that she'd devoted many years beyond the call of duty to her mother's whims and that it was now her turn. She didn't want to do anything that would be intentionally hurtful to the old lady but realized that Charlotte had damaged her throughout her life. A child should be nurtured to someday go into the world unafraid, to be encouraged to pursue whatever path she's chosen with confidence and without guilt. Charlotte had failed her daughter in this. By making her feel inadequate and guilty, Lori had been afraid to fulfill her dreams. She would never let this happen again.

"So what do you think of the gambling capital of the world?" Blake asked between bites of pepper steak and fried rice. Although Blake's winnings that afternoon had totaled over a thousand dollars, they'd decided to save the steaks and lobster until the following night, which would be their wedding night. It had been a long, busy day and exhausted, they opted to have Chinese food delivered to their room. They were sitting at the table by the window, where they could look out on the city. The lights seemed to go on forever, or at least as far as the eye could see.

"It's quite indescribable, and I'm glad I've had the chance to experience it," Lori answered. "I guess there's nothing quite like it anywhere else."

"There are lots of places that allow gambling now," Blake said between bites. "Atlantic City is probably the next largest casino town, but it doesn't even begin to compare. And, of course, there are Central City and Black Hawk in Colorado, but they're not on a par with Vegas either."

Lori helped herself to some almond chicken, her favorite. "Don't they have gambling somewhere up in South Dakota?"

"Yes, Deadwood is quite popular. And more recently the Indians are building casinos across the country. When all of this started happening, I understand the guys in Vegas were worried. But it actually seems to be working in their favor. People who might have never had the chance to gamble get the fever once casinos are opened in their areas. With their appetites whetted, they can't wait to come to Vegas where the real action is."

"I don't think I could ever become addicted. I hated to lose that fifty dollars. I doubt if I'll try it again."

Blake laughed. "No, my darling, I doubt if you will. I don't think you have any vices, unless you're hiding them from me. Oh, that's right, you're an ungrateful daughter, who has deserted her poor invalid mother. I forgot about that."

"Please don't joke about my mother, Blake. I do get angry at times, but was I really a victim? I didn't have to let her manipulate me. You could say the fault is mine, that I was weak."

"I'll admit one could argue that point. The important thing is that you've made a mature decision to no longer allow her to control you." He reached out and touched her hand. "The proof is you're here with me now."

"Let's make a pact to not discuss my mother for the rest of our time here. Anyhow, I do have some other weaknesses. Shall I confess?"

"I think this would be the time. Otherwise it could be grounds for annulment."

"Okay. Well, I have this bad habit that once I start a book, even a bad one, I'm unable to lay it down. It's a kind of addiction. Sometimes I'll read until three in the morning and then I have to get up and go to work, and it's awful."

Blake buried his face in his hands. "Oh no, not that. If you'd told me you were addicted to heroin or cocaine, I could have dealt with that. But this is too much."

Lori laughed. Around Blake, she had begun to lighten up, to have a better sense of humor. "But if you really love me, you can work with me on this."

"You're right, I do love you, and I'll help you to overcome this terrible obsession. I'll buy a large safe and lock all your books away. Then if you've been real good, I'll get one out and let you read a chapter or two. But come to think of it, that won't work. Remember, you work in a library. No, I think this is too big for me to deal with. We'd better call everything off."

"How about you?" she asked in a bantering tone. "Do you have any despicable habits, such as marrying women and disposing of them for their money?" It just popped out, probably as a result of her conversation with Charlotte. But she was a little taken aback to notice he didn't immediately comment. Suddenly, he seemed to be the one who didn't realize she was joking.

Finally he said, "You've guessed my secret. I suppose now that you know, you won't want to go ahead with the marriage ceremony tomorrow either, especially when I tell you I've heard rumors that your grandfather never really lost that money, that it is buried underneath a tree on your oil field."

He jumped up and, grabbing her, carried her over to the bed and threw her on it. For a brief moment she didn't know whether to laugh or scream. He straddled her, pinning her arms down and kissed her long and passionately.

Then his mouth moved around to her ear, and he began to nibble on it. "What I do, my pretty one," he whispered, "is to love my victims to death."

Later they lay there, her head cradled in his arm, their half-eaten dinner forgotten.

Lori felt she could lie this way forever. Never had she felt so warm and secure. Finally, Blake broke the spell. "My arm's going to sleep, " he apologized.

She sat up and looked down at him. "We've never discussed our financial situations. Contrary to rumor, I don't think Grandfather buried any money. But I do have a small retirement fund and some savings, which would be yours if I die. That's about all I have except for the oil royalty, which . . ."

He reached up and covered her mouth with his hand. "My sweet Melora.

I don't care what you have. Besides, I don't have much to offer you in the way of material assets. That's going to change. But at this point you'd better be marrying me for love, because that's about all I have to give you."

Lori looked down at him lovingly. She kissed him gently. "It's all I need or want from you, my darling. By loving me you have given me something more precious than all the riches in the world. That sounds kind of corny, but it's true."

Blake rubbed his hand lightly along Lori's cheek. "I'm glad you feel that way. But there is something you could do for me if you mean what you say, a kind of wedding present."

"Anything within my power."

"I'm kind of embarrassed to ask, since my father owns a store where they sell all kinds of them."

Lori was completely perplexed but curious. "Blake, what is it you want?"

"A shovel. I don't have one, and I want to get started digging for that money as soon as we get back to Platte Valley."

She picked up the pillow and put it over his face, laughing. "Blake Johnson, you're impossible," she said.

They were married the following morning. Lori wore a white street length dress with simple lines, which Sarah had helped her pick out at Joslins in Denver. The couple who stood up for them were employed by the chapel. As she looked into Blake's eyes and repeated the words of the chaplain, Lori prayed that if this were all a wonderful dream, she would never wake up.

Everything about that day was perfect. After the ceremony they took a taxi back to the hotel. They had a champagne breakfast sent to their room, which they ate between their lovemaking. Blake joked that he couldn't keep up with her—that she was insatiable.

And she was beginning to think he was right. "Must have been all those years I did without," she said, pulling him down on top of her.

"I may not survive this," he said, groaning. But as she rolled him over and began kissing him on the lips and working her way down, she could feel him begin to respond.

It wasn't until late afternoon that they emerged from their room. They wore light jackets over their shorts and tee shirts. Blake had warned Lori that Vegas sometimes had violent winter storms. But on their wedding day the gods smiled on them and sent a crisp, sunny day. As evening approached, though, it had become quite cool. Lori was glad they'd thrown the jackets in their suitcases, along with their swimming suits and shorts.

147

As they strolled leisurely through the hotel grounds, hand in hand, Blake explained how the owner, Steve Wynn, had transported the huge palm trees from Hawaii and other south sea islands at a tremendous expense. Set among the other beautifully landscaped trees and shrubs, the result was a virtual wonderland.

Later, after a light nap, they sat in the Jacuzzi—and made love again. It was almost seven before they stepped on the elevator to go down for their wedding supper. For this Lori slipped on a pale blue dress, one she'd bought at Joslins, along with the white one. Perhaps it was just her imagination, but she felt that the eyes of every male in the restaurant were on her, admiring her, and especially those of her husband.

The following morning a limousine drove them to the airport. Even here there were slot machines. One last attempt to send the tourist home with a lighter wallet, Lori thought.

Blake reached in his pocket and pulled out a handful of silver dollars, part of his winnings he hadn't cashed in. "Want to try your luck one last time?" he asked.

Lori shook her head. " I couldn't be more lucky if I won a million dollar jackpot," she said.

As they stepped off the plane in Denver, it seemed that it had been only yesterday that they'd left. Lori didn't mind, as she felt Las Vegas and everything that had happened there was just a prelude—that her wonderful new life with Blake was just beginning.

"Hi, Sweetheart. How was your day?" Blake asked. He had come out to the car to help Lori with the groceries.

Lori was exhausted, but as soon as she saw her husband, she felt her fatigue evaporating. "It was good, because I spent the whole day thinking about you and how nice it was going to be to come home."

"What a smoothie! Have you been taking charm lessons on the sly?"

"Now where would I find the time for that?" Lori asked.

Lori couldn't remember a time when she had been busier. Her mother seemed resigned to the fact that Mrs. Jacobs was now doing most of the things her daughter formerly attended to, but Lori tried to get over for a short visit each day. By the time she stopped off at Isley's and picked up some things for dinner, it was usually seven before Blake and she sat down to eat. On weekends she sometimes prepared dinner for her mother and herself. Once Blake had joined them, but Charlotte's hostility turned the evening into a fiasco, one Lori didn't want to subject him to again.

In spite of her busy schedule, she was happier than she could ever remember being. Marriage to Blake these past two months had been everything she had hoped for and more. He was loving and considerate. Several times he had surprised her by telling her not to worry about dinner. Just yesterday he had called as she was leaving work and said, "Ze great chef is concocting one of his world renowned secret recipes, so you may visit with Madame Charlotte a leetle longer."

She did insist that he leave the household chores for her. Just because he wasn't working in an office didn't mean he wasn't extremely busy. Lori knew he was working hard to get his business going and, beyond this, he had parents in ill health to think about. Often he spent the entire day at their house working on a project. This above all convinced Lori what a good and caring person he was.

She, herself, hadn't spent any time with the elder Johnsons. Blake seemed a little hesitant about accepting his mother's persuasive dinner invitations. "I see so little of you as it is," he explained. "I don't want to share you."

They put the groceries away while they chatted about the day's events. How had she ever lived without this man? Coming home from work used to be so lonely. Charlotte had seldom asked about her day. When she'd volunteered little tidbits, her mother usually had no comment, or, if she did, it was to say something negative.

"Hey, your mind seems a hundred miles away," Blake said. "Have you already met someone more interesting than your boring, stay-at-home old man?"

"Oh, Blake, no," she said, embracing him. " I was just thinking how lucky I am." His lips sought hers, and as they kissed, she felt her desire heighten.

"I feel the same way," he said in a husky voice. "I wish you'd quit your job so we could be together all the time."

Lori stepped back and looked at him tenderly. "We've already been through this, darling. I love my work at the library. Besides, you wouldn't get anything done if I were here all day."

Blake reached for her again "You're right about that. Why don't we skip dinner and go right to bed."

"Even if I told you we're having lamb chops?"

This time it was he who released her. "In that case, let's eat and then go to bed."

Lori began the dinner preparations, while Blake set the table. "By the way I have to go to Denver tomorrow," he said in a casual tone.

"Oh, Blake, can't it wait? The weather is so bad."

"It's supposed to start clearing tomorrow. I won't have to leave till around ten, and I'll take it slow. But I'd better plan on spending the night there. The meeting could last until five, and I don't want to drive in the dark if the roads are still bad."

Lori tried not to show her disappointment. She knew he needed to make these trips to talk to investors and line up companies to work on his project. She just hated the idea of spending even one night separated from him. And now she would have an extra worry with the hazardous road conditions. During the past six weeks Blake had made several business trips to Denver, sometimes being gone two or three days.

Lori walked over to the counter and began to chop up vegetables for a salad. She didn't want him to see her face just then. "I know you have to go, but I'll miss you," she said.

Blake followed her over and leaned against the counter. "And I you. But let's not spoil our evening together by brooding about it." He reached over and touched her arm.

"Will it always be like this or once the business is off the ground will you be able to cut down on your trips?"

"That's a good question. I'm not sure I know the answer, but I think they'll be much less frequent. Say, how about those lamb chops? I'm starving."

Lori stepped over to the stove and raised the cover on the skillet. "They'll be ready in a few minutes. By the way, how are your negotiations going with the owner of the Adena field?"

She felt it was important to show an interest in his work. She had seen her father's hurt look when Charlotte had cut him off while he was telling her of a field he had plowed or a crop he had sold. Besides, she was genuinely interested in everything Blake did.

But a pained look came over Blake's face. He walked over to the door without answering, his hands stuffed in his pockets.

"I was just wondering about it. You have made the owner an offer, haven't you?"

Blake's voice was strained. "We have so little time together. If you don't mind, I'd prefer not talking business."

"But I'm interested. I want to be a part of everything you do, so I need to know about how things are going."

He walked over to the table and picked up a plate, which he held up and seemed to be studying. "Things are going well. Now, can we just leave it at that?" Suddenly he threw the plate on the floor, shattering it, and stalked out of the room.

Lori stood in shocked silence for a moment. She finished chopping the vegetables for the salad and placed them in a bowl; then stood frozen, trying to decide what to do with it.

Before she could decide, Blake was back. He took the bowl from her hands and placed it back on the counter. "I'm sorry," he said, putting his arms around her." But the way you interrogate me makes me think you doubt my ability to conduct my business. I have a pretty good success record, and I know what I'm doing. We have been managing to pay all our bills, haven't we?"

It was true. He had insisted on paying most of their living expenses. Obviously, he had carefully planned this career change and had put money away to tide him over. She admitted to herself that perhaps she had been subconsciously worried about finances. Blake had the added expense of supporting her. She just wished he would let her help more.

"I'm sorry, too, Blake. I didn't mean to upset you," she said.

But even though he had apologized, Lori couldn't shake her feelings of uneasiness, and later she carried them to bed with her. She wished she could understand what was going on with Blake. Perhaps things weren't going that well and her questions had hit a sensitive chord. Everything had been so good between them, but it could be the honeymoon was over. She had heard the first year was difficult, a period of getting to know another human being on the most intimate level and learning to adjust to that person.

I'll just have to be careful to not ask questions about his business, she thought. But it will be difficult. If things are not going well, I want to share his worries. Maybe he doesn't feel he can trust me. I'll just have to show him how much I love him, regardless of whether he's ever successful. He can be a garbage man for all I care. Lori almost smiled at the thought of Blake in this career role. She sighed and turned on her side, snuggling against his back. He moved away from her, which surprised her, but she could tell from his breathing that he was asleep.

Chapter 18 - Blake

Janice made her way to 6th Avenue through the heavy traffic. Blake was in the passenger seat beside her, and he couldn't take his eyes off her. She was wearing a new full-length leather coat, maroon to match her suede boots. They looked expensive, which was sexy. He was more interested, however, in what was underneath.

"So how is the job, going?" he asked, realizing they had a few miles to go before he could start living his fantasy.

"It's a job. The pay is good and they treat me okay. They wouldn't dare do otherwise, since Daddy's a close friend of the owner. The main thing is I'm finally out of Platte Valley, and there's almost as much to do in Denver as there was in Chicago."

"Like what?"

She turned and smiled at him. "Like concerts and clubs. I've been meeting a lot of interesting people."

"Really. These interesting people wouldn't happen to be other men, would they?"

"Blakie Boy, I do believe you're jealous. But I'd say it's none of your business. You lost that right when you got married."

"It's my business whether or not I put myself in the position of contacting AIDS or some other disease." His mouth was tight.

"Let's don't fight. We only have this one night together."

"Do you still not understand what this has all been about, why I moved back to Platte Valley, my marriage, my oil project?"

She was driving too fast for the city traffic, and another vehicle had to swerve to avoid missing them as she turned onto the freeway. "Please slow down a little," Blake said, after he had recovered. "It would be embarrassing, among other things, to be involved in an accident with you."

Ignoring his plea, she continued on at her present speed, moving into the far left lane. "I like to live in the fast lane, sweetie, and in answer to your question—yes, I understand, but I don't have to like it. Put yourself in my place. How would you feel?"

"Lori means nothing to me. She's just a means to an end, but this thing can't be rushed. I don't blame you for not hanging around Platte Valley. I know Tonia was getting on your nerves, although I'm sure you instigated a lot of the problems yourself."

Janice opened her mouth to protest, but he continued. "You can't help it, darling. It's in your nature to be a little beast." His mouth twisted into a crooked smile. "That's what makes you so sexy, your animal nature. You scratch and claw for whatever you want, and God forbid if anything or anyone gets in your way—like your father's new wife."

Janice made a hissing sound through her teeth, and then laughed. She seemed to accept this description as a compliment. "Ah yes, sweet Tonia, who thinks she has the perfect setup, until the old fool's offspring shows up and starts to wreck havoc on their little domestic scene. She knows I'm on to her, that her only interest in my father is his money, and that's what makes her so uncomfortable." She laughed. "I guess we're a lot alike, and she picked up on this. It was fun for a while, making her sweat. She never knew what little seeds of doubt I might be planting with her adoring husband."

"Damn it, move it or get off the highway, grandpa," she yelled, laying her hand on the horn." The driver of the car in front, who had been going the speed limit, finally moved to the middle lane. Janice accelerated and as she passed the slower moving vehicle, she raised her middle finger.

Blake laughed. "You're a dangerous lady in more ways than one. Don't you realize that's not a smart thing to do these days?"

"You mean with that old man? They ought to yank everyone's license once they reach fifty."

"You were saying about your stepmother . . ."

"Yeah, well after awhile it got boring keeping her off-balance. Or maybe I just got bored being stuck in Platte Valley. It was getting where you were tied up with your little bride most of the time. While we're on the subject of unprincipled people, what makes you so different? I think the three of us belong to the same little club, Tonia, you and me."

"You're right, we are all alike, at least in our ambitions. The difference with you is that you don't bother to be subtle about it. Tonia and I play the game closer to the chest, so to speak. But I'm more like you in that I do admit my motives, that I'll do anything to get what I want short of getting caught. I doubt if Tonia is that honest with herself. She's like most of the people out there who lie, cheat, and steal, but then sit in church on Sundays and feel good about themselves."

Janice nodded in agreement. "Amen."

"But that's why we need each other. We don't have to put on pretenses. We both know what we are, and in this respect, we're more honest than most people."

Janice nodded again. "And how is the project going? Does Lori know anything?"

"No, and she's not going to. I can work around her."

They were both silent for the rest of the trip. She turned onto East 1st Street and pulled into the driveway in front of one of the condominiums on 1st and Cherry Creek Boulevard. Blake grabbed his suitcase and followed her up the stairs.

As she flipped on the lights, she said, "You know the way. Put your luggage in the bedroom and freshen up if you want, while I mix the drinks."

"In a minute." He grabbed her and began unbuttoning her coat. When he had finished, she shrugged it off, letting it fall to the floor behind her. To his pleasant surprise he found she was wearing nothing but a seductive smile and maroon suede boots.

His eyes traveled hungrily down her fabulous body. "Very nice, but I feel a bit overdressed. Hold that pose, and I'll be right back." He carried his suitcase into the bedroom and threw it on the bed. Remembering what awaited him in the other room, he decided to unpack later. "I'm going to take a quick shower," he yelled. "Care to join me?"

Later, as they lay on a blanket in front of the fireplace, he said, "I did actually have a meeting with some investors today. Their office is on Union Boulevard, where you picked me up."

She sat up and reached for her drink, which was on the coffee table beside them. "At least you didn't have to lie to little wifey for a change. How does it look? Are they going to come through?"

"It looks good. Eric Anders, the expert in the field, gave an impressive presentation. You could see their minds clicking up the dollar amounts of the profit they'd make. And when I took the floor, told them I was the sole working interest owner as well as the royalty owner, which, of course, makes the project even more attractive, you could see them beginning to drool."

"Why is that? I mean, why does your owning the thing make it better from their standpoint?"

"Because, my love, I don't have to overburden the project. So many of these operations have to pay out so much to royalty owners, they wind up not having enough capital to do the job right. This makes the guys putting up the money nervous."

She laid back her head and gave a long, throaty laugh. "I see. You're in the somewhat unique position of owning the whole enchilada, and all because of your ingenuity, shall we say."

"Yes, I like that word. It sounds better than some you might have used."

"Blake, you're priceless." She raised herself on one elbow and looked down at him. "You know there hasn't been anyone else. Sure I go out with friends, dance, have a good time, but you're the only one who really turns me on. You've ruined me for anyone else."

"That's what I want to hear, baby. Just go on being a good little girl, and daddy will soon bring home the bacon. He pulled her down on top of him, his hands moving slowly down her back. She bent over and began licking his face, working her way down. He lay there inert, letting her do her thing. Then he suddenly flipped her over and straddled her, pinning her arms over her head with one hand. With the other he slapped her hard on the face. "You're mine. Do you hear? You just go to your job and forget the night life."

Her eyes were flashing, defiant. "That's not fair. I told you there's no one else."

"And I told you we're in this together. If I hear you've been screwing around with anyone, we're finished. And believe me I'll find out."

"Blake, let me go. You're hurting me."

He released her, and she put her arms around his neck, pulling him toward her. "It's only you I want, daddy. I promise I'll be a good girl."

The next morning Janice dropped him off at the parking garage where he'd left his pickup. As he edged his way toward the interstate, he was deep in thought. Some of the side roads were still icy in spots and traffic was slow. He had called Nathan Martin this morning from Janice's place and was told the words he wanted to hear. They were ready to go with him. The contract would be sent within a few days. Everything was moving along without a hitch, just as he'd planned.

And yet he couldn't seem to shake the dark mood that had settled over him. He supposed part of it had to do with Janice. It was becoming increasingly difficult to arrange these trysts. Beyond this, his meeting with Martin had revived the old rage he felt at having to work so hard for what was handed to others. Why was it so easy for those born into wealth and social status? Martin was one of these. You could smell it on him. Sure, Blake was eventually accepted into their elite society, but he had to fight for it, while they were accepted merely because of an accident of birth. He could never figure out what cruel trick of fate had landed him in Platte Valley with those peasants, Betty and Bud Johnson as parents. He had always figured some error had been made.

Fate, though, had tried to make amends by giving him a keen, razor-sharp mind and by sparing him any tiresome scruples that might have stood in his way. He was convinced he had every right to use whatever means necessary to take what was rightfully his. This had been his philosophy for as long as he could remember. Early on he had realized some of the people in Platte Valley, such as the Hollingsworths, lived better than his family. His dear little mother had tried her best to make sure he got every new toy his friend, Jimmy, was given, an expensive bicycle, and later an automobile. Jimmy's parents had bought him a Corvette for his sixteenth birthday, so Blake, whose birthday was three months later, began to work on his mother immediately. The result was a red Camero. He smiled when he thought of how she had managed this over his dad's protests.

This realization, that his family's position on the social ladder was close to the bottom, was only reinforced when he started college and ran into all those Ivy League boys. No matter that they had chosen the mining school at Golden rather than Harvard. They were still the same. So he had struggled to bury his past – and, at times when necessary, to invent a new one. He had even managed to marry well. But that frigid little phony, who never put out, had expected him to live like a monk. And when he couldn't, when she'd found out about his affair with Morgan Russell, one of the Pierce executive's wives, Andrea had had the nerve to get upset, gone crying to her daddy, and her old man had convinced her to get a divorce.

In retrospect, he knew he should have been more careful, found someone outside their circle, but Morgan had been so available, made it so obvious she was his for the taking, he'd found her invitation irresistible. Several times they'd slipped away in the midst of a party with both of their mates present. The memory of a hot and heavy moment in their host's guest room or in an automobile parked by the golf course aroused him still. But his feelings had been purely physical, and when she'd become demanding, as they always did, he was able to walk away without a backward glance.

After turning his pickup onto I70 East, he took it up to seventy and hit the cruise control button. The heavy traffic had taken care of any ice on the highway, but Blake wasn't in a hurry. He had much to think about. He hadn't called Lori last night as was his usual practice when he was out of town. What if she'd called the hotel where he was supposed to have stayed? Then there was the dinner coming up with his parents. Next Wednesday was his dad's birthday, and he'd told his mom they'd try to make it. She'd become increasingly persistent in her demands that he bring Lori for a visit, and he was running out of excuses. Women! he thought. They were the cause of much of his grief. Although he made a conscious effort to choose women who were the exact opposite of his meddling mother, cool, independent women, they all wanted a piece of him the end. Denise, the buyer from Chicago, whom he'd met on the airplane, was a typical example. When she didn't hear from him, she'd started calling his parents' house. It wasn't too difficult to find him, as there were only six Johnsons listed in the Platte Valley phone book. His little, Christian mother couldn't bring herself to lie and tell the woman she didn't know his whereabouts, so his only recourse was to refuse to speak to her or return her calls. Even after all these months and after his mother had conveyed to Denise he was now married, she still called once in awhile.

Blake noticed an oil field off to his left, and his mind drifted back to the project. Nothing could happen until spring, but his money supply was starting to dwindle again. A big chunk had gone to Anders, and he'd put a deposit on the compressors. And then, of course, there were the every day expenses of living, plus the child support.

Perhaps the dinner at his parents wasn't a bad idea. If he could get a few minutes alone with his dad, he could press him about selling his business. The person he didn't want to be alone with was his mother. She was nervous about loaning him that money without his dad's knowledge, always calling and whining about how he never came to see her and then asking in her "subtle" way how things were going on the project. He would casually mention to Lori that Betty measured a woman's worth by her domestic skills, that the way to impress her new mother-in-law was to insist on helping her with the dinner.

It was so easy to manipulate his unsuspecting, little wife. She was almost as gullible as his mother. But he would have to be more careful. That incident with the plate had been a mistake, even though she'd provoked him with her incessant questions. And then to top things off, he'd forgotten to call her last night. This role of playing the loving husband was a real strain on him, but he couldn't show his hand, not yet. He'd toyed with the idea of being up front with her, telling her about the project and how it could make them both rich, but this approach would merely postpone the inevitable.

Blake looked over as a BMW whizzed by on his left. An image of Janice flashed into his mind. He couldn't visualize her ever driving below ninety on an open highway. She told him she was in danger of losing her license because of all her speeding violations, but the threat didn't seem to worry her.

He smiled to himself. Janice literally lived life in the fast lane, and Blake knew this was part of her appeal. Crazy or not, he had to be with her. And this was becoming increasingly difficult. She hadn't figured in his original plan and even when he became involved with her, he'd viewed her as merely a pleasant diversion, someone to be dropped when he tired of her. It was ironic to find himself in this position, a real role reversal. Even though he'd pulled his tough guy act with her, he knew it was really Janice who was calling the shots. The thought that she may tire of waiting, meet someone else, caused a tightness in his chest.

Blake noticed the highway sign, indicating the exit to Platte Valley was a mile ahead. He touched the brake lightly and swung over to the right lane. As he turned off the interstate, he tried to focus on what story he was going to tell his wife. But he couldn't get Janice off his mind. Damn her, he said under his breath. I don't need this complication. She's jeopardizing my whole plan. Then a cynical smile crossed his face. The fact is Blake, old boy, you get off on living dangerously. Well, up until now, they could take everything away but they couldn't lock him up. This time the stakes could be higher.

Chapter 19 - Lori

Lori looked at her watch. In just an hour she would be with her husband. That is if she didn't have to stop by to see her mother on the way home from work. She picked up the phone and started to dial Charlotte's number. Then she impulsively hit the off button. She felt like a coward as she punched in the Jacobs number, but sometimes she didn't feel up to Charlotte's cynicism. And this was one of those times.

Pauline Jacobs answered on the third ring. "Hello, Mrs. Jacobs. This is Lori. I was wondering if you could give Mother a message when you take over her dinner tonight. I'd call her myself, but she may be resting. Blake was out of town overnight. He called me here at the library to tell me he made it back. I'd like to go home as soon as I get off work."

"No problem, Melora. We were over there this morning. I did the vacuuming and the kitchen, and George shoveled the walk and driveway. Now I'm fixing a big pot of chicken and homemade dumplings for dinner. There will be plenty, so I'll take her over a plate. She shouldn't turn up her nose too far."

"Has she been giving you some trouble?"

"Oh, you know your mother. She bitches and complains. Says she can't afford to pay me and that I don't get the corners good anyhow."

"Oh, Mrs. Jacobs, I'm sorry. She knows that I'm the one paying you. She's just trying to give you a hard time, I guess." Lori wanted to add "since I'm not around as much for her to kick around." But she thought better of it.

"Don't worry about it. I've known Charlotte since we were girls. I can handle her. And I told her it wasn't coming out of her pocket so she could just quit being so critical. She pretty much shut up after that," Mrs. Jacobs said with a chuckle.

"I don't know what I'd do without you. I did think it would be nice to have a whole evening at home with Blake. And tell Mother I'll be over first thing in the morning. Since it's Sunday I'll be able to spend some extra time with her to make up for tonight."

Lori was relieved to hear Mr. Jacobs had shoveled her mother's sidewalk and driveway. Blake had been over there twice to do it for her. And Charlotte had never so much as acknowledged his thoughtfulness, let alone thanked him. She would rather pay Mr. Jacobs than be embarrassed by Charlotte's bad behavior.

As she drove home from work, the incident with the plate was on her mind. Lori admitted to herself that this was her primary reason for wanting to hurry home. She needed the reassurance that everything was still all right between them. There was something else bothering her. When Blake had stayed over in Denver on previous occasions, he'd called her. But last night the telephone was silent. So about nine o'clock she impulsively dialed the hotel where he said he'd be staying and was told they had no one registered under his name. She had debated all day whether or not to ask him about this but decided there was probably a logical explanation. They might have been booked up or he simply decided to stay somewhere else. And she didn't want him to think she was checking up on him.

After dinner they sat on the couch, while Blake told her about his trip. "I'd say it was most successful. I met with some investors, and they must have been impressed. They even took me out and wined and dined me. That's why I didn't call you. It was late when I got to the hotel. By the time I'd registered and gotten settled in my room, I was afraid you'd be in bed. Anyhow it looks like they're going to loan me the money for the project."

"That's wonderful, Blake." Lori breathed a silent prayer of thanks she hadn't grilled him about his whereabouts. She was curious about the loan for his project and what it all meant but was reluctant to ask.

"Lori, Lori, you remind me of a scared little doe with those big eyes." Blake took her hands in his and held them tightly. "You're not going to run away like one are you, now that you've seen my dark side? To tell you the truth, I had this meeting coming up and guess I was nervous. That's why I jumped all over you. No excuse, I know, and again I'm sorry."

Before she could formulate an answer, he continued. "But I really don't want to talk about my project. I need to get away from it, relax a little. Do you know what I'd like? I'd like to get out one of our poetry books. Could we do that?"

162

"I'd like that too. I know just the book," she said.

After fixing tea and pouring it into her favorite china cups, Lori walked to the bookcase. Her eyes traveled over the books until she found *Library of Poetry and Song*, the one she'd been carrying that day at the lake so long ago.

When she returned with the book, she asked, "How about this one? It's always been my favorite. I think every great poet is represented in it."

"Isn't this the book that has 'A Portrait' in it, the one by Barrett Browning? I used to know it, but I guess I've forgotten it after all these years. Remember, I recited a couple of stanzas for you once."

Lori had marked the page with a bookmark. "Yes, I remember. Will you read it to me?" she asked.

He took the book, and began to read,

I will paint her as I see her,
Ten times have the lilies blown
Since she looked upon the sun . . .

The next morning before she left for her mother's house, Lori walked into Blake's study. He was sitting at his desk, engrossed in paper work. "I meant to tell you something last night but forgot. I guess we got busy with other things."

He looked up and grinned. "Don't remind me, or you'll never get out of here. By the way, tell your mother 'hello' for me and that I'm sorry I didn't get over to shovel the snow for her."

Lori hugged him impulsively. "It's okay, Mr. Jacobs took care of it. Why you'd even want to help her again is beyond me. She's so unappreciative."

"I don't need her to thank me. I doubt if she knows how."

"Yes, you're probably right. But what I wanted to say is that I called Rusty Reardon yesterday. Now that things are settling down a little, I thought his grandfather could bring him by for a visit this afternoon. You know I told you what good friends Rusty and I have become, and I feel as if I've deserted him lately. He seemed thrilled to hear from me."

"This afternoon would be fine. Do you want me out of the way while you're entertaining one of your male admirers? I don't want to put a cramp on things."

"Rusty does seem fond of me, but I don't think it's that kind of affection. I think he's looking for a mother, poor little guy."

"Does he ever hear from his own mother?"

"Rarely. It's probably been over a year since he's seen her and then, only for a short time."

Blake didn't respond, and as she turned to leave, she noticed he seemed distracted, his eyes fixed on some point beyond the window above his desk. She wondered if he was thinking about his own son, whom he hadn't seen since he moved back to Platte Valley.

As she walked to the car, Lori was glad she'd worn her boots. The sun had been warm the previous afternoon melting much of the snow, and her feet swished through the brown slush. She'd worn a skirt and sweater, as she planned to take Charlotte to church. This was something she'd done each Sunday while she'd lived with her mother. Since moving out, she was making an effort to keep up the practice. Besides, she liked to go to church.

Lori had asked Blake to go with them once. He'd declined, and it wasn't so much his words, but the look he'd given her that had kept her from asking him again. She hadn't really expected him to go. He'd told her how he hated having to go with his parents while he was growing up and said he hadn't "darkened the door" of a church since he'd left home, except, of course, when Andrea and he had married. "And look how that turned out," he'd added. The quick service at the Las Vegas chapel when Lori and he had exchanged vows had been just about right, according to Blake. The chaplain's sermon had been limited to a few words about having a long and prosperous life together.

Lori waved to the Matthews children as she passed their house on Crawford. . The remains of a snowman sat in their yard, his further demise inevitable in the bright morning sunshine. She braked at the stop sign at Crawford and Main and then swung the car onto Main and the deserted downtown area. Unlike most cities, the merchants of Platte Valley still observed Sunday as a day of rest. Isley's Grocery Store had yielded to current trends to the point it stayed open from noon to four, but the other businesses remained closed throughout the day.

Charlotte was dressed and sitting in her recliner, when Lori arrived. She wore a flowered dress with her good sweater over her shoulders. Lori noticed she was wearing her black oxfords and hoped she intended to change into boots as they went out. It hurt to see how thin her mother had become, even thinner than before Lori had married and moved out. She fought the pang of guilt that was moving its way to her chest. Charlotte's weight loss could be caused by many things, she told herself.

"How did you like Mrs. Jacobs' dinner last night?" she asked as she sat down in the chair opposite Charlotte's. "I remember going for dinner to the Jacobs as a child and how happy I was when I learned we were having chicken and homemade dumplings."

"It was all right. I don't think she puts the time into the dumplings she used to. They were a little lumpy. She gets in a hurry and adds them to the broth too quickly."

Lori decided to drop it. "Are we having coffee with Phoebe after services?"

"No. Her niece from Golden is here visiting. She can't be bothered with me when she has something better going."

"Now, Mother, you know that's not true. We don't have many out-of-town visitors, but if we did, I'm sure we'd be the same. It's a lot of work having house guests." Lori was secretly a little relieved. The day was going to be full enough. This way she could be home in time to bake a quick batch of cookies for Rusty. She'd planned to stop off at Isley's and buy some packaged snacks but this wouldn't be as special.

"I don't know how you could possibly know that. We've seldom had anyone visiting, except your father's cousins from Iowa while he was alive. You were always off doing your own thing and never had to worry about entertaining them. Since he died, they've never bothered to come back to visit us."

Lori felt her mother was just being contrary. Still, Charlotte's words stung, and she retorted before she had a chance to think about it.

"That's not quite true. I remember working to have the house sparkling before their arrival and then cleaning up afterwards. And I did try to keep the boys entertained, in fact, you never knew about it but . . ."

Charlotte was looking at her expectantly, but Lori decided there was no point in bringing up her harrowing childhood experience. And if her mother chose to brush the incident aside as insignificant, she felt it would just add to her hurt.

"I was just going to say, it wasn't easy to keep them entertained."

"Those were wild boys. I hear neither one of them has amounted to a hill of beans."

Lori wasn't surprised to hear this. They had come back a few years after the incident involving the outhouse. Her dad had taken her aside and told her she didn't need to spend any time with them if she felt uncomfortable, but her mother had insisted that it was her duty to play with them. Lori got out the cards and some board games and set them up, but she was careful not to spend anytime alone with them.

Charlotte had moved on to other relatives. "Even my only sister has never once come back to see me since she moved to New York. She didn't even come to your grandmother's funeral. Had a big bouquet of flowers sent over and thought she'd done her duty."

Lori suddenly felt sorry for her mother. She knew how hurt Charlotte had been by her younger sister's neglect. It made her realize that she was all the old lady really had. "I know how difficult it's been for you, but Sophie does keep in touch. She's been writing more in recent years, hasn't she?"

"She's a widow now like me, and her children have gone off and left her alone." She looked pointedly at Lori, "so now she knows how it feels."

Lori didn't know how to respond to this, so merely said, "We'd better get started for church or we'll be late."

After church Lori had planned to stay and visit with her mother for a while, but Charlotte picked up the remote control and turned on the television. After a few moments, Lori felt she might as well leave. Charlotte seemed to be absorbed in a program on the pros and cons of air bags. She kissed her mother on the forehead and promised to see her the following day.

As she walked toward the door, Charlotte turned her head and said, "I know what a burden I am. Maybe one of these days my heart will just give out, and you won't have to bother with me anymore."

"Oh, Mother, why do you say such things?"

Charlotte didn't answer. She seemed to be once again absorbed in the television program.

Lori sighed. "I'll see you tomorrow then. Be sure to call if you need anything."

Rusty was to arrive at three o'clock, and it was almost that time when Lori took the cookies from the oven. Blake came up behind her as she was lifting them from the cookie sheet and rubbed against her back provocatively. Before she could say anything, he reached around her and grabbed a handful of cookies.

"Blake, these are for Rusty." Lori tried to sound outraged, but her smile betrayed her.

"I'm just trying to act like a typical jealous husband. Why don't you ever bake cookies for me?"

"Out! Take your cookies and get out of here. I have exactly five minutes to put this kitchen back in order."

Lori ran water in the sink and immersed her baking utensils. As she began to wash them, she reflected on how full her life was these days. Sure, she was busy, but she didn't mind. There were little nagging worries, which kept her from being completely happy, most of which involved her mother. But she always came to the same conclusion. When she had lived with Charlotte and had spent most of her time at her mother's beck and call, the woman had been unhappy, anyhow. It was a choice Charlotte had made, and Lori was coming to realize she wasn't responsible, nor could she do anything to change her. She hoped Charlotte would somehow come to realize that, even with her poor health, she could broaden her world and find some pleasure in life. But Lori was doubtful this would happen.

The doorbell rang just as she finished sweeping the kitchen floor. The first thing she noticed as she opened the door and saw Rusty's upturned little face was that he had two shiny front teeth. They looked out of proportion, since his face needed to catch up with his new adult-sized teeth.

She bent down and gave him a big hug, which he didn't seem to mind. Switching her attention to his grandfather, she noticed Larry wasn't in uniform. His smile seemed a little strained.

"Can you come in? Blake is here, and I'm sure he'd like to say 'hello.'"

His response was abrupt. "I have some errands to do but thank you. I'll just pick Rusty up in an hour or so if that's all right."

Perhaps because Blake found her desirable, she had a new image of herself, that of a desirable woman. Lori wondered if Larry could possibly be a little jealous. She thought his terse refusal of her invitation was more like the response of a surly little boy, than that of a man who patrolled the streets of Platte Valley, protecting its citizens.

Looking down at Rusty and seeing his apparent happiness at being here wiped thoughts of his grandfather from her mind.

"I've been doing a lot of stuff on our new computer, even some of my school work." His face shone with pride. "Grandpa is learning to use it too. Sometimes he plays games with me. And guess what? My mom wrote me a letter, and she's going to school in Denver. She took this test so she could get her high school diploma. I forget what you call it."

"I believe it's called a G.E.D test."

"Yeah. That's it. Anyhow, now she's going to this school in Denver to learn to be a secretary. And she's got a new apartment there and says when she gets some more furniture and a bed for me to sleep in, I can come and see her and spend the night. And something else better, when she gets done with her school and gets a job, I get to go live with her."

"That's wonderful, Rusty." Lori hoped Cindy would follow through with her plans. She would hate to see Rusty disappointed again.

She led him to the kitchen, and his eyes lit on the plate of freshly baked cookies.

"Are some of those for me?" His face was bright with anticipation.

"They sure are. You just sit down and help yourself. I'm going to see if my husband will join us."

He was happily munching cookies and sipping lemonade as she left the room and walked toward Blake's office. "Rusty is here," she said. "How about taking a break and joining us for a few minutes?"

He held up his hand as a signal he was in the middle of something. Looking over his shoulder, Lori noticed he was working on some equations. Finally he laid down his pencil. "Sorry, but I'm in the middle of some complex stuff and don't want to lose my train of thought. I'll have to meet him another time. You two have a nice visit together."

"I'm sorry you couldn't join Rusty and me this afternoon." Lori hoped by bringing up the subject of Rusty and his visit Blake would be encouraged to talk about his own son. They'd finished dinner and were having tea in front of the fireplace. Blake had been unusually quiet during dinner. He'd stayed in his office during Rusty's entire visit, had even shut the door. The more she thought about it, Lori was sure his behavior was connected with Josh. She decided the reason he never spoke of his son was because it was too painful. But she also knew it wasn't healthy to keep these feelings bottled up.

Lori took a deep breath and plunged ahead. "I'll bet you miss Josh. You haven't seen him in awhile, not since you've been back here, have you?"

For a moment she didn't think he was going to answer. Then he said in a strained voice, "His mother has made it very difficult. Not only does she have the court on her side, but she's managed by telling him vicious lies to turn him against me."

"Oh, Blake. I'm so sorry." She reached over and touched his hand. "I didn't mean to upset you. It's just that he must be about the same age as Rusty, and I would love to meet him."

"You're not the only one. My mother gets very depressed about it. I'd hoped to bring him here so she could have time with her only grandson." His jaw tightened. "Well, I haven't given up yet. Money talks and once my business takes off, I'll be extremely verbose."

"It's hard for me to believe they won't let you see Josh because you don't have enough money."

"You've led a very sheltered life in this little hick town." His face was one she hadn't seen since that day at the lake when they were still in high school, hard and cynical.

It made Lori cringe to hear him speak of Platte Valley as a hick town.

"Take my word for it, without money you're powerless and can get stomped into the ground. That thing about all men being created equal is a crock of bull. I wasn't fortunate like Andrea to have been born into wealth." His tone was bitter. "She not only had to bankrupt me, but she had to castrate me, as well. Well, that bitch hasn't won yet. Things are about to change. One of these days soon I'll have enough money to hobnob with the best of them."

Lori sat in shocked silence. She sensed his feelings about his deteriorating relationship with Josh were only partially the cause of his bitterness, that there were things and events unknown to her that had warped the way he viewed the world. It struck her that he was no longer thinking of his son but of his own disappointments.

"I thought money wasn't that important, that you just wanted enough to be able to stay in the area so you could be close to your parents."

He looked at her as though he had forgotten her presence. Then he smiled, but his eyes were still cold. "Did I say that? Well, my little lamb, it just goes to show you can't believe everything people say."

Lori decided it was time to drop the subject. Trying to sort out their conversation later, she concluded Blake didn't really mean the things he'd said. His disappointment at not being able to see his son had caused this strange mood.·

The next morning they were both unusually quiet. Blake had poured his coffee and taken it into his office, declining her offer to fix breakfast. Lori had settled on toast. But as she sat there alone at the kitchen table, she had trouble eating it. She drank a glass of juice and put the toast down the disposal.

The hot water of the shower restored her sense of well being somewhat. Before leaving for work, she stepped into Blake's office. He seemed to be hard at work on his computer. Lori bent over and threw her arms around his shoulders, hugging him long and hard. She hoped that through a process of osmosis she could absorb some of his pain. She loved him so much, she knew there wasn't anything she wouldn't do for him.

Blake didn't get up but put a hand on her arm. "I'll see you when you get home," he said in a noncommittal voice.

Chapter 20 - Joe

When the bus pulled up in front of Brooks Drug Store at around seven-thirty in the evening, there was no one there to meet him. The bus driver waited a little impatiently as he struggled to get his large duffel bag from the overhead compartment. It was all he owned in the world, except for his two dogs and Pa's old place, which was now his.

Joe hadn't really expected anyone to be here. With Pa dead who else would come to meet him? He had kind of hoped his Uncle Luke would, since he had written to him about getting out. But he hadn't been that close to his uncle. He was probably too busy trying to run the store, just like he always was in the old days, too busy to even say "Hello, Joe," when he saw his nephew at the store. Most times he didn't even see Joe. The clerks all got to know him, so when he went to the back, they didn't even stop him, didn't even ask, "Hey, where do you think you're going?" except maybe when they were new. He'd go back of the store where they kept all the food before they put it on the shelves and find the carts with the bakery goods that had gone a little stale but were still good when you put them in the oven for a few minutes. And he'd find the squishy brown bananas and the cereal and cookies in the crushed boxes. Joe would take what he could carry out and put it in the wagon tied to the back of his bike.

He didn't have many friends in town when he left all those years ago. He doubted if any of them were still around or if they'd still be his friends after what had happened. He slung the duffel bag over his shoulder and started walking. He didn't know what shape the old house was in. How long since Pa had passed on? He couldn't remember too good, but it was real cold. He'd stood out at the graveyard with the guards right there behind him and wished his coat were warmer. There were just a few people there. A few more had come to the funeral, mostly old ladies, and Joe guessed maybe it was too cold for them to come out there and stand by the grave when they put Pa in it. Uncle Luke was there, but he didn't look at Joe, and afterwards, after they put Pa down in the ground and Joe had stood there with the tears freezing right on his face, he'd looked up and everyone but him and those guards was gone. Even Uncle Luke was gone.

The house hadn't been in the best of shape then. But he and Pa had made out all right. It would be strange to go home and have him not there. Joe wasn't sure what had happened to the dogs. The lawyer hadn't said anything. He'd gotten a letter from the lawyer after Pa died. The lawyer said it was a pro bono case. Joe's best friend in the place, Jay, said this meant when poor people couldn't afford to pay for lawyer work they did it for free. That was Pa all right. The letter said Henry Isley, that was his Pa, didn't have a will, so Joe got to keep everything, which the lawyer said was the house and the land. He didn't say anything about the dogs and the goats and the chickens. When Joe had written back to the lawyer at a place in Sterling, asking about the dogs, he'd never gotten anything back. He guessed someone took them and was looking after them. Their names were Shotgun and Bullet, and they were the best dogs in the world, as well as being his best friends. They used to listen to him when he talked better than most people did. He hoped whoever was looking after them was being good to them. Joe remembered he had been gone a long time. Maybe the dogs had died, too. They hadn't even let him go over to the house when he'd come back for Pa's funeral. He wanted to ask Uncle Luke about the dogs, but he had looked up and Uncle Luke was gone.

Thinking hard like he was doing, he'd walked the two miles before he knew it. He stood for a minute before the old gate, hanging loose from the hinges. Nothing much changed there, the gate had always hung this way. He used to fix it sometimes, but he guessed the wood was too rotten, and that's why it didn't hold. He could barely make out the house in the darkness. He hoped there was some kerosene or candles, 'cause he knew the lights weren't going to be on. Even back in the old days, him and Pa had to use kerosene lanterns a lot, 'cause the electric company was always shutting off the lights when they couldn't pay the bill.

When he tried the door, it swung open. They'd never locked it. Pa said if anyone could find anything in that place they wanted, they were welcome to it. But no one had ever bothered, or if they thought about it, the dogs made them think better. The dogs weren't barking now. Of course, they'd only barked at Joe 'cause they were happy to see him, not like with other people. They could be real mean when someone else came around. Once they'd taken a chunk out of the man from the electric company when he'd come out to shut the electricity off. Pa didn't call the dogs off him right away. He just stood by the window kind of chuckling. Then when he went outside and called the dogs, the man said he was going to sue Pa. Pa just laughed and said, "Go right ahead."

Joe found some kerosene on a shelf and lit the lantern. He walked through the rooms, looking them over. Not much changed, he thought. He was anxious about what was going to happen to him now that he was back in Platte Valley. He didn't like to think about this. The dreams were still there, but he'd told the doctor they were better. The doctor seemed to want him to say this, and Joe wanted to please the doctor. He finally even agreed with the doctor that it wasn't the stranger who killed Norma, that he'd made it up about the stranger. He didn't like to lie, but when Joe kept telling him about the stranger, the doctor looked unhappy. He'd look down at his desk and put his hands on his head. When Joe finally said there wasn't really a stranger, the doctor had smiled at him. The next time when he went to the office, and the doctor asked him if it was him who'd killed Norma, Joe said, "Yeah, I guess it was." He liked the doctor and didn't want him to put his head down and sigh. The doctor was real happy that day. He said they'd made a big breakthrough.

But Joe was kind of surprised when they told him he could go home. He'd gotten used to being there, and he wasn't sure if he wanted to go home since Pa wasn't going to be there anymore. But then he remembered Shotgun and Bullet. He needed to find out where they were. He still didn't like to think about why they'd sent him to that hospital. He didn't like it that they thought he'd hurt a nice lady like Norma. He'd never really had a girl friend before her, and she acted like she really liked him. Whenever he went into the restaurant, even though there were a lot of guys sitting at the counter talking and laughing with her, she'd just leave them there and come over and talk to him real nice.

Joe found some cans of beans and opened one, eating them right out of the can. There was no water. He'd have to check the well out in the morning. Suddenly feeling very tired, he walked to the other side of the room and held the lantern out. The blankets were still on the beds in a heap as always. Taking off his boots, he stretched out on the one that had been his. As he drifted off, he thought how quiet it was without the sound of Pa's snoring from the other bed and about how lonesome it was without the dogs there

173

lying on the floor between them. He thought he'd go looking around for the dogs in the morning after he'd checked the well.

Chapter 21 - Lori

"Where has that boy of ours been hiding you? I had to throw a regular fit before he agreed to bring you over for dinner."

Lori smiled at the plump, friendly little woman. "I've been wanting to come, Mrs. Johnson."

"Please call me Betty. Or if you want to, you can even call me mom. I'd like that. I'm just real pleased to finally have a daughter. I always wanted one, but it just never happened. The good Lord knows best, I guess. But no matter, I have one now. I hope you and I can be real close, do things together." Betty looked up at her, beaming. "But listen to me going on. Let me take your coats."

As she walked over to the hall closet to hang up their coats, Lori glanced at Blake and noticed a strained look on his face.

His mother continued talking. "Of course, it may be best to just call me Betty for now. After all you do have your own mother, and I wouldn't want her to think I was trying to take her place. You just call me whatever feels comfortable to you."

Bud Johnson, who had been sitting in a recliner, came over and put out his hand.

"How are you, Lori? Glad you could make it." When he shook Blake's hand, Lori noticed he was a little more restrained. She hoped she might be instrumental in easing the tension between the two men, but at this point, she had no idea how to go about it.

Bud was clearly the quiet type, or perhaps it was because he hadn't had much of a chance to talk through the years. Betty seemed to hardly take a breath between sentences. Lori remembered going to the Johnson's store with her father several times. Bud had always had a warm friendly smile for her. She thought now that he reminded her a lot of her father. She'd never expected to be visiting the Johnsons in their home, especially as their new daughter-in-law. But she felt welcome and looked forward to having a close relationship with them.

Betty declined her offer to help. "It's all simmering on the stove. All I have to do is dish it up. You two just go on in and keep Dad company."

As Lori sat on the sofa next to Blake, she took in the warm, homey atmosphere. In one corner of the room stood an old piano covered with photographs. Lori walked over to look at them more closely, and found, not surprisingly, that many of them were of Blake. She smiled when she saw his high school class pictures. Although of average build, he seemed to stand out by force of personality, his blonde hair cut in a long shag. In each of them was a skinny, studious looking girl with dark hair. Lori's eye was drawn to her own image only because she was familiar with the photo.

After dinner, while the two men visited in the living room, Lori helped Betty clear the dishes. Blake had hinted she should offer to help, and Lori was surprised he felt he needed to mention it.

"Blake didn't exaggerate when he said you were the best cook in town," Lori said as she rinsed off the plates.

Betty's entrée of stuffed pork chops was a culinary delight. She had served it with acorn squash and creamed asparagus. The meal had left little need for scraping the plates. By the time she'd finished the last bite of chocolate mousse, Lori was glad for the opportunity to move around.

"I hope to reciprocate one of these days, when things are a little less hectic," she said, wondering what in the world she could cook that would measure up.

"Oh, that's not at all necessary. I know you kids are busy. Blake is trying to get his company going and you're working. I just hope you'll come back here for dinner soon. I do love to cook, and it's not as much fun just cooking for Bud and me. By the by, my neighbor goes to the same church as you, and she tells me she sees you there a lot with your mother. How's her health these days?

"She's doing okay. It's been a big adjustment for her to not have me around. Mrs. Jacobs next door is working for us, fixing her meals and cleaning. I do try to get over there after work each day, if only for a little while. On weekends I'm able to make my visits longer."

"Well, I think that's real nice. Of course, Bud and I are in good health and don't need Blake to be looking after us, but I'd hoped we would see more of him since he's living right here in Platte Valley."

A frown had come over her usually cheerful face. "When he first got back, he was at the store a lot helping out and did some things around the house, you know, little repair jobs. But we haven't seen him much since the two of you got married. Oh dear, that didn't come out the way I intended. Of course the two of you being newlyweds need your privacy. But now that it's been a couple of months, maybe we'll start seeing you a little more."

Betty looked at her expectantly, but Lori was too stunned to respond for a moment. Blake had led her to believe he was at his parents' house frequently. He'd also told her their health was failing. When she finally spoke, it was to ask, "You don't have any health problems then, you nor Bud?"

"Not yet, thank goodness, and hopefully, we will continue to enjoy good health for some years to come. Oh, I have a little problem with my blood pressure being too high, but I take medicine for that and . . ."

"How is your heart?" Lori asked. Her own heart seemed to have momentarily stopped while she awaited Betty's answer.

"No problems there. I do have a few aches and pains when I get up in the morning but guess that's only natural as one gets older."

Just then Blake walked through the door. "What are you two ladies up to in here? I need to take my bride home so she can get her beauty rest."

Lori thought he looked a little sheepish and wondered how much of the conversation he'd heard. "We're just finishing up. Is there anything else I can help you with, Betty?" Her voice sounded cool to her own ears in spite of her effort to conceal her disturbed feelings.

Betty didn't seem to notice. "Heavens no. You two run along now. But don't forget, I want to see more of you. Why don't you plan on coming for dinner again next Sunday?"

"We'll have to let you know, Mom. It depends on my schedule. You know how busy I am." Before Betty could make a further plea, Blake turned to Lori. "I'll get your coat," he said.

As they drove home, Blake was unusually quiet. Lori was thankful, as she needed time to think. She wished she'd had the opportunity to ask Betty about her husband's arthritis. Surely if Blake thought his father needed to retire, his condition must be quite serious. But Betty said they were both in good health. She tried to recall her past conversations with Blake concerning his visits with his parents. Perhaps she'd misunderstood. What had he said specifically about helping out with projects at the Johnson's home? Then she remembered that early last week before the storm Blake told her he was tired because he'd worked most of the day moving things to the attic, a task his father couldn't do because of his arthritis. Could it be Betty was just forgetful? Or maybe, like her own mother, she had a negative outlook and no matter how much her son visited her or did things for her, it was never enough. This image certainly didn't seem to fit the pleasant little lady, however.

The nagging doubts persisted when they arrived home. She waited until she knew Blake was asleep before retiring herself. Lying in the dark next to him, she forced herself to think of more pleasant things, like how much she liked Blake's parents and what a pleasant evening she'd spent at their house. Finally she drifted off to sleep.

The next morning, though, Lori's troubled thoughts returned. She didn't feel she should confront Blake about the discrepancies in what he'd told her or ask him why he had fabricated these stories, so she kept silent. If he noticed she was cool toward him, he didn't say anything. For the first time since their marriage, she didn't kiss him goodbye—just called out that she was leaving.

Once at work, Lori sorted the returned books as she put them on carts. So familiar was this task that she hardly had to think about it. Her mind was still on her husband. Another thing that bothered her was that he suddenly seemed so cynical. This was not the Blake she thought she knew. Her mind was in turmoil as she wheeled the first cart of books to the fiction section and began replacing them on the shelves.

Then around ten o'clock she got a call that swept all thoughts of Blake from her mind. Mrs. Jacobs telephoned to tell Lori that when she'd gone over that morning, she'd found Charlotte lying on the floor by her bed, unable to move or talk. The medics were there now and were getting ready to move her to the hospital at Fort Morgan. She'd evidently suffered a stroke.

Lori stood frozen for a moment, unable to fathom what to do next. I need to get over there, she thought finally. If I can just get a hold of Kristen . . . . Being in good health, she seldom needed to call on anyone to fill in for her. During the five years she'd been in charge, if she needed to take a rare day off, she'd been able to make arrangements in advance, either with Mrs. Moran or with one of the succession of part-time high school girls.

Luckily she was able to reach Kristen at school. She assured Lori it was no problem to miss her afternoon classes. When Lori arrived at the hospital Blake was already there, since she'd called him immediately after contacting Kristen. The hospital personnel had just settled her mother into a room and they were able to go in immediately. She had to hold back the tears when she saw her mother, looking so small and pale in the large hospital bed. There was a tube connected to her hand, which was attached to a bag of fluid. They were feeding her intravenously. They also had her hooked up to a heart monitor.

Blake walked over and laid his hand on her shoulder, a look of compassion on his face. Lori needed no further encouragement to let him envelop her in his arms.

She spent the next few days at the hospital, going home only to sleep. At first her mother's words were slurred when she tried to talk, and she was unable to even sit up without help. The doctor assured Lori this condition was not necessarily permanent, that with a little time and physical therapy, Charlotte could experience an almost one hundred percent recovery.

Dr. Bob wasn't much older than Lori. She remembered him as being one of the big high school kids when she was still in grammar school. After he graduated from medical school, he'd come back to Platte Valley and gone into practice with his father. Then when the older Dr. Jefferson died, most of his patients had stayed on with his son. He was well liked and respected, like his father before him.

During the days that followed, Blake was wonderful. He put everything he was doing on hold. Lori herself had taken a leave of absence from work, getting Mrs. Moran to come in and take over for her. She'd met the older woman at the library to explain the computer system. Jon's mother was over sixty, but her mind was still sharp and she caught on in a couple of hours. "I have a computer at home, you know. I'm even on the Internet," Mrs. Moran said proudly.

Charlotte was in the hospital for a week. During this time the feeling in her face returned and she was able to enunciate her words more clearly. She also regained some of the use of her arms, but was still unable to walk. Dr. Bob said there was a good chance this condition was temporary but that, in the meantime, he could send her home in a wheel chair if there were someone there to look after her.

This presented a real dilemma. Lori knew she couldn't ask Mrs. Jacobs to stay with Charlotte full time. Since she helped her husband out with the farm chores and was getting up in years, their neighbor couldn't take on anymore than she was already doing. Neither could Lori expect Mrs. Moran to do more than fill in for her for a week or two at the library. And Kristen was not a possibility either, since she had to be in school and spring break was still over a month away. When she voiced her worries to Blake, he surprised her.

"It's simple. I can take my laptop with me and do my work there during the day. Then you can stay with her at night."

"Are you sure, Blake? I really hate to burden you with this. And besides, taking care of an invalid is not something you've had any experience with. I'm not trying to say you're not competent at what you do. You're an extremely talented engineer, but this is so different that..."

"I know how to cook, Lori, and there are a lot of other things I can do, which you obviously have no knowledge of. And if your next statement is that your mother harbors a resentment towards me that will make my job even tougher, I can handle her. Okay? Besides, according to the doctor, this will only be for a few weeks. We have to keep a positive attitude, plan on her making a complete recovery soon."

The last vestige of doubt that Lori had begun to harbor about Blake disappeared with his generous offer. They had simply hit one of those rough spots all newlyweds experienced, she told herself as she hugged him.

"Platte Valley Library. May I help you?" Lori asked, as she picked up the telephone.

"Hi, Lori. How's your mother doing?" Sarah's voice came over the wire.

"Everything's going well. She seems much stronger. She's regained almost all of the feeling in her arms, although her legs don't seem to be much better. By the way, thanks for your work in getting that physical therapist to come out from Denver. She's just been there once, but I'm very hopeful after talking to her."

"Just doing my job, Ma'am. Actually I keep pretty close tabs on your mother's case, since that's part of my job. What I'm really curious about is how that husband of yours is holding up."

"I never would have believed it if I wasn't seeing it with my own eyes. Blake is wonderful with Mother. Oh, she tries to give him a hard time, but what's new? The fact that she has some of her old spunk back is encouraging in itself. But unlike me, Blake seems to be able to keep his perspective, not take her insults and bad humor personally."

"This man can't be for real. You're beginning to make me feel bad I didn't set my sights on him years ago when we were in high school."

"I know you're joking. Jon is a rock and you know it. But this is what makes me happy about Blake—the fact that he views this as our problem, not just mine. We'd been having a few small problems before this happened, but I suppose all couples do. This crisis seems to have brought us closer together."

"That's great, and I'm glad your mom's doing better too. Another unrelated item, in case you haven't heard about it. Joe Isley has evidently been released, because he's back in town. He's living at his dad's old place."

"No, I hadn't heard. Phoebe has been by to visit Mother a couple of times, but if Phoebe's feeding Mother any gossip, she hasn't passed it on. I suppose that's a sign she's not completely recovered yet. That is surprising about Joe. Guess his being released means he's been cured."

"Let's hope so." Sarah's tone was apprehensive. "Oh yes, before I hang up, guess who else is back?"

Lori laughed. "You're a gold mine of information. I don't have a clue." Normally, she'd be impatient with her friend by now, but even Sarah's bent toward gossip couldn't disrupt her sense of well being today.

"Karen called to tell me Janice Hollingsworth was in the store this morning. She's been working in Denver, you know. Guess she must have gotten some time off and come home for a visit."

"I didn't know Janice has been living in Denver. I knew she'd left town but assumed she'd gone back to Chicago."

"Oh, well, I guess that's no concern of yours. But Joe walking around the streets of Platte Valley may be. Be sure you lock up good at night, since you and your mother are alone in the house. Maybe you should have Blake stay over there with you."

"I'm sure there's nothing to worry about. Besides, I don't want to ask him. He needs a break after being over there all day. By the way, I've missed our weekly lunches, but for now I feel I should go by Mother's during my lunch hour to see how everything's going."

"I've missed our lunches, too, but I understand. I've got to go. My other line is buzzing. Talk to you soon."

Lori paused a moment after hanging up, reflecting on the conversation. In spite of her earlier feeling, a sense of uneasiness came over her. She had mixed feelings about Joe. How could one help but feel sorry for the guy, murderer or not. She wondered what Larry Reardon's reaction to Joe's release had been. It was almost lunchtime. She had called Dora's and asked them to have a take-out lunch ready. It took a little extra time to pick it up but made Blake's role a little lighter.

As she turned on her car's ignition, Lori became aware of a nagging little thought that had been gnawing at the edge of her consciousness—the passing remark Sarah had made about Janice living in Denver. And what this remark meant—that she had been there during those times Blake had made his business trips to that city. I'm acting like a jealous schoolgirl, she told herself, as she shoved this thought and all other thoughts of Janice Hollingsworth from her mind.

Late that afternoon, as Lori was replacing books on the shelves, she sensed someone's presence. As she looked up, she had to stifle a scream. Standing at the end of the row staring at her with those strange eyes was Joe Isley.

She fought to regain her composure. "Hello, Joe. I heard you were back in town. Is there something I can help you with?" She hoped her voice reflected the casualness she was attempting to convey. Thank goodness Sarah had warned her that he was back in town or she might have been even more shocked.

Joe continued to stand there looking at her. He was dressed in faded jeans and an old jacket, which Lori thought was probably a leftover from his Army days. His hair was long and greasy looking. Finally he said, "I wanted some books."

Lori stood there expectantly, waiting for him to continue. When he didn't, she asked, "What kind of books are you looking for?"

"I don' know. They took my dogs away when Pa died. I couldn' find out where they took 'em, so I asked everybody. Then I find out they had 'em put to sleep. I need a book to see if they can do that. Those dogs was all I had left, now with Pa gone."

Lori felt a pang of sympathy for the man. She was also relieved to learn Joe was actually here for a legitimate purpose. She had been devising a plan to alert Kristen to call for help. "I think what you need are some law books, Joe. But since this is a small library, we may not have the right one. I am sorry to hear about your dogs."

"Well, the thing is they was gettin' kind of old. But it still makes me real mad they killed 'em. They was good dogs. Somebody coulda' took care of 'em."

"I'm sorry the authorities, people, who did this, didn't consider that alternative. Perhaps you could give . . ." Lori hesitated. She had been about to suggest he call Sheriff Reardon to learn what his rights were but then realized this was the last person Joe should contact for help.

"What I mean to say is, even if you find out it was not legal for them to put your dogs to sleep, that won't bring them back. Perhaps it would be best to just put this behind you. You may want to get a new dog—a puppy maybe.

I'll bet if you called the veterinarian, Dr. Cooper, he would be able to help you find one. Sometimes he takes in strays, dogs that people have dropped off just to get rid of."

Joe seemed to be pondering this. Lori hoped she hadn't said the wrong thing. She didn't want to make him angry. But when he spoke it was to say, "Yeah, that's a good idea. I'd like to give a home to some poor little guy nobody wants. I know how that feels. You're the first person that's even talked to me since I got back to town."

Lori couldn't think of a response, so she just stood there waiting.

"I think I'll just stay aroun' for awhile and look at some of the books. I like books. They had a library at the hospital, the place where I was, and it got to where I used to read a lot."

"That would be fine. We're open for another hour. I can issue you a library card so you can take some books home with you if you'd like."

Lori helped Joe with the application, as he had difficulty understanding it. When she typed up his new card and handed it to him, the look on his face told her it had been worth the extra trouble. She was still indecisive about her feelings towards him. Years ago, before Joe was convicted and sent away, Lori had only seen him from a distance, usually riding his bicycle. From her experience with him today, though, she concluded he was no killer. And if she was right, an innocent man had been locked up for fifteen years, been deprived of being with his father during his last days and lost his closest companions, his dogs. And, even worse, the murderer of Norma Reardon was out there walking around somewhere.

Chapter 22 - Blake

"I'm coming, you old bitch," Blake murmured under his breath. How did he get himself into this fix? Charlotte was ringing the little bell she used to summon her daughter or Blake whenever she needed something. He took his time, but finally the incessant ringing drove him up the stairs to see what the old lady wanted.

"Yes, Mother dear, what can I get for you?" His voice was sarcastic.

Charlotte was sitting in her wheelchair beside the window. Ignoring his tone, she said, "I need some fresh water."

Blake walked over and picked up the pitcher. After he had filled it, he slammed it down on the stand beside her, spilling some of the water. He knew she needed help pouring it, as her arms were still weak. It would have made it easier for her if he had held the glass while she drank. But he walked off. He couldn't help but chuckle a little. Whenever the old lady told her daughter about how neglectful Blake was, Lori got a glazed look in her eyes and merely nodded her head. Since Charlotte had always been a complainer, Lori didn't take her mother's grievances about his treatment of her seriously. It was the old story of crying wolf too often.

He resented being here but felt it was the perfect stratagem. Lori had been decidedly cool before her mother suffered the stroke. He had to admit he had made some major errors, such as the story he had told her that first night they were together in Denver. It hadn't been just idle chatter. He needed her to think of him in a different light. That's why he had told her he was moving back to Platte Valley to be near his ailing parents, when the truth was they had few health problems. Since then, he had built on his role as the dutiful son by telling his wife how he spent a lot of time doing little chores for them.

He hadn't heard all of the conversation as he stood outside the kitchen listening the night they visited his parents. What had his mother said to Lori? He wasn't sure, but he knew from the look on Lori's face the little chatterbox had said something disturbing. There was another mistake, leaving them alone together, if only for a few minutes.

He also regretted his cynical remarks the day before Charlotte had her stroke. But sometimes the little do-gooder got on his nerves. She was so damned obvious, trying to use her misguided psychology on him by getting him to talk about his hurt over not getting to see Josh. Well, guess she got an earful on that subject and a couple of others. Still, it wasn't too smart of him to show his hand this way.

So this was his punishment for being careless, a way to restore Lori's faith in him. It was also a good way to set the scene for the future. It was important the people in this town think well of him. And it seemed to be working. Lori was again looking at him in that adoring manner of hers, and when that old battle-ax, Phoebe Gibbons, had visited, she grudgingly told him she was grateful he was looking after her good friend. "Don't you mind Charlotte," she told him on the sly. "She'll come around. It's just her nature to be difficult." Blake wasn't surprised they were friends, as they both seemed to have the same sour nature.

There was a third reason he thought it may be beneficial to spend some time alone with Charlotte. He was hoping she would reveal further information concerning a conversation they had had when he had come over to shovel her snow. While he was playing dutiful son-in-law, Charlotte had come out on the porch and stood there watching him, clutching an old shawl tightly around her. Curious, he had laid down the shovel and walked over to where she was standing. He had gone over their conversation numerous times, and now, as he sat in front of his computer, his fingers idle, he went over it again.

"I just want you to know, you're not fooling me. I don't know what your game is, but I'm going to make it my business to find out."

Blake had feigned a look of injured innocence. "I have no idea what you're talking about."

"No? Well, we'll see. Whatever it is, I know you didn't marry Lori for love. You're a user, and she has something you want. As I said, I'll find out. By the way, you may be interested to know she had an appointment with a lawyer a couple of weeks ago. Told me she was having a will made. Just in case it's her oil royalty you're interested in, I thought you might like to know."

Blake had been about to say, it takes one to know one, but Charlotte's last words left him speechless. She had walked back in the house, giving him no further details.

He hadn't told Lori about the little "visit" with his mother-in-law, although he longed to confront her. What if she had cut him out of her will, or even part of it? He didn't care about a little insurance policy or whatever small savings she had. What he was worried about was the override.

He had gone home that day and immediately made a thorough search of their house, hoping to find a copy. Lori kept some important documents in a small file in their bedroom, but his search turned up nothing relating to a will. If there is such a will, she must have the copies at her mother's house or at the library, he concluded. He toyed with the idea of suggesting they retain a lawyer for the purpose of making wills now that they were married. Surely this would prompt her to tell him she had recently made one and what was in it. He knew he had to be careful, however. Charlotte might have mentioned their conversation to Lori, and if so, such a move would look suspicious. Better to bide his time on this.

As a last resort Blake paid a visit to the county courthouse. After introducing himself to the clerk in his most charming manner, he asked if there was a copy of Mrs. Johnson's will on file. The clerk had fallen all over herself trying to be helpful. She said a will had been filed for Melora Johnson just last week. But when Blake asked to see it, the clerk informed him that only the testator, that is the person who made the will, was allowed to unseal it. "What you can do, though," she told him in an apologetic voice, "is get your wife to sign something giving you permission to look at it, or she probably has a certified copy you could see." Blake had thanked the girl with one of his radiant smiles.

The ringing of Charlotte's bell broke into his brooding. Damn her. She would have made a great slave owner had she not been born too late for it. From what I can gather, she's had people waiting on her all her life. The woman isn't stupid. He realized he had a strange sort of admiration for Charlotte. He didn't care much for noble, self-sacrificing people. Thought of them as fools.

"What is it now, Mother?" he asked.

"I have something I want to ask you. I have my little network and I found out there have been some people fooling around the oil field. My report is that it looked like they were taking some measurements. Just what do you have to do with this?"

"If your sources are correct, you'd better ask your daughter about it. It has nothing to do with me." Blake was sure Charlotte's "sources" was Phoebe, since she had called earlier.

"I intend to do just that, but I thought you might want to discuss it with me first, since I'm sure she'll be as surprised as I was to hear about the activity out there."

Blake decided to make an attempt to dissuade her, although he doubted it would work. "It was probably something Malcolm Murphy ordered. Doesn't he own the working interest?"

Charlotte looked a little doubtful. "Yes, he does as a matter of fact, but I don't know why he would have a bunch of people fooling around the field. I'm going to tell Lori about it just the same. She can call Murphy, and if he doesn't know anything about it, I'm pretty sure I know who's behind it." She looked at him accusingly. "What I don't know is what your scheme is, but you can bet I'll find out."

As Blake turned to leave the room, he said in a noncommittal voice, "Do whatever pleases you."

His mind was whirling as he walked downstairs. He sat down in the den next to the desk where his computer was hooked up. The old lady was dangerous. She was too smart, not as educated as her bright daughter, but without Lori's hang-ups. Unlike her daughter, Charlotte never let sentiment cloud her judgment. Blake couldn't be sure what Murphy would say to Lori. He was one of those simple, straightforward types. It was one thing for him not to disclose something, but quite another when someone started asking questions. And Blake knew his wife. She wasn't going to accept a simple "yes or no" answer. Murphy would probably break down and tell her the truth, that he had sold the working interest to none other than her brand new husband.

He needed time. Charlotte could be calling Lori right now. He reached over and picked up the telephone. Assured that no one was on the line, he laid the receiver down on the desk. As he removed his coat from the hall closet, he heard the sound of Charlotte's bell. It seemed to grow louder and louder as he walked out the door.

Chapter 23 - Lori

When Lori arrived at her mother's house shortly after noon, Blake's truck wasn't parked in front. Her heart fluttered a little. Something must be wrong. When she tried the door, it didn't seem to be locked. Then, as she walked into the living room, she saw her mother's crumpled body lying at the foot of the stairs.

What happened next was unclear. She remembered stooping down and feeling for a pulse. She must have called the emergency number, because she had a vague remembrance of the phone being off the hook and having to hang it up to get a dial tone. Soon Larry Reardon and a lot of other people filled the house, Dr. Jefferson, Sarah, some medics. Mr. and Mrs. Jacobs, and Phoebe Gibbons were there for a while. At one point Blake arrived. His arm was around her, asking what happened. He said he'd left to get medicine for her mother. What medicine? Lori wondered.

Later, after Charlotte's body had been removed to the funeral home, and everyone but Blake, Larry, and herself had gone, Blake fixed her a cup of tea and brought it to her, wrapping a blanket around her legs. Then with Blake sitting next to her, his arm protectively around her, Larry sat across from them and gently asked some questions. It's just routine, he explained. We need these things for our records. What time did she find her mother? What did she do next? Then he addressed some inquiries to Blake in a less amiable tone. Where was Blake? What time did he leave? Why did he leave?

Then Larry was gone. Lori let Blake bundle her into the car and take her home. He said he thought it best they not spend the night there. Her sleep was intermittent, but each time she awakened she felt Blake's arm around her and his voice next to her ear whispering, "It'll be all right." The following morning he led her to the table and watched her as she drank a glass of orange juice and forced down a piece of toast.

Her voice felt full of cotton as she spoke. "I guess it hasn't registered yet exactly what happened, why mother was out of her chair, why she was evidently trying to get down the stairs. And I don't understand this thing about her medicine. She wasn't out of anything that I know about. It was all there on her nightstand. I remember our talking to Sheriff Reardon about all of this last night, but I guess I was kind of out of it."

Blake's look was sad. "As you must know, I feel terrible about what happened. If I hadn't left her alone . . . but she said she'd be all right. I was just gone for a short time. What happened, as I told Sheriff Reardon, was that she rang her bell and I went up. She said she was feeling a lot of pain. I told her the pain pills were right there on her stand and asked if she wanted me to open the bottle. But she got upset, said those weren't working, that she needed this other kind. God, I can't even remember the name, but it will come to me. Anyhow, I had the same problem when I went out to get them. I pulled up in front of Brooks and couldn't remember what it was I was supposed to get."

"She used to have me get her some pain pills called Quik-Relief but then she decided she liked the other kind better. She did seem to switch her non-prescription medicines quite frequently, never satisfied with what she was using." Lori's voice was sad, as if this trait, once so exasperating, was now an endearing quality to be remembered with fondness.

"That was it, Quik-Relief. That's the name of the pills she insisted I buy for her. But since I couldn't remember the name, I went to the phone booth across the street, the one in front of the post office, and called. I could have gone down to the store to use the phone, but I knew I'd never be able to get away from Mom even if I told her I was in a hurry."

Lori nodded to let him know she understood his reasoning, although she wondered why he just didn't go into Brooks and use their phone.

"Anyhow, the line was busy. I stood there for several minutes redialing. I remember wondering who she may be talking to, thinking if it was Phoebe, I may as well forget it and just go home."

Lori's mouth curved in a little smile, thinking of Phoebe and her mother's marathon telephone conversations. Now, she thought, all the little gossip Charlotte seemed to thrive on no longer mattered to her. At this very moment, they were laying her out in her coffin at Harmon's Funeral Home. Lori forced her mind back to what Blake was saying. "Yes, I remember, when I tried to call for help, the phone was off the hook. But how did that happen?"

"This is the part I really feel awful about. I could lie and say I have no idea, that perhaps I accidentally pushed it off when I moved a file, but I need to tell you the truth. You may hate me, but I'll have to risk it."

Blake carried Lori's dishes to the sink and stood there a moment. Then he turned around and faced her, a determined look on his face. "I don't know if you knew about it, but Janice Hollingsworth is back in town. Damn, this is tough. She won't leave me alone, Lori. She calls and calls. She evidently found out from someone that you've been staying at your mother's house at night, so she's been calling me at home in the evenings. I keep telling her I'm not interested, that I'm a happily married man, but it hasn't convinced her."

Lori was looking at him intently. *Why would Janice keep calling him if he told her he wasn't interested?* she wondered. Was he encouraging her, perhaps subconsciously? Perhaps he was flattered. Lori knew that life in Platte Valley wasn't too exciting. Maybe he was getting bored with her.

As if he had read her thoughts, Blake said, "I'm beginning to think the woman has some serious mental problems. Yesterday morning she called me at your mother's house. I finally hung up on her, but when the phone started ringing again, I just took it off the hook. I didn't think Charlotte would be using it, as she was napping when I looked in on her earlier. Then when she summoned me and told me she was in a lot of pain, I was concerned and simply forgot about it."

Blake walked over to the table and sat down across from Lori. "I've gone over and over what might have happened. Did she start feeling really bad and try to call someone, perhaps Dr. Jefferson? And not being able to get through, did she panic? Or maybe she thought there was someone in the house and became frightened." Blake buried his head in his hands. "I don't know," he said softly. "I guess no one will ever know for sure."

Seeing his torment, Lori was moved. "Please don't blame yourself," she said. "What happened wasn't your fault. I do wish you'd told me about Janice, though."

"I wanted to, but with your mother being so ill, I hated to add to your worries. I thought I could handle it. And I can. I plan to tell Janice the result of her harassment, and if this doesn't do it, I'll get a restraining order."

Lori reached over and touched her husband's hand. "I love you, Blake, and I need you, now more than ever," she said.

Lori chose her mother's favorite dress to bury her in and, although it was now too large for her, with the extra material pinned underneath this wasn't noticeable. Everyone said she looked lovely. As she laid there, her hands positioned around her favorite prayer book, Lori thought she looked peaceful in a way she hadn't often seen her in life.

Blake was there for her, helping to make all the arrangements, meeting Charlotte's sister, Sophie, at the airport when she arrived in Denver. Her family now scattered, she came without them. Charlotte was buried in the Platte Valley cemetery next to her loving husband, John. Blake was there through it all and was the perfect host at the wake. And in the weeks following, when she awakened from a bad dream, she would reach out for him, and he was there. Lori's recurring nightmare was of her mother sitting in her wheel chair at the top of the stairs calling to her for help. Sometimes, like Blake, she wondered why Charlotte had tried to get downstairs. Lori reasoned it must have been something very important, or disturbing, for her mother to have taken such a risk. Eventually she'd drift off to sleep. But mornings brought little relief. The visions and unanswered questions continued to batter her consciousness. Eventually, Lori felt the best therapy was for her to return to work. Mrs. Moran had once again filled in for her after her mother's tragic death, and Lori saw no reason to impose on this gracious lady any longer.

Blake continued to treat her as an invalid, and she knew his work was suffering also. She convinced him the best thing for both of them was for her to return to her job. After a few days back at the library, Lori knew this was the right decision. She buried herself in her work. As good as Mrs. Moran was at filling in, there were some things only Lori could do. The library accounts needed updating, and there was a huge stack of telephone messages to respond to.

But something that posed a bigger challenge was going to her mother's house. Blake had been going over every few days to check on things. One evening he gently brought up the subject of what they should do with the house. "I know this is difficult, but even though we're from a small town, and there isn't much vandalism, you never know with it being vacant like that. Besides, with an old house like that a pipe could burst. I don't even think the insurance would cover it when no one is living there."

"I know you're right. I've been thinking about it, too. I thought maybe we could rent it, but realized that doesn't make sense. We need to move in, since we're just renting here ourselves."

"I agree with you, that is if you're sure. There would be no hurry as we have a couple of months left on the lease here. But, let's face it, we could save money by moving over there."

The next evening after work she forced herself to drive over and walk through the house. The hardest part was going into Charlotte's room. Everything was neat as a pin. Some kind person, Sarah or Mrs. Jacobs, had made up Charlotte's bed and put away all her personal belongings. Still, Lori was overcome by the thought she would never see her mother lying there again. Standing there alone, she allowed herself to give vent to her emotions. Then, wiping her eyes, she left the room.

After that she began to go over to the house after work and on weekends to sort through Charlotte's belongings. Lori kept some of her jewelry, most of which was costume, and some of her other more personal items. There was her parents' marriage license and a tarnished medal her mother had won as a girl for coming in first in a spelling bee. The rest she boxed up to give to the church for distribution to the needy.

And when she had finished there, she slowly started packing for the move to the Wyatt house. All this kept her busy and helped get her through her grief.

Lori wasn't sure when it started; it was a gradual thing. But Blake started pulling away, and she began to catch glimpses of that look on his face, so fleeting she questioned whether she had imagined it. Was it irritation, scorn? He was hard at work again. Many times she was on the brink of asking him about the project, but she remembered that day when he had been so angry and thought better of it. She hoped he would start confiding in her, but he was as close-mouthed as always. She supposed he had been successful at buying part of the Adena field and was moving ahead rapidly now that spring was here. Perhaps this was all it was. He had a lot on his mind and was bound to be feeling the effects. She must learn to not take things so personally.

Chapter 24 - Lori

The day Lori returned to work, Joe Isley came in, his arms loaded down with books. Lori thought he looked different, his appearance less disheveled, his eyes not quite as haunted.

"I been comin' here a lot while you was gone." He lowered his head and studied his feet for a moment. "I was sorry to hear about your mother. That's somethin' I can understan', losin' my pa an' all."

"Thank you, Joe." Lori felt his sympathy was genuine, and it touched her. "So you've been using your library card then?" she asked, wanting to move on to something lighter.

"Yeah, like I said, I like books a lot. Some of these here ones is about dogs, puppies, that is. Hey, can you come out front for jest a minute?"

Lori followed Joe out the door. There, tied to one of the posts in front of the library was a beautiful dog, not more than a few months old. He appeared to be predominantly German Shepherd, but his hair was a little too long for a pure breed.

"Well, whad'da you think? I went over to the vet's like you said, and he had this little guy there. The folks that brung him in said he'd been hangin' aroun' their place. Dr. Cooper says lots of folks do that, bring the dogs to him, 'cause they can't keep 'em.."

"He's wonderful, Joe. I'm so happy you have him." She reached down and petted the puppy, who wiggled with delight. He seemed to be all legs.

Joe didn't stay at the library for over a few minutes, just long enough to check his books in. He said he didn't like to keep his dog, whom he had named Lucky, tied up too long.

"I don't usually bring him with me. I kep' askin' Miz Moran when you was comin' back an' she said today, so I jest brung him by so you could see him."

In the days that followed, he was a regular at the library, coming in every few days.

Lori was no longer apprehensive. If he had ever been mentally ill and committed a terrible act because of it, he seemed to be cured.

But when she mentioned Joe's visits casually to Blake one evening, her husband was not convinced the man was harmless. "I guess there's not much you can do about him using the library," Blake said, "but I wouldn't be too friendly. He's liable to get the wrong idea. Look what happened to Reardon's wife."

"That wasn't the same thing. Norma was supposedly being flirtatious. I'm just trying to be kind."

"Guys like him don't know the difference. Promise me you'll do what I ask, Lori. Be polite, but don't encourage him by talking to him beyond what's necessary."

Lori decided not to pursue the subject. After the way he'd been acting lately, she was touched. *I guess he does still care.* She told him she'd be careful.

He seemed satisfied with this, even though she hadn't promised to do what he asked. How could she suddenly snub the poor man? This was the treatment he got from most of the Platte Valley citizenry. Lori had been reading up about mental illness lately. From what she could surmise, these poor afflicted people, who sometimes committed violent crimes, did so because they were extremely troubled, not out of malice. But Lori wasn't sure Joe fit the description of any of these people she read about. From what she had seen, he wasn't capable of murder. She didn't plan to do anything foolish, but he needed a friend, someone to believe in him.

After Lori had been back at the library for several weeks, she resumed her weekly lunches with Sarah, something she had missed during the past couple of months. And Sarah was good for her. Her friend had the ability to make her laugh in a way no one else could, not even Blake. Since today was Wednesday, at a few minutes before twelve she started toward the back to get her purse. Just then Phoebe Gibbons walked in the door.

Lori was a little surprised. She'd only seen Phoebe at the library a few times over the years. "I like to read," she said, "but my eyesight has gotten so poor, I just can't do much of it anymore." Lori thought at the time that Phoebe always seemed to do fine reading the menus when the three of them, Phoebe,

Charlotte, and herself had dined out. She suspected the real reason Phoebe didn't read much was that it would cut into the time she spent watching her soap operas.

"Hello, Phoebe. How are you?" she asked.

"Thanks for asking, but I'm not doing all that well, Melora."

Lori noticed the woman did look rather gaunt. Although smiles did not come easily for Phoebe, her lips seemed to be drawn together into an even tighter line than normally. Although Phoebe had never been one of Lori's favorite people, she felt a sudden warmth for her. She was touched that Phoebe's feelings for Charlotte had run so deep.

"Is there someplace we can have a little chat? Phoebe asked. "Something's been bothering me, and I need to get it off my chest."

"Sure. It's time for my lunch hour. I'm supposed to meet Sarah in a few minutes at Dora's. Let me give her a quick call first. We can go out and sit on the bench in front of the library. It's such a pretty day."

Lori was disappointed at having to cancel her luncheon date, but something in Phoebe's manner bothered her. She had a feeling this could involve more than the woman's usual idle gossip.

The well-manicured grounds were beginning to lose their beige winter coat, and the hardened ground had started to relent, allowing the bulbs buried beneath to give birth to shiny new life. Phoebe went on ahead, while Lori made her call. When Lori joined the older woman, she noticed that Phoebe seemed oblivious to the lovely spring weather. She sat on the bench, clutching her jacket tightly around her and for once, seemed at a loss for words. The two sat in silence for a moment.

Finally Phoebe spoke in a voice that seemed a little apologetic, as if she realized her words could bring a dark cloud to the clear sunny day. "I've had this on my mind since I learned of Charlotte's death. I'd called her that morning. I have a friend, Jane Abernathy, who lives on a farm out by where your oil field is located. You may know her. She goes to our church." Phoebe glanced over at Lori.

Lori nodded to indicate she did indeed know Jane. Her daughter, Angela, was Rusty's teacher at Platte Valley Elementary School. Lori knew her better than she did her mother, since she had a working relationship with all of the teachers. Angela was especially likeable.

Phoebe went on. "Jane and I were talking earlier that day, and she asked kind of casual like. 'What's going on over at the Wyatt lease?' Seems she'd driven by there, and there were all kinds of people at the field, measuring and such. So I called your mother as soon as I hung up. I didn't know, thought maybe she was aware of what was going on. But she acted real surprised. Said things like, 'So it finally comes out. Blake Johnson is behind this. I knew he was up to something from the time he showed an interest in Melora. Now it's beginning to make sense.' Those might not have been her exact words, but it was words to that effect. Anyhow, she said Blake was downstairs and she was going to confront him that very minute. I had some other stuff to tell her, like Janice Hollingsworth being back. How she had a good job in Denver, but didn't find it fulfilling, so she decided to move back here again, sponge off her father. But Charlotte didn't want to hear anything about that. She just zeroed in on what I'd said about the oil field and said she had to go. That was the last time I ever talked to her." Phoebe dabbed her eyes as she delivered the last sentence.

"I can fill you in on what was going on," Lori said gently. "Mr. Murphy called me a few days after Mother's funeral. He said he'd decided to drill some new wells. I wasn't sure of the wisdom of this, as from what I've learned, drilling new wells is often fruitless. But since he owns the working interest, I don't have any say so in what he does. I guess the only thing that bothered me is that in the past Mr. Murphy has always informed me in advance when he's going to start something new."

"Well, did he tell you that the activity out there has increased in the last week or so, that they're moving in all kinds of new equipment. Jane called this morning and filled me in."

"I appreciate your concern, Phoebe. And it is puzzling. I mean what Mother said about Blake being behind all this. Her mind was evidently not functioning properly, because of the stroke. It's probably because she never really accepted Blake or the fact that he could be interested in me just for myself. She thought he had some devious scheme for marrying me, and in her condition she'd become irrational." Lori's voice caught a little. "What makes it sad is that she was wrong. Malcolm is undoubtedly moving the equipment in to drill the wells. But if Mother was upset, she evidently kept it to herself, because Blake never mentioned anything about her confronting him."

While Lori was talking, she noticed Phoebe looking at her strangely. Now she said in a voice that was barely audible, "Well, I suppose you're right, but I still think it's a little strange. I mean that it was such a short time after we'd talked that she got up out of her wheel chair and tried to go down those stairs."

"What are you saying? That her fall was somehow connected with the oil activity."

Phoebe braced her shoulders, as if she had come to a decision. "I shouldn't be telling you this since I promised Jane I wouldn't, but I owe it to Charlotte. There is something funny going on, but I don't know if Blake's involved. Virginia Murphy is a friend of Jane's, and she told Jane in strictest confidence that they're planning to move out of the area, that her husband sold the working interest to someone, but he wouldn't tell her who. She said Malcolm told her not to breathe a word of it to anyone. But Virginia and Jane are pretty close, and she felt she needed to tell someone."

This time it was Lori who pulled her jacket tighter around her. The day suddenly felt chilly.

Phoebe continued relentlessly on, hardly pausing between sentences. "Of course, Jane thought she ought to pass this on to me, since she knew I'd told Charlotte about the activity at the field that day before she died. Jane thought it was strange, too, about Charlotte's accident right afterwards." Phoebe took a deep breath. It was as if these secrets had expanded inside her ready to burst, and now that she had gotten them out, she had breathing room again.

Lori was suddenly anxious for Phoebe to leave. "There's probably a perfectly logical explanation for all this. I'll get in touch with Malcolm Murphy and clear it up. But thanks, Phoebe, for coming to me about it."

Phoebe looked like she wanted to say something else but thought better of it. As Lori watched her hobbling down the street toward town, she wished she could stuff the words back into the old lady's mouth. Her first thought was to call Malcolm right away and confront him. She looked at her watch. There were still forty minutes of her lunch break left. She walked purposefully into the library and grabbed her purse, reaching inside for her car keys. She would talk to Blake. He may have some advice concerning Malcolm's strange behavior.

Lori never went home for lunch. Blake had his own schedule. Sometimes he was over at his parents' house. Or at least this is what he said. Her conversation with Betty, which seemed a hundred years ago, flitted across her mind.

As she pulled up in front of the house, she caught a glimpse of something shiny, like chrome, sticking out from in back of the house. She got out of her car and walked around to investigate. What she saw caused her to half run back to her car. As she turned on the ignition, Blake came out of the front door. He seemed to be waving his arms, signaling her to stop. She couldn't be sure as tears blinded her eyes. What she had seen parked in back of the house was what she had known would be there. Even in her agitated state, she noticed the top of the Monte Carlo convertible had been up. It was still a little too early in the season for Janice to be driving around with the top down, her nose high in the air, her long platinum hair flying in the breeze.

Lori wasn't sure how she got back to the library that day. She willed herself into a robot-like state in order to get through the afternoon. Several times when she picked up the ringing telephone and answered "Platte Valley Library. May I help you?" she recognized the responding voice as Blake's. Each time she hung up before he could speak further.

Later, as she drove to her mother's house, she told herself she must start thinking of the Wyatt place as hers. This is where she would live out her days, becoming more and more like Charlotte, a bitter old lady. But what did Charlotte have to be bitter about? She had a loving, loyal husband, while I have...Lori stifled a sob, forcing her mind to move onto something else. She noticed how the trees lining the streets of the neighborhood were starting to bud. Everywhere she looked, the earth was putting out new life. Just as mine is ending, she thought.

That evening Sarah and Jon went over to Blake's place, the home she had so recently shared with him, and picked up some of her things. Later, as Lori fixed them tea, Sarah reported that Blake was in a terrible state. "He told me to see if I could just get you to talk to him, that he could explain everything. He said he'd told you that Janice was crazy. He mentioned that you were aware that she'd been calling him and that he'd been trying to get rid of her. But he said it wasn't working, that the more he put her off, the bolder and more desperate she got. Then today she just showed up at the door."

Lori listened with a cynical smile. "And in a mad frenzy she forced her way in, following one rational moment during which she parked her car in back of the house out of sight."

From the look on her friend's face, Lori could tell Sarah was skeptical, also. After assuring her friends she was fine and declining Sarah's offer to stay the night, Lori sent them on their way. She continued to sit at the kitchen table long after they departed, unable to erase the memory of the day's events and what they meant. One of the traits she prized in herself and worked hard at was her ability to look beyond peoples' behavior for underlying causes. With her mother, it had been her illness, with Blake, his father's disappointment in him. Now, Lori feared Blake had made it impossible for her to retain this generosity of spirit. Perhaps it was true Bud was tough on his son, but hadn't her own mother been equally critical? Yet, she hadn't used this as justification for becoming a deceitful person. Blake had been blessed with good looks and intelligence but thought nothing of using these gifts to his own selfish ends.

Lori knew she didn't have the luxury to sit there and brood much longer. She checked her watch. It was eight thirty. Not too late to make that call.

"I felt real bad about not saying anything, Miss Wyatt. Sorry, I guess it's Mrs. Johnson now. But Mr. Johnson insisted I keep quiet."

Lori assumed it was something in her voice that had prompted Malcolm Murphy to level with her.

"And the phone call about your drilling new wells? Did you get paid for that?"

"I was strapped. Things have been real bad. I don't know if you knew about it, but Ginny was in the hospital. She had to have her appendix taken out. It had burst on her, so she was real sick. Well, the hospital bill took most of the money your husband paid me for the lease. I let my insurance lapse, which I realize now was a big mistake."

Malcolm went on, as if now that he had finally been forced to come clean, he wanted to be sure to not leave anything out. "After the two of you got married, I told Mr. Johnson I figured it was all right to let folks know I had sold him the working interest. But he said I should still keep it confidential. I thought it was unusual, but guessed he had his reasons. You know, some kind of business strategy. But I honestly thought he'd told you. Then, after your mother died he asked me to call you about the new drilling. None of it made sense to me, but again I supposed he had his reasons."

Lori detected the curiosity in his voice but ignored it. "So you're still looking after the field for him."

"Yeah. I mean I have been. But I don't think this'll be for long. Mr. Johnson says he's starting a big project out there involving a new type of enhanced oil recovery, something called high-pressure air injection. I ain't never heard of it, but he says it's supposed to get a lot more oil out. Hope he's right for your sake. It could mean as much as . . . ."

She cut him off. "Can this be done without the royalty interest owner's approval?"

There was a long silence. "Well no, not normally," Malcolm finally responded. "But since the land's been unitized and water flooded, permission was probably given by the state to your father back when this was done."

"I don't understand."

"Did your dad ever tell you about how they came in and did the water flooding? This was back in the seventies as I recall."

"Yes, he told me about it. He said it really increased the oil production for a while. He also told me that even after the water flooding peaked out, there was still a lot of oil they didn't get. Is that what Blake's new method will do, get this oil out?"

"That's right, leastwise that's the idea. The oil remaining is called oil in place. Through geological studies they can estimate if there's oil still in the ground and how much is down there. But getting back to your question, on most of these projects permission is given the first time around. Your dad probably signed something that said the working interest owner had permission to use whatever method, water flood or anything else."

Lori's head was spinning when she hung up, so many lies, so much deception. Now that she had confirmed Blake had bought the working interest on the Wyatt lease, she could no longer delude herself about his reason for marrying her. It wasn't enough for him to own part of it. He wanted the royalty interest as well.

And all along her mother had tried to warn her. Suddenly, she remembered Phoebe's visit. How long ago it seemed, and yet it had only been about eight hours since they'd sat on the bench in front of the library. Perhaps her mother had confronted Blake, as was her intention according to Phoebe. Lori had a vision of Blake heaving Charlotte's wheel chair down the stairs. No, this was too horrible to contemplate. She covered her face with her hands in an effort to blot out this scene and everything else that had happened that day. How could she have been so blind? Was it her naiveté or her vanity that had kept her from seeing Blake's devious motives?

Either way, she had to put it behind her. She couldn't let others, who depended on her, suffer because of her mistakes. She would be at the library tomorrow morning, fresh and ready to do her job.

As she lay in the bed in her old room, however, sleep refused to come. Finally in desperation, she got up and went into the bathroom. Rummaging through the medicine cabinet, she found what she was looking for, a bottle of her mother's sleeping tablets.

Soon, she fell into a fitful sleep filled with disconnected dreams. One was a variation of her recurring nightmare about her mother. In this one Blake was pushing Charlotte's wheel chair, but it was not her mother whom she saw falling from the chair and landing limp and lifeless at the bottom of the stairs. It was herself.

Chapter 25 – Lori

"Good morning. How are we today?" Lori opened her eyes. Hannah, the heavy-set day nurse, was standing by her bed with a thermometer in her hand. Lori was barely able to get a "fine" out before Hannah popped the thermometer in her mouth. She realized she must have drifted off toward morning.

"We slept in this morning," Hannah said in her usual cheerful voice. "The breakfast cart is just down the hall."

Lori knew the nurse meant well but her manner was irritating, especially after just waking up.

Hannah removed the thermometer and placed it on her tray. "How about if we raise your bed to sitting position?" she asked. Without waiting for an answer she reached for the button on the side of the bed.

Lori's eye caught an Easter lilies plant with a balloon in the center setting on her bureau. The balloon said "Get Well Soon."

"When did the plant arrive?" she asked.

"Your boyfriend was here earlier. Didn't want to wake you," Hannah replied.

Lori realized Hannah's reference to her boyfriend must mean Larry. She let the misnomer pass.

Hannah walked over and took the card, which was tucked in the plant, and brought it to Lori.

"Look's like he wrote you a poem," she said. "Now ain't that sweet!"

The plant and the card were from Rusty. Her eyes clouded up as she read the large, uneven words, so typical of a seven-year old.

These flours are white
And they are just right
And I got you a balloon
So get well soon.

Hannah was standing there expectantly. "Yes, it was sweet of my boyfriend to write me a poem," Lori said. "He's just seven years old by the way."

After Hannah left Lori swung her legs over the side of the bed. After two days in the hospital, she felt her strength returning. Her face, as she examined it in the bathroom mirror, looked less gaunt. She cleaned her face and teeth and ran a brush through her hair.

When Larry arrived later that day he had a big box of chocolates under his arm. "You're spoiling me beyond any hope of rehabilitation," she protested. "I'm already hooked on the afternoon soap operas. Now I'll be munching chocolates as I watch them."

He handed her the box. "Wrong on both counts. The chocolates are from my mother, and you won't get a chance to be spoiled any further. I just talked to Dr. Bob and he told me he's kicking you out of here tomorrow."

Lori had gotten the news from her doctor that morning. She wasn't sure she was ready to face that empty house yet but had attempted a weak smile.

As if reading her thoughts, Dr. Bob had said with a twinkle in his eye, "Sarah told me she was going to play hooky from my office so she can stay with you for the next couple of days. Since I can't spare her any longer than that, you'd better take care of yourself and follow my orders. And Sarah informed me her mother-in-law will fill in at the library until you're ready to go back."

Lori knew if she was ever going to get through this it would be because of her good friends. She was apprehensive about going back to her house but was also anxious to confront the ghosts awaiting her there. Only then would she be able to get on with her life.

She felt that Larry over the past few months, and especially since she'd been in the hospital, had become one of these good friends. She wanted to say something to this effect but was having a problem getting the words out. Instead she remembered Rusty's gift. "Rusty's plant is lovely." She glanced over at the flowers, thinking of the role lilies had played in her life and wondering if there was some significance. "Did you see the poem he wrote to go with it?"

Larry nodded. "He bought the plant himself and asked me to bring it to you."

"Tell him I love it. I'll write and thank him when I get home. You hinted earlier that things had not been going well between Rusty and his mother."

Larry pulled up a chair and sat down. He was quiet for a moment, but she could feel his eyes on her. She filled the time by working open the box of chocolates. When she finally turned toward him to offer him one, he seemed to have reached a conclusion.

"He did have some disturbing news from Cindy. He got a letter from her. She's in Germany."

Lori couldn't help but cringe when Larry mentioned the word letter. Seems that the last couple of days, letters or notes had had a dire impact on her life, as well as on the lives of those she loved. "Germany? But I thought she was going to school in Denver."

"She was, but she quit to get married. The brother of one of her classmates was home on leave. He's in the Air Force. Her friend introduced him and Cindy, and it seems it was love at first sight." This last was delivered in a cynical tone. "Things must have moved pretty fast. Cindy didn't tell Rusty all of these details. But she told him he could come for a visit sometime."

"Well, that's something. Isn't he excited about going to Europe?"

Larry's smile didn't spread beyond his mouth. "She wrote me also. My letter took a little different tone. She said she hasn't broken the news about Rusty's existence to her new husband. She's waiting for the right moment, whenever that will be. She said Rusty is better off with her grandmother and me. I agree, but it's tough on him. He's been counting on going to live with her once she finished school and found a job."

Lori almost wished she hadn't pressed him about Rusty. She wasn't sure how much more bad news she could handle. It was one thing for an adult to have to go through pain, but she hated it when a child had to suffer, especially this little boy who was so dear to her. "How awful for Rusty," she said. "I don't know if it will help but tell him I'm going to be just fine."

"You bet. And it will be a big relief for him to hear you're all right."

Lori held out the box of chocolates and Larry's attention seemed to focus momentarily on choosing one. After taking a bite, he said, "It's caramel, my favorite, but sometimes they fool you – look a lot like those crème-filled ones. But look at me, eating all your candy. Aren't you going to have one?"

"My appetite has improved but these are a little rich. I'll take them home and enjoy them later."

"During my little chat with Dr. Bob, he told me it would be okay to answer your questions about the – things that happened last Sunday – that is if you're up to it."

Larry's statement caught Lori off guard. Since her arrival at the hospital, she'd been in a dreamlike state. Was she ready to be awakened? Her voice sounded far away to her own ears. "My first question has to do with Joe. I thought you'd taken him back or at least that you were meeting someone in Denver who would escort him back to Pueblo. When Suzie called and told me you were on your way there, I concluded this was what your trip was about."

"Yes, I can see where you might have gotten that idea. And that was my intention when I talked to you that morning. It was while I was waiting for you to come back on the line that something clicked. When I went out to Joe's place and had that little chat, he kept rambling on about Norma. I think it bothered him, my belief that he'd murdered her."

"I'm confused. You said what he told you convinced you more than ever he was unbalanced. Something must have happened to change your mind."

"That's right. Joe told me he liked Norma, and she'd shown an interest in him. He'd been spending a lot of time at Dora's, but then he started hanging around our house. He never got the nerve to go to the door. Said he was working up to it. Well, one day he saw a car drive up, a big black one. There was a man driving it. Joe didn't recognize him and concluded he wasn't from around here. Later he saw the license plates closer and verified the car was registered here in Colorado although he didn't remember the number. A few minutes later, Norma came out and got in the car. Well, this worried Joe, especially when they sat there smooching for a minute. After all, she was supposed to love him."

"But you said you didn't believe any of the things Joe told you."

Larry held up his hand. "Wait, there's more. I didn't at the time. Joe told me some other things about that day. Eventually the guy drove off with Norma in the car. Joe said he followed them for a while on his bicycle, but he couldn't keep up. He thought they might be heading out toward the lake, because he saw them turn north on Mylanders' Road. When he arrived out there, he saw the car parked down close to the water. He kept out of sight, but even at a distance he could hear them. They seemed to be having a confrontation. Norma got out of the car first. When the man then got out, he had something in his hand, but Joe couldn't see what it was—said it looked like a piece of rope. Whatever it was, he used it to strangle her."

Larry paused for a moment, a far-away look in his eyes. Lori knew this was difficult for him, bringing up old painful memories.

"When he told me this story, I took it as just a lot of gibberish and further proof that he needed to be locked up again. But then, as I said, I suddenly had this flash of memory, and it had to do with that big black car. You see, I remembered the car also. It was a sleek black Buick, a real beauty, not something you'd ordinarily see on the streets of Platte Valley. I guess that's why it made such an impression on me. As you'll recall I used to work at Johnson's. This salesman came in there a couple of times, the one who drove the Buick. I couldn't remember what he was selling, but I was pretty sure we had done some business with him."

An orderly came in with a tray for Lori. He was a cheerful young man, working to save money for college. His parents, who were farmers, had been unable to put aside the money for tuition. If Matt carried any resentment, he hid it well. "No more of that delicious broth and pudding for you," he said, uncovering the silver tray with a flourish. On her plate were chicken, rice and broccoli. Lori had to admit the dinner smelled rather good. Could it be her appetite was returning?

"Please go on," she said when the orderly had left. "I can eat while you're talking." She cut a piece of chicken and popped it into her mouth, hoping this would encourage Larry to continue.

Larry stood up and stretched. "How about if I run down to the cafeteria and get a cup of coffee while you're eating? I can come back in about fifteen minutes."

"Of course. If you want to get a bite to eat, I understand the food is pretty good for hospital fare."

"I'd better not. Mom usually has something on the table for me when I get home. Be back in a few."

Lori tried to concentrate on her dinner. Nonetheless, she was only able to eat about half the plate contents. She swung the tray to the side of her bed and leaned back, her mind filled with the implications of what Larry had been telling her. Was Joe innocent of Norma's murder, after all? The first time he'd come to the library she'd begun to believe he wasn't capable of this terrible crime. Then, that day he'd stayed late, after everyone else had left and she was alone with him, he'd really frightened her.

During the weeks following her separation from Blake, Lori had managed to hold herself together, at least through the days. She could see from people's faces that the news about her separation from Blake had circulated quickly through the small community. Their manner toward her was polite but cautious. She wondered if Phoebe had been the instigator of much of the talk and hoped that for once her mother's old friend had held her tongue, leaving this task to others.

Lori noticed a little absently that Joe seemed to be spending more time at the library. In fact, he was coming in almost daily and staying longer. Joe's manner, rather than becoming more reserved, was more open. Lori wondered if the gossip about her might have caused him to feel a certain kinship now that they were both objects of pity or scorn.

He always sat at the same table, the one closest to her desk, a pile of books spread out in front of him. Lori knew his level of reading ability was inadequate for him to do much more than skim through these books. Often she looked up to find him staring at her. Sometimes she would smile, hoping to convey the message that he had at least one friend in this town. Later, Lori realized this had been a mistake, that she should have used better judgment. Perhaps normally she would have, at a time when she was less distracted.

One evening she was tidying her desk in anticipation of closing up for the night, when she looked across the room and noticed Joe still sitting at "his table."

"It's after five, Joe," she called out. Her voice, as it carried across the large room, sounded strange to her own ears, so accustomed was she to speaking softly during regular hours.

Joe closed his book and, picking up his worn canvas satchel, walked toward her. As he drew closer, he said, "I was hangin' around on purpose. I thought we could go over to Dora's and get somethin' to eat."

His invitation caught her by surprise. Whatever had prompted it, she knew she must decline firmly. "Thank you, Joe, but that isn't possible."

Rather than accept this, however, Joe moved closer until he was standing only inches away. His expression was cocky. "Well, why not?" he asked.

As Lori instinctively stepped back, an image of Norma in her pink waitress uniform and crisp white apron seemed to float between them. She looked around nervously. Kristen had left five minutes earlier and was probably half way home by now. The library sat on a large lot of at least two acres and the building itself was solid brick. It was unlikely if she screamed for help, a passer-by would hear her. She had only her own wits to get her out of this one.

When she spoke, her fear made her voice sound harsher than she'd intended.

"Because I'm a married woman for one thing, and because . . ."

"But I thought you'd want to go out with me 'cause you like me. And I like you, too," he said stubbornly, closing the distance between them again.

"I do like you as a friend." She searched desperately for something to say that would convince him to back off. "Remember I helped you get a library card and told you how to get a new dog."

He seemed a little less certain. "But you and your husband ain't together no more, and I thought you liked me better."

"I'm sorry if I somehow gave you this idea. It's true, I'm separated from my husband, but I am still married."

Joe still didn't move, and Lori attempted a tone of authority, one she didn't feel. "I really have to close up now."

Finally he moved past her toward the door. It wasn't until they were outside and Joe was walking toward his bike that the pounding of her heart subsided a little.

Chapter 26 - Lori

Lori wondered if Larry had decided to have a snack or had run into someone he knew. He had been gone almost an hour. Her thoughts migrated back to Joe and the events following that day at the library. She remembered how relieved she's been to see him riding away on his bike. On an impulse she'd decided to go by Larry's house. She needed some reassurance and wasn't ready to go home to that empty house just yet. She offered a silent prayer of thanks as she pulled up in front of Larry's house. His patrol car was parked in the driveway.

She recognized the woman who answered the door as Larry's mother. She was a pleasant looking woman in her mid-sixties. Her gray hair was pulled back in a bun, and though her dress was casual, slacks and a cotton shirt, she had a neat, well-groomed appearance.

"Hello, I'm Melora Wyatt. I hope I'm not calling at a bad time, but I need to speak to the sheriff."

"He's just finishing his dinner but please come in. Are you all right?

"Yes, I think so."

She followed Mrs. Reardon into the living room. A faint scent of lemon oil permeated the air. Lori noticed the house was modestly furnished but, like it's mistress, clean and orderly.

"Please have a seat, and I'll tell him you're here. Can I take your coat?" Mrs. Reardon looked concerned.

"No thank you. I won't be here long and I don't want to interrupt his dinner. Be sure to tell him I can wait." Lori walked over to the brown frieze sofa and sat down. She thought she should at least say "hello" to Rusty, no matter what her state. "Could you also tell Rusty I'm here?"

Mrs. Reardon smiled. "Now, I remember who you are. You're the lady from the library, who's been so nice to Rusty. I'm afraid you're going to miss seeing him. He's at his Cub Scout meeting, and this being a Friday night, he's going home afterwards with his friend, Cody, to spend the night."

Lori breathed a little sigh of relief. She wasn't keen on having to put on a front for her little friend.

After Mrs. Reardon left the room, her eyes traveled to the photographs on the mantle above the fireplace. There were several of Rusty, as a baby with bright copper curls surrounding his chubby face, as a toddler of about three or four standing beside a tricycle, and a recent one, a larger version of the one she carried in her locket. Lori suffered a pang of guilt as she felt the locket around her neck. Rusty had called her about ten days ago, wondering if he could come for a visit. She'd promised to have him over soon to help her plant some flowers, which she'd started indoors in little boxes.

Her eyes moved to the last picture, one of Cindy at around the age of fourteen. She had the same copper-colored hair and fair complexion as her son. But her face, heavily made up, had begun to lose some of its innocence and the smile on her lips seemed tentative. Lori couldn't help but wonder how much effect Cindy's mother's violent and sudden death had on the little girl. She hoped the stable influence of Larry and his mother would be enough to break the cycle for Rusty.

In a couple of minutes, Larry appeared. He looked worried as he sat down beside her on the couch "Mom said you looked like you'd seen a ghost, and she was right. What happened, Lori?"

"I hate to bother you when you're off duty, but I did have quite a scare. I think I need to report the incident. You've finished your dinner, haven't you?"

He laid his hand on her arm. "Sure. It's okay. Besides, I'm still on duty. I just took some time off for dinner. Wait just a minute. I want to get a report sheet out of the car."

Before going out to his car, he walked toward the back of the house again. When he returned, he said, "I asked Mom to make us some coffee. You look like you could use a cup."

After Mrs. Reardon brought the coffee, she disappeared to the back of the house. Lori told Larry about her experience with Joe. As she put what happened into words, it seemed less ominous. Maybe because of the strain she'd been under, she might have overreacted. After all, Joe didn't actually do anything, and he left when she'd insisted. "I may have jumped to some conclusions here," she said. "I can see where Joe could have innocently mistaken my efforts to be friendly for something more. Everyone else has shunned him and . . ."

Larry cut her off. "Like with Norma?" His eyes were fierce, like she had seen them years ago. "I don't think you should take this lightly."

He'd been writing steadily while she told her story and now his eyes returned to the pad, and he continued to write for a moment.

"I'll tell you what I'm going to do. I'm going to follow you home, make sure everything's secure at your place, and then I'm going to bring him in. I can't make a battery case against him, as he didn't physically touch you. Isn't that what you said?"

"No, he didn't touch me and . . ."

"But I can charge him with assault."

"Don't you think we should wait, see if he does something else? If you do charge him with assault it's not all that serious. He'd be out soon and may be angry with me. Wouldn't this put me in even greater danger?"

"Not if I can convince the people over at the mental health institute at Pueblo that he needs to be committed again."

"I don't like it. I don't want to be the cause of his going back there, especially if I mistook his motives. You need to have me sign a complaint, don't you? What if I refuse?" Lori picked up her purse on the floor beside her and stood up. "I shouldn't have come here."

"Just why did you come?" His voice was soft, but there was an iciness to his words. This was a side of Larry she hadn't seen.

"Because . . . I don't know, I was frightened. But I realize now I could have made too much out of what happened. I've had a lot on my mind lately, which might have caused me to overreact." Why was she fighting him on this? It was just that he seemed so positive, so ready to believe the worst. And then it came to her. Ordinarily Larry, who was experienced in the workings of the criminal mind, would be able to make a sound decision, but not in this case. How could he be objective, when the person involved was the man whom he believed murdered his wife?

"I'm sorry I seem so indecisive, but a grave injustice may be done if Joe is sent back there, when his motives might have been innocent. He's been coming to the library a lot lately. I'll admit he's a little strange, but this is the first time he's given me cause for alarm. Don't you think I'm right?"

"No, I don't. I can't do much if you won't sign a complaint, though. You're right about that. But you need to understand my position. As a law officer I have a responsibility to protect the people of this town. I don't want that lunatic doing to you or to anyone else what he did to Norma. You may not know this, but I never agreed with the verdict. I think the man should still be behind bars but not in a hospital. He should have been sent to prison for life with no chance of parole."

Larry put his head down and rubbed his fingers through his hair. "I thought I'd put this all behind me. But now when I see him, free to walk the streets, it's started eating at me again. I suppose I'm not completely unbiased where Joe Isley is concerned, but I'd a whole lot rather do him wrong than take a chance by letting him off."

"I know, Larry," Lori said gently. "I promise I'll be careful, and if you still want to, I'd like it if you followed me home."

"Sure." He stood up and walked over to the coat rack in the corner of the room and removed his jacket. "I doubt if I could have made an assault case against him anyhow, since he didn't threaten you with bodily harm. But I am going out to his place in the morning and have a little chat with him. I don't need a signed complaint for that." His eyes were challenging.

Lori didn't respond.

He walked back toward the kitchen as he put on his jacket. "I'm leaving, Mom," he called.

Mrs. Reardon came back into the room. "I'm happy I finally got to meet you. I hope you'll come back to see us sometime." Her look was intense as she took Lori's hand. "And I hope whatever problem you're having will soon be resolved."

Larry walked Lori to her car, and as he opened the door for her, he asked, "Did we just have our first fight?"

She looked at him, puzzled. But when she saw his mouth turned up in a small smile, she realized his question was an attempt to be droll. The man has a sense of humor, she thought. This was a side of Larry she hadn't seen.

Later, Lori was glad she hadn't declined his offer to follow her home. He accompanied her through the house, checking the doors and windows. In spite of her strong proclamation that Joe should be given the benefit of the doubt, she wasn't as sure as she'd let on of what he may do.

"I notice you have a dead bolt on the front door but not on the back," Larry said as they completed their tour. "I'll go by Johnson's..." he hesitated. "That is, I'll pick one up and come by and put it on tomorrow afternoon."

"That's not necessary, really. I mean, you're right, I should have one put on, but Mr. Jacobs next door can take care of it. I pay him to do some handyman jobs around here."

"Please, Lori, at least let me feel like I'm doing something, beyond just waiting for Joe to make another move."

She nodded. "All right, if you're sure you have the time, and if you'll bring Rusty with you. Maybe he and I could get some plants in the ground while you're putting on the lock. I promised him he could help me with it."

"That's a great idea. I'd ask you to go out to dinner with us afterwards, but maybe that's not such a great idea." Larry had that little smile on his face again.

Lori laughed out loud for the first time in weeks. "I see what you mean. Who would I report you to? But perhaps another time."

Larry looked hard at her. "Seriously, Lori, I was sorry to hear about your separation. Any chance of patching things up?"

"No, I don't think so, but I'm all right with it." Lori knew Larry wasn't asking out of idle curiosity, that he was genuinely concerned. Still, she had trouble confiding in him. She hadn't even talked to Sarah about it that much. She felt like such a fool. Everyone had tried to warn her. Yes, even Larry. "Thanks so much for everything. But I'm awfully tired."

"And it's no wonder. I'll just check around the grounds before I leave."

Another effect of the strain she'd been under was her loss of appetite. Her clothes were beginning to hang on her. Lately, she'd been frequenting the frozen foods section at Isley's. It had never been her practice to buy TV dinners, but she had neither the stamina nor the interest to prepare anything more adventurous. Now she popped one of these into the microwave. Her breakfast had been just tea and toast, and she hadn't eaten since. Even so, she had trouble finishing her dinner.

Before climbing the stairs, Lori pushed back a corner of the living room blinds. Larry's patrol car was still parked in front of the house. She had a feeling it would be there until dawn.

Lori had hated Charlotte's heavy reliance on pills as a means of solving problems. She didn't like the thought of becoming dependent on sleeping pills, so after toying with the idea, decided to tough it out. Surprisingly, almost as soon as her head hit the pillow, she fell into an exhausted, dreamless sleep.

Chapter 27- Lori

At around eleven the next morning, Larry called Lori at the library. "Can you talk for a few minutes?" he asked.

Lori glanced around. Karen Matthews' oldest daughter, Heather, was working on a term paper for her senior English class. Lori had helped her with some books on her chosen topic, American women artists. Heather now seemed settled in at a back table.

The only other people in the library were Beth Jacobs and her two preschool children. Beth had headed for the romance section about five minutes ago, her children in tow. She had stopped to chat with Lori for a few minutes. "I used to be able to leave these two with Diana, my thirteen-year old, on Saturdays," Beth had confided. "But she's baby sitting for my neighbor on weekends now. Says she gets paid better. These kids never take into account the amount of money it takes to feed and clothe them. I figure she owes me around fifty thousand to date," Beth had added, laughing.

A glance in the direction of the fiction section assured Lori that Beth was still looking for books. "I think I'm free for a few minutes, " she said.

"I need to fill you in on what's going on. I drove out to Joe's place this morning and had that little chat. I don't want to upset you, but I'm afraid I was right about him. I plan to call his doctor over at Pueblo but thought I should touch base with you first."

Lori felt the sense of well being she'd experienced since awakening from her restful night's sleep evaporating. "What's happened?"

"The reason Joe felt you'd be receptive to his advances was because he supposedly received a note from you."

"What note?"

"That's what I figured. You didn't send him one. I was sure you hadn't sent him anything or if you had, it was something innocent, such as a line or

217

two telling him about a book you thought he might like or even that he had an overdue book that needed to be returned. But this was more personal, according to Joe."

"There was no note, at least not one written by me. Did he show it to you?"

"Unfortunately, he no longer has it. According to Joe, there were instructions in the note telling him to destroy it. As to the contents, he told me it said you liked him a lot, that you didn't love your husband anymore, words to that effect."

"That explains his odd behavior. But who would have played such a cruel joke?"

"Probably no one. It's my belief he imagined it. This is one of the things I want to discuss with his doctor. But there's more. He told me some other disturbing news that had to do with Norma."

"Oh, Larry, how awful." Lori knew this must be painful for him.

Just then Beth walked toward the front desk, one arm loaded with books, while her little boy tugged at the other. The younger child trailed behind. "Someone's coming to the desk. Can you hold the line a minute?"

Laying the telephone receiver down, Lori turned her attention to Beth. "All ready to check out?"

"I just wound up grabbing a bunch of books. When I'm by myself, I try to scan through them but not today. These two are having too good a time playing hide and seek among the shelves, and I can't concentrate. But I promised Jared he could get some books, too. May I just lay these here?"

Lori nodded, and Beth laid her books on the counter. Jared immediately started pulling his mother toward the children's section. But the other child, a little girl around two, who had been staring up at Lori, remained standing there, her thumb in her mouth. Beth retraced her steps and scooped her daughter up, laughing. "She seems fascinated by you, Lori." She held her daughter's arm and pumped it in a waving motion. "Say 'Hi' to the nice lady, Sierra."

"Hello, Sierra," Lori said in an encouraging tone. Ordinarily she enjoyed such exchanges, but today she was preoccupied. Her eyes wandered involuntarily to the telephone receiver.

"You're busy. Sorry to interrupt. I'd better get over there. Jared will have all the books off the shelves."

When Lori finally picked up the receiver, Larry had hung up. She quickly dialed the station. But, Suzie, the dispatcher, told her Larry was sorry he'd had to cut her off but that he'd get back with her later.

Shortly after lunch, Suzie called. "Larry told me to call and let you know he had to make a quick trip to Denver."

Lori wondered if the trip had to do with Joe and was about to ask, but Suzie continued. "He told me to give you a message. He said he'd pick up a dead bolt and put it on tomorrow when he gets back, but it could be late afternoon. Something else he wanted me to be sure to tell you is that the immediate danger has passed. He said you'd understand."

Lori felt a lump in her throat. No need to question Suzie further. Larry's message could mean only one thing. He'd gotten a court order and was on his way to Denver with Joe. He'd evidently made arrangements to meet some of the people from the institute there; people who would take Joe back and lock him up again.

"Yes, I think I know what Larry meant. Thanks for relaying his message."

After hanging up, Lori stood there hugging herself. A chill went through her, even though a minute earlier the room had been warm and toasty. Even though she knew logically she wasn't responsible, that her friendliness to Joe hadn't caused the recurrence of his illness, she wished she hadn't been instrumental in his having to go back to the hospital. If possible, her heart felt even heavier than it had that awful day when she discovered Blake and Janice together.

That evening when Lori checked her mailbox, among the bills and advertisements was a letter from Blake. Several times he'd shown up at her house, first ringing the bell. Then banging on the door when she refused to answer. She'd watched from the window as he walked away, his shoulders in an uncharacteristic slump. He'd continued his calls to the library, two or three times day, but each time she heard his voice, she hung up.

As she saw the familiar handwriting, once so dear, her eyes clouded. This is the same hand that formed the words to that lovely poem, "The Fractured Stem," she thought. Not for the first time, she wondered how someone so callous could be capable of writing with such sensitivity. But the feelings he'd conveyed in the poem were meaningless, as were the words in the unopened letter, she concluded. She quickly tore the letter into pieces and carried them to the wastebasket by the kitchen door.

Later, sitting in Charlotte's old chair, it occurred to Lori that it wouldn't be long until her own body molded into the curves made by her mother's small frame. But, unlike the times when Charlotte sat there, no voices emanated from the television set across the room. The only sounds to be heard were those made by the old house, which went unnoticed before. Now, in the night's stillness, they reverberated throughout the room in an eerie, disjointed melody. And the words of regret she'd been able to hold in check played over and over in her mind—if only he'd been the man she thought he was, if only he'd really loved her.

She wasn't aware of getting up or going to the wastebasket, but a few minutes later, she was standing at the kitchen table, laying out the pieces of the letter. Then, like an addict who succumbs to a burning need, she began to devour the words spread out before her.

My dearest wife,

How do I make you understand that everything that's happened has been a nightmare for me. I telephoned Sarah. Like you, she hates me, but at least she talked to me. She said you not only believe there's something going on between Janice and myself, but that you are now aware I bought the working interest in the Wyatt lease. And that you've come to the conclusion my reason for marrying you was to somehow get your royalty interest as well. This idea was so shocking, I was momentarily speechless so, therefore, couldn't explain to Sarah how wrong you are. I would like to do so now.

I was approached by Malcolm Murphy some time ago. He'd heard I was looking around the area for possible oil sites. At the time, I'd just learned about this new enhanced oil recovery method and thought the Wyatt field could be a good prospect. Murphy was real anxious to get out from under it and offered it to me for a good price.

In retrospect, I know I should have told you, but my reasons for keeping it from you seemed sound at the time. First, I wanted to make sure the process would work. Call it male ego, but I wanted you to be proud of me. Secondly, once I was sure the project would be successful, I wanted to surprise you, make it a sort of wedding present. My idea was to take you out to the field, perhaps take along a picnic basket as we did before. Ironically, this venture could be the one thing to turn out well or me. The project looks great so far.

So can we still do this, Lori? If you can find it in your heart to give me this chance to convince you of my love and good intentions, meet me at the gazebo at one o'clock on Sunday. I can also explain why Janice was at the house that day. I can see why you'd misinterpret her reason for being there, but there's nothing going on between us of a personal nature.

Your loving husband, Blake

Lori scooped up the pieces, and carrying them to the bathroom, threw them into the toilet. Lies, all lies, she thought. But even as the last fragment was flushed away, she knew she hadn't destroyed the words of the letter, that the time and place of Blake's proposed rendezvous was etched on her mind. She also knew she'd spend a turbulent night wrestling with her desire to see him, to touch him just once more, and that tomorrow she'd don the silk slacks and matching sweater he'd bought for her "because they cast flecks of emerald on her dark eyes." And getting into her car, she'd head north.

Chapter 28 - Lori

As she approached the Wyatt field, Lori saw the evidence of recent activity, a trailer with a truck parked beside it, as well as several large pieces of equipment. Today, however, the field looked deserted. Of course, it's Sunday—the workers would be gone for the day, she told herself. As she continued down the road, her heart began to beat a little faster, her hands becoming clammy on the steering wheel. She hadn't rehearsed what to say, what to do, when she saw him. She'd timed her drive to arrive late and had envisioned Blake walking toward her, his face somber but grateful, while she stood there, cool and detached. But as she pulled up in front of the little gazebo, nestled under the willows, there was no sign of Blake's truck—nor of Blake.

Lori checked her watch as she walked toward her familiar childhood haunt. It was ten past one. Where could he be? As she sank down on the bench, a feeling of anger, mixed with humiliation, came over her. Was this just another one of his schemes? Or perhaps she was confused. Had she made a mistake about the time or place where they were to meet? She reread the letter in her mind, picturing it's physical equivalent as it had lay in pieces on her kitchen table. Or perhaps there had been no letter. In her disturbed state of mind, could she have imagined it? No matter, she thought, I'm not hanging around here another minute.

As Lori stood up, she could see movement off in the distance, a small cloud of dust down the road from which she'd come. But what she saw was too small for a truck. A motorcycle? No, it was a bicycle. It's probably someone coming with a message from Blake, she decided, one of his field employees with a message telling her to come back to the project area. She breathed a sigh of relief, mingled with exhilaration.

Too late she recognized the man getting off the bicycle as Joe Isley. Lori grappled in her purse, searching for her car keys, although Joe was already walking toward her, was between the gazebo and her car. She stood helplessly waiting as he continued purposefully toward her.

It all happened so fast she had difficulty fathoming the sequence of events. There was a loud noise like a small explosion. And after that Joe was lying motionless on the ground about ten feet from where she stood. Then Blake was there, a few feet to her right, had seemingly appeared from nowhere. And he had a revolver in his hand.

Lori couldn't hold back the anguished scream, which permeated the silence. She felt if she could just reach the safety of Blake's arms, everything would be all right. She seemed to be moving in slow motion but finally she was there, her head and arms pressed against his chest. "I'm so glad you came," she said between muffled sobs. "I was so afraid. But did you have to shoot him? Couldn't you have just warned him?"

There was no answer. Slowly a cold realization came to her as, nestling closer and closer to him, she sought the reassurance that wasn't there. There were no arms encircling her, no hand stroking her hair. The voice she needed to hear, telling her this insane moment would pass, that they would face this nightmare together, was silent.

Lori drew back, saw his arms hanging stiffly at his sides, still holding the gun. She looked into his eyes but found no comfort there.

"Hello, dear wife," he said in a strange, distant voice. "Too bad about your secret admirer, but you understand, I had no choice."

He walked past her and stooped over Joe's lifeless form, searching for something. He pulled a folded piece of paper from Joe's jacket pocket, opening it and scanning it briefly. "Good. I thought I might find this. It saves me a possible complication. He was supposed to destroy it, but I couldn't be sure. I'd have had to go over to his place."

"What is it?" She already knew the answer. A blessed numbness was beginning to set in.

"It says 'Dear, Joe, I can't stop thinking about you. I know now it's you I love. If you feel the same, meet me at my little house on my oil field at one-fifteen on Sunday.'" He refolded the paper and tucked it in his own jacket. "It also has a post script that tells him to show the letter to no one and to get rid of it."

Blake looked down at Joe. "I assume he followed the first part of the instructions. Since you were his only friend, there was no one he'd have shown the note to. I'll take care of the last part, myself."

"Yes, I can see where this would be necessary." Lori marveled at her calmness. "Did you kill my mother, also?"

"No, Lori, at least this is not one they can pin on me, if it comes to that. She had me pegged, you know." There was a note of admiration in his voice. "She confronted me that day about my interest in the oil property. And that wasn't the only time. Earlier, when I was shoveling her walk, she told me you'd made a will and hinted you'd left your oil property to her. Not that it matters now but did you, Lori?"

Lori nodded.

Blake seemed agitated, waving his arms about. Lori kept her eyes on the gun still in his hand.

"She threatened to call you," he said. "I needed time to think things through, so I took the receiver off the downstairs phone and walked out. Not one of my smartest moves, but it turned out all right."

Of course, Lori thought. With Mother and me both dead he'll get the royalty. That's why he has to kill me. Otherwise he could just divorce me to be with Janice.

But she had forgotten something. Now it came back to her. That day in Bill Caldwell's office when she'd made out her will, he'd been concerned about adding a provision. He advised her there was a good probability she'd outlive her mother and that she should provide for this. He'd suggested that she might want the royalty to revert to her husband.

And she'd sat there thinking this sounded reasonable. But she'd remembered the locket on the chain around her neck, the locket carrying the picture of the little boy who'd wanted her to be his mother. The royalty was virtually worthless, anyhow, but perhaps someday, as her dad had said . . .

Now as she stood there, realizing that the reading of her will could be much sooner than she'd envisioned, the words came back to her—"And if she shall predecease me, it is my wish that any and all property bequeathed to Charlotte Wyatt hereunder shall devolve to Michael Lawrence Reardon."

Should she tell this man, this stranger who was her husband, who'd been her lover, someone she'd called friend? No, not a stranger—a stranger wouldn't need to take her life. Could she use this information as a bargaining tool? Agree to give him the royalty in exchange for letting her go?

She needed the right moment, the right words that would make him see he could still have it all without killing her. Or if she could stall him, maybe someone would come. But who? Larry was in Denver. Keep the subject on the royalty, she thought. "So now, as one hundred percent owner of the Wyatt lease, you and Janice can live happily ever after." It was a statement, rather than a question.

Blake didn't answer immediately. His eyes softened and when he finally spoke, it was with a note of regret. "No, Lori. I doubt it. Believe it or not this is difficult for me. You're a nice person, decent. I meant all those things I said about you, and I liked it you found something in me to love. For a while, I actually thought it might work, that I could become the guy you thought I was. But it wasn't in the cards. The pressure became too much. As for Janice, the pressure will become too much with her as well." He laughed but it was hollow – a strange, cynical laugh that twisted his face. "But not in the same sort of way."

Lori felt a faint glimmer of hope. This man who was always so methodical was obviously not thinking straight. Perhaps she could use this knowledge to dissuade him.

"I don't understand what you're saying, "she said.

His voice was flat, emotionless. "Janice has an insatiable need no one can fill. Eventually she'll become restless, just as with her other relationships. And I'll encourage her to move on because I'll get tired of the effort to keep her happy."

"But if you know that, why would you go to these lengths for her – even commit murder." Lori's eyes moved involuntarily to where Joe lay in a crumpled heap, and a shudder passed through her.

He didn't answer immediately, as if he was searching for the right words, the words that would give meaning to the events that had led them to this place in time. "I guess it all has to do with destiny," he said finally.

"It's too late, Lori. You see that, don't you?" He put the gun in his pocket and pulled out a piece of rope. His eyes were hard again and his jaw had a determined set.

Lori was too tired to resist. She realized absently this was the way he had to do it. He had to strangle her to make it look like Joe had murdered her—and that his reason for killing Joe was self-defense when he happened upon the scene. She glanced down at the body of the man, who like her, was but a pawn in the hands of this monster. And yet, didn't she share the guilt? Hadn't she played a part in his tragic death? Yes, she thought, it was indeed too late. Suddenly, she just wanted it to be over.

She felt as if she were someone standing apart, an actor ready to move on stage. Soon it would be time to play her role. As he moved closer, the rope grasped tightly in both hands, it dawned on her that this would be the last time she would see him in this life. "I'm not going to make it easy for you, Blake," she said.

No response, no applause, as Lori turned and walked slowly toward her car.

Chapter 29 - Lori

Larry returned from the cafeteria, jolting Lori back to the present. "Did you decide to have a bite after all?" she asked him.

"I ran into Jim Thompson. He'd just brought in a guy who was stabbed. It wasn't life threatening, but they had to hospitalize him. He was involved in a fight at a bar and they jailed three other guys who weren't that bad off. This guy will probably join them at the taxpayer's hotel in the morning. But in answer to your question, I did decide to try one of their specials, a Mexican plate. It wasn't too bad." He glanced at her half-eaten dinner as he sat down but didn't say anything.

Lori nodded politely. She was anxious for Larry to continue their earlier conversation. "Before you left, you told me about a salesman you'd suddenly remembered," she said.

Larry sat down in the chair by her bed. "Yeah, that's right. After I remembered him, for the first time I began to have doubts about Joe being the one who murdered Norma. And I knew I had to pursue it. I'm afraid I forgot everything else, including the fact I was waiting for you to get back on the line. I went over to Johnson's and asked Betty how far back their records went. She said they had all their old sales orders in a storeroom in the back. She was good enough to take me back there and even helped me look through them. It took the better part of an hour, but we finally the found the ones I was looking for. When I saw the name of the salesman, a Ralph Winslow, I immediately connected it with the owner of the Buick. And one of the sales orders matched the date of Norma's murder. What's more, Winslow lived in Denver."

Lori had been listening intently to what Larry was saying but when he mentioned Betty, she had to make an effort to keep her mind on the remainder of his story. That poor lady, so kind and cheerful. There she was, trying her best to be helpful to Larry, and a day later she learns her only son is dead and in such a horrible manner.

"Did you have to break the news to Betty about Blake?'

"No, I was fortunate to be able to delegate that responsibility to Jack Matthews, one of the deputies who found the bodies. I was concerned about you at the time and didn't want to leave."

"Were you here all night, Larry?'

He looked a little sheepish. "Well, at least physically. I did manage to catch forty winks now and then. Let's see, where was I?"

"You'd found out about the existence of Ralph Winslow, the man who drove the Buick."

"When I left Johnson's, I headed for the interstate, put the pedal to the metal so to speak, not breaking any speed limits, of course. I called Suzie on the way out, letting her know my plans, but I also needed her to verify Winslow was at the same locale. She reported back that a Winslow was still at that address, but the listing was under a Margaret only. When I found the house, there was no one home. It was about two o'clock and I hadn't eaten, so I drove back to a shopping center a couple of blocks away and had lunch. While I was there I went into K-Mart and picked up that lock for your door. Then I went back there and waited. Finally at around five-thirty, a woman showed up."

"Was it Mrs. Winslow?"

"It was she all right. And she was most helpful. Invited me in, even offered to fix me a drink. Of course, I declined, being in uniform. She told me she'd divorced Ralph about five years ago. Seems she discovered he'd been having an affair with a gal in Grand Junction, which was also on his sales route. The relationship went along fine for a couple of years, but the woman started putting pressure on him to leave his wife. So the thing turned sour. He got nasty and roughed her up. The woman said he would have killed her if her son, a high-school kid, hadn't come in. The boy ran next door and called the police. When the police arrived, Ralph was gone. He'd gotten worried when the kid came in, so he left. The woman went ahead and filed charges. It made the local papers and got back to Margaret. Seems she had a friend in the area who saw the newspaper report. She said she'd suspected he'd been unfaithful for years. After this happened, she questioned the secretary at the home office and found out he had gotten calls regularly from a lot of different women through the years."

230

Lori could empathize with Margaret. "And this is when she divorced him?"

Larry nodded. "I asked her if she'd gotten the names of any of these women, if the name Norma rang a bell. Margaret said she was almost sure she was one of the women the secretary had mentioned. The secretary still works at the same place. It's a company called Bradbury Manufacturing, but Ralph lost his job over the scandal. He still lives and works in Denver. Margaret didn't know where he was employed but gave me his home address."

"Oh, Larry, it looks like poor Joe was innocent." Lori couldn't hold back the tears, and it seemed like once she started, all the pent-up feelings of the past few weeks came flooding out. "I'm sorry," she said finally, making an effort to regain control. "But don't you see, they locked him away for fifteen years for a crime he didn't commit. And then he becomes involved in another one. But this time he wasn't even given that much of a chance."

"I know. It's been heavy on my mind ever since I found all this out. I think I convinced Joe that if he'd gotten a note, it wasn't from you. I told him if he got another one, he should bring it to me immediately." Larry bowed his head, as if he couldn't look her in the eye. "When I called in from here at the hospital, Suzie told me he'd come by the office looking for me on Saturday afternoon after I'd left. She told him I was out of town and asked if he'd like to talk to someone else. According to her, he looked confused, hesitated for a minute as if pondering what to do. But finally he declined without telling her what it was about. I wish he had. Suzie evidently didn't think it was important enough to radio me, just another crazy story concocted by an unstable mind. But if she had seen the note and Joe had been able to explain to her what it was about, I'm sure she would have contacted me, and I would have come back."

The orderly returned for Lori's tray, and Larry paused until she had left.

"Suzie feels pretty rotten, also, after she found out about Joe's death. Anyhow, I thought I'd stay over and see if I could find Ralph the next morning. But when I went over to his house Sunday morning, he wasn't there. I waited around several hours, but he never showed. I wanted to talk to the secretary at Bradbury Manufacturing, but since it was Sunday, I knew the office would be closed. So I came on back."

"If Joe thought the note was a hoax, why did he come out to the field?"

"I think, as with Norma, he was worried about you. He figured something was going on, and when he was unable to make contact with me, he decided to go out there at the time designated in the note—and walked right into the

231

trap Blake had set for him. He said something else the morning I was at his house. Again, I didn't take it too seriously—something about letting his buddy down in Vietnam, and then running away when he might have saved Norma. Perhaps he saw this as an opportunity to make amends."

Lori could feel the tears welling up again and reached on her tray for a tissue.

"Joe told me he tried to tell Sheriff Nelson about the car and the stranger back when it happened, at the time of the murder. But Nelson wouldn't listen. It was never brought out at the trial. Evidently his own court-appointed attorney didn't give any credence to Joe's story, either. But how can I find fault with them, when I didn't believe him?" Larry added in a voice heavy with self-reproach. "Like Nelson and Joe's attorney, I thought it was the ramblings of a lunatic and would have seen he was locked up again if I hadn't remembered the car."

"And if you had taken him back as you'd intended, he would still be alive," Lori said softly. Then realizing how this sounded, added, "You can't blame yourself, though. How could you foresee what was going to happen? The action you took at the time was the right one."

Larry was looking at her intently. "I suppose you're right. But I'm not going to let this drop just because he's dead. The least I can do for Joe is to try to clear his name. I'm going after Winslow. With all the new DNA testing and other developments in forensic science, I should be able to get enough to charge him."

Lori felt almost envious. At least he could take some action to help alleviate the pain. All she could do was lie here and think. Suddenly she remembered Lucky. "Larry, Joe has, or had, a dog, a mixed-breed puppy. Someone needs to look after him."

"Yeah, that's right. I saw him when I was there—a friendly little guy. I'll have someone go out and see to him."

"The poor dog must be in a terrible state. Joe and he were close. All they had was each other. Would it be too much of an imposition for you to keep him at your place tonight? Then you can bring him to my house tomorrow."

"Sure, I can do that. But do you want to keep him?"

"As you said, it's the least I can do for Joe."

Conclusion

Lori was due to go back to work on Monday. Sarah had stayed with her three full days. After that, she came by with Jon every evening. Her good friend had been both discreet and compassionate, letting her talk only when she felt up to it.

Jon was less tactful. One evening he remarked the only thing that surprised him about Blake was his suicide. "Guys like him think too much of themselves. It would have been more in character for him to just disappear, then resurface somewhere else with a new identity and try to scam some other unsuspecting woman."

Lori didn't say anything. She certainly didn't feel a need to defend the man who had coldly calculated an elaborate plot to murder her. But perhaps seeing Joe lying there brought home to Blake the horror of what he'd done and rendered him incapable of carrying out the rest of his plan—and in the end he couldn't live with the guilt. Lori knew she should hate him, but if she could hold on to the thought her husband wasn't totally without scruples, she knew it would hasten her recovery.

Sarah and Lori decided Blake's reluctance to get together with her friends was because he was afraid they would see through him. It was safer for him to keep Lori isolated, although it wasn't possible to keep her away from her mother, the one person who was constant in her distrust of him.

"But it is ironic," Lori observed.

"What do you mean?"

Lori's look was sad. "The reason Mother didn't trust Blake was not because she was a great judge of character. It was because of her belief no one could be interested in me for myself."

Sarah reached for her friend's hand. "But then she needed to hold on to this idea. Her motive might have been purely subconscious, but it was her way of trying to keep you from leaving, and when you did leave, of getting you back."

One evening Larry and Rusty joined them. Once Rusty was reassured she was on the road to recovery, he deserted the rest of them to play with Lucky. There were others who stopped by during the week, Jon's parents, Karen and Jack Matthews and their daughter, Heather, who said she was almost finished with her term paper, and Phoebe, who brought her a lovely little throw pillow with a crocheted cover. Sarah's mother and father were traveling in Europe but asked Sarah to order a plant to be sent to her. Mrs. Jacobs had been plying her with food until finally Lori convinced her she was going to be so fat she'd need a whole new wardrobe.

It all seemed a plot to keep her from brooding, and it was working to a point. Sarah had destroyed all the newspapers, which Lori assumed carried the news of the murder and suicide. Lori was thankful. She wasn't ready to deal with the rehashing of the sordid details and doubted if she would ever be. She and Larry had agreed to split the costs of a nice funeral for Joe. She hadn't been strong enough to attend, but Larry had gone and reported there was a large crowd there to pay their respects. Although Larry was still in the evidence gathering stage of charging Ralph Winslow with Norma's murder, the word had no doubt gotten around about the case being reopened. And many of the town's people had shown up, Lori suspected, to assuage guilty consciences.

But try as they might to keep her from being alone, her good friends couldn't always be there. When she was by herself, Lori spent much of her time sitting on her screened-in back porch. There she could view the trees and flowers as they hailed the coming of spring with their lovely new garb of blossomed finery. And she could think.

Something Larry had said the evening he and Rusty had dropped by kept coming back. Sarah and Jon had left, and they'd taken a stroll around the grounds. Rusty and Lucky ran ahead, experiencing the pure joy of the here and now, as only the young can do.

Lori had mentioned this to Larry, and he said, "Yes, childhood is a wonderful thing. Too bad we all have to grow up. Where once we accept others on blind faith, life teaches us this isn't always wise. Rusty is getting his first lesson now. He's finding out his mother can't be trusted to keep her promises."

Lori had started to say something but couldn't find the words.

"But he'll be all right. Look at him. He doesn't look that disturbed, does he?"

"What I'm getting at, Lori, is that I think in a sense this is what happened to you. Because of your feeling of obligation to your mother, heightened of course, by your father's death, you never allowed yourself to go through that period most of us go through. At a certain age, as a normal function of growth, we begin to question whether or not adults have our best interests at heart. For instance, your experience with Blake was something a lot of us go through at an earlier age. Oh, maybe it's not so drastic for most of us, but it's a lesson we all have to learn sooner or later. But there's one thing I know about you, Lori—you're strong. You proved this when you were facing death. Most people, many of them who consider themselves really tough, would have gotten down on their knees and groveled. But you didn't. I'm not sure if you would have been alive today if you had. I think it's what made it impossible for Blake to carry out his carefully laid plans."

He stopped and took her hands. "Look at me. I'm giving you my fifty-cent psychology lesson. All I really wanted to say is that I think you're one hell of a lady."

The afternoon sun was beginning to set, and Lori pulled her sweater around her shoulders. Whether or not Larry was right about her, she liked what he'd said. *I have no choice but to prove him right,* she thought, *by putting this thing behind me and going on.*

"May I please speak to Melora Johnson."

"Yes, this is Melora." The voice wasn't familiar.

"My name is Eric Anders. I was working with your husband at the time of his death. He'd hired me as a consultant. First, let me say I was sorry to hear about your loss. This is a little awkward. I hate to bother you, but I need to talk with you. Did your husband ever mention me?"

"No, he didn't like to discuss business with me."

"I'd been working on this project with him, the one he was doing out at the Wyatt lease. We were all primed up to go and, of course, now everything's come to a standstill."

"I really don't know how I can help you."

"Well, the thing is Mrs. Johnson, something's going to have to happen out there. The state will want those non-producing wells plugged if the project doesn't move ahead. I know you can't discuss it now, but I thought you might meet me for a cup of coffee somewhere after you get off work. I live in

Grand Junction, but I can get there by five."

What Anders was saying made sense to Lori. "All right. I can do that," she said. "I'll meet you at Dora's Diner. Its right on Main and not difficult to find."

When Lori saw the distinguished-looking gentleman sitting in the booth toward the back, she knew it had to be Anders. He had a head of beautiful white hair and there were lines around his eyes, which indicated he saw the humorous side of life. She thought immediately, this is a man to be trusted. Was she finally learning how to judge character, or was she still being naive?

They ordered their coffee. Anders also ordered a hamburger, but Lori declined.

"Dora makes a really good hamburger," Lori said. "You'll not be disappointed."

Anders smiled. " I often stop at fast food places when I'm on the road since they're convenient, so this will be a treat." He looked around. "This place is nice and clean, too, and the waitress was friendly."

As pleasant as the man seemed to be, Lori was anxious to get down to business. "As I told you on the phone, I'm not sure how I can help you. I own the royalty to the Wyatt lease. But you'll need to get permission from the working interest owner to move ahead—and, of course, that's not possible."

"Did your husband leave a will, Mrs. Johnson?"

"I've gone back to using my maiden name of Wyatt, but you can call me Lori."

If Anders was taken aback by this, he didn't let on. "All right, Lori. And please call me Eric."

"To answer your question, the answer is 'no.' His estate is being handled by a court appointed administrator."

It suddenly dawned on Lori what this meant. Without a will, the working interest would go to her, along with anything else that was Blake's. "I guess that means I'm the working interest owner. His death was so recent, it hadn't occurred to me that I now own the lease one hundred percent." An unexpected tear slid down her face.

Eric looked at her sadly. "You must think I'm a terrible heel to put you through this, and if there were any other way . . ."

Lori braced her shoulders. "No, I understand something must be done about the project. What do you need from me?"

"You can get the court's permission to move ahead, even though the estate hasn't been settled."

Lori nodded. "I'll made an appointment with the administrator first thing tomorrow."

"Good. Now, since your husband didn't talk about the project, he probably didn't go into its potential. It involves a new form of enhanced oil recovery that is proving to be tremendously successful on certain types of reservoirs, and the Wyatt lease is a good candidate."

"Yes, I talked to the former operator, Malcolm Murphy, and he told me about this new method and said this is what Blake was working on."

The evening waitress, a high school girl whom Lori didn't know, brought Eric's order.

"It seems you do know something about this after all," he said. "Well, I have a proposition to offer you, but first I'd better eat this hamburger. If it's as good as you say, I don't want it to get cold."

After he'd finished, Eric wiped his mouth on his napkin. "I see I can trust your judgment, young lady. That's the best hamburger I've had in years. Now, here's what I propose. I'm so convinced your oil property is an excellent site for this method that I'd like to purchase the working interest myself. I'd be able to finance part of the operation. And I've contacted the people who were backing the project for your husband. They're still willing to put up the rest of the money."

"This all comes as pretty much of a surprise. I'd like to think about it."

"Of course. I'd expect you to do this. He reached into a brief case on the seat beside him and pulled out a file. I have made copies of everything I think you'll need. There's a copy of a paper I authored about high pressure air injection, plus copies of data about the Wyatt lease, figures showing the amount of oil in place, projections, et cetera. I've included some references, people in the industry you can contact about me."

"I don't know how much of this I'll be able to understand," Lori said, scanning through the documents in the file.

"What I'd advise you to do is to contact the bar association in Denver. Ask them for the names of attorneys who work in this area of the law, and get one of them to look over this material for you. We'd like to get back to work as soon as possible, but I want you to be comfortable with it, be assured this is the way to go."

"The thing is, Mr. Anders, from glancing over these figures, it looks like we're talking about a lot of money. This may sound phony, but I don't really have a great desire to be wealthy." She looked down, before proceeding. "The desire for money has . . . well, let's just say I don't think having money necessarily brings happiness."

Lori fought for composure. Raising her head she looked Mr. Anders directly in the eye. "So you see," she said, "there's no great incentive for me to go ahead with this, other than this business about the state wanting to plug the wells. I understand this could be a big expense."

"Believe it or not, I can understand where you're coming from. My motive is not solely financial either. I believe this new process will catch on once they see how successful it is, and it will be good for the country, make us less dependent on foreign oil." The lines around his eyes deepened as he smiled. "So you see, if for no other reason, you need to consider this for patriotic reasons."

"You say your process will be a good thing for the country, and I know you're probably right. There is one thing I'm not sure I understand, and perhaps you can explain this to me. If oil production is good for the country, why are there so many new regulations hampering the production of oil?"

"You've asked a very complicated question, young lady, and I think I'd need more time than we have today to fully explain it. But in a nutshell, many of the new laws are good. Contrary to popular opinion, most people in the petroleum field are not anti-environmentalists. As with any industry, in the past there were a lot of abuses, and so laws were needed to keep unscrupulous people from polluting the air and waters. Sometimes, however, people who don't fully understand the effects of oil production on the ecology pass these laws intended to protect the environment. Therefore, some of the laws are not only unnecessary but are a burden on oil producers. Does this help answer your question?"

"Yes, but now I have another more specific one. What's the purpose of plugging the non-producing wells? Is this one of those unnecessary laws you're talking about?"

"No, I believe this law has merit. When a well is active, we are required to test it periodically to insure oil is not seeping into the surrounding water supplies. But when it's no longer active, this is no longer something we're required to do. For one thing, the expense would be tremendous. The state governments thought they had a simple solution. That's when they decided to require the operators to plug these wells that were no longer producing. Sounds reasonable, except they don't understand there is still a lot of oil in those wells and that an enhanced oil recovery method such as the one I developed can get this oil out. But if these wells are plugged, the cost of going in and recompleting them, or in laymen's terms, unplugging them, would be prohibitive. This would make my method a lot more expensive to implement."

"But can't you explain this to the state?"

"Of course. We've done so many times, and once they understand, they back off. They're very reasonable and willing to work with us as long as we have a plan to get those wells producing again."

Before they parted, Eric shook her hand warmly. "I'll be looking forward to hearing from you, Lori."

As he opened the door of her car for her, Lori was sure her first instincts about this man were correct.

"Lucky, quit that." Rusty pushed the dog away in mock exasperation. "He's trying to dig up these flowers as fast as we get them planted."

"Well, I guess we'd better put him in the house then." Lori walked over to where Rusty was working. "Come on, Lucky," she said sternly.

"No, no. He'll be good, wont'cha, boy?"

It was early May, and Lori thought if she was going to get any planting done this year, she'd better get started. She'd talked to Rusty on the telephone several times during the past month, but this was the first time she'd seen him. She hadn't seen Larry either. He was coming over after work as she'd invited them both to stay for dinner.

She finished putting the last of the geraniums in the hole Rusty had dug and stood up, brushing the dirt off her jeans. She noticed that Rusty was covered with mud from his face on down, but decided not to mention it. He seemed to have had such fun helping her and she didn't want to spoil the experience.

"Well, now that we've finished, I'd better go in and check our dinner before it burns to a crisp," she said. "What do you think your grandfather would say to that?"

Rusty giggled. "Aw, he wouldn't care. He'd just say, 'Them's mighty tasty vittles, Ma'am.' Then he'd go home and ask Grandma if she'd fix him something to eat."

Lori, who'd just removed her gardening gloves, reached down and rapped him playfully over the head with one of them. "I think a certain young man has been watching too many TV westerns."

"I'd rather watch Alien Space Wars, but Grandma won't let me. Grandpa likes all those old John Wayne movies. Borrrring."

Just then Larry walked up. "What's this?" he asked in a voice of mock outrage. "Am I going to have to take you in for picking on my young partner, here?"

Lori laughed. "It was justified, honest, Sheriff."

"Oh well, in that case I'll let you off this time. But can I help with anything? I'm not looking forward to an overcooked dinner."

"I was about to check my dinner, as you no doubt overheard. You can come in and keep me company."

Lori fixed a glass of iced tea for Larry, and he sat at the kitchen table while she tossed a salad to go with her chicken casserole.

"It should be ready in another five minutes. We'd better call Rusty and have him wash up."

"Okay, but there are a couple of things I want to discuss before he comes in."

"Sure, I'll just turn the oven down a little. What is it you wanted to say?"

"First, I wanted to tell you they've taken Winslow into custody. Without going into a lot of detail, the results of the DNA tests have put him at the scene of the crime."

Lori abandoned her salad and walked over to the table. "That's great news. I know you've worked really hard on this."

There was a look of pride on his face. "The department gets a lot of credit for letting me go ahead with it. I also put in a lot of off-duty time. But I did it for myself. I had to finish this, you know."

"Yes, but now Joe's name will be cleared, and you've made the world safer for other women with Winslow off the streets."

"I'm extremely pleased about that."

"But you said there were two things on your mind. What was the other thing you wanted to discuss?"

The sheriff suddenly looked like a tongue-tied little boy. Lori had an image of him at Rusty's age and thought he must have looked a lot like his grandson.

When he spoke, it was in a voice that sounded rehearsed. "If you'd let me, I'd like to spend more time with you. The thing is, what you're going through is pretty similar to what I'm experiencing, and I think we can help each other."

Lori sat down across from him. "What do you mean, Larry?

"I've been thinking about this. You were in love with someone who wasn't worthy of that love, and it's pretty tough to face. I think I can understand this more than most people. All the time I was married to Norma and during the years since her death, I've had an image of her as this faithful wife. Maybe this is why I didn't want to believe Joe when he told me about Winslow." He bowed his head. "You see, I'm having to face the same thing you are, only with me much more time has elapsed. In a way, I guess it's easier."

"No, I think it must be even more difficult. You two were married for a long time. I'm sorry I've been so wrapped up in my own problems, I didn't even think about what you must be going through."

"I didn't bring this up to make you feel guilty. Anyhow, I'm probably just using it as a ploy to be able to see you more often. I'm very fond of you in case you haven't noticed."

"I know, Larry. And I like you a lot, too. I don't know if I've told you how grateful I am to you for being there when I was going through that terrible ordeal. The thing is, I've thought a lot about what you told me the last time you were here, just after I got out of the hospital, about how I was going through some growing pains a little belatedly. And I think you're right. I was ripe for someone like Blake. When he started to pursue me, I reacted like a sort of star-struck kid. I had a crush on him in high school, but a mature person would have outgrown this teen-age fantasy long ago, moved on with her life. And fifteen years later, seeing this old flame again, would have wondered what she ever saw in him, even chuckled fondly at her youthful naiveté."

Lori searched for the right words. "But now I need time to go through the things I missed. I need to find out if the rest of what you said was right, that is, that I'm strong enough to take my lumps and go on. I have to concentrate for a while on getting to know Melora Wyatt. Do you understand?"

"Sure. But I needed to say it." He reached up and pretended to mop his forehead. "Now that I've gotten that off my chest, when do we eat?"

Lori laughed and got up to finish the salad. "First you'd better get that boy in and start scraping the mud off."

He headed toward the back door. Then turned around. "When and if you find you have room in your life for someone else, will you let me know?"

"Of course. You'll be the first."

As she walked to the refrigerator to get out the salad dressing, her eyes lit on Rusty's poem, held in place by a butterfly magnet. The balloon had long since lost its helium and the lilies had died, but his poem would be there for a many years time to come, eventually yellowing with age. This is one poet she could trust, one whose words came straight from the heart. For now, this would be enough to sustain her.

* * * * *